P9-CKY-419

WITHDRAWN

ZZT is the place to be!

Camille whizzed Lora-Leigh into the sorority house's living room, cleared of furniture so everyone could move about. While there was still the normal "hello my name is" and quick pace, Lora-Leigh noticed these girls more. The one with the long red hair had a cool set of dangle earrings like ones Lora-Leigh had seen at a downtown thrift store a couple of weekends ago. Another girl had a small diamond stud in her nose. They didn't seem pretentious or judgmental.

Being steered around by Camille, Lora-Leigh met a Megan, a Sarah, an Amy, an Erin, and two Nicoles. Girls were all over the room, weaving in and out, shouting louder and louder. Lora-Leigh's heart pounded to the cadence of the room and the kinetic energy being generated. Out of the corner of her eye, she caught glimpses of Jenna and Roni, both seemingly enjoying themselves.

All right, I admit it . . . this is a bit of a rush!

The lights started flickering, just like they had in the previous houses. Only this time, Lora-Leigh wasn't as eager to leave. She wanted to stay longer. Hang out with Camille and get to know her better.

Camille leaned in. "You did a great job, Lora-Leigh! I think we met everyone twice. I *really* hope to see you again!"

"Thanks, Camille. Great meeting you!"

And then Lora-Leigh did the last thing she expected herself to do. She turned and squeezed Camille's hand.

"Good luck," the ZZT whispered.

Lora-Leigh was surprised to find herself hoping that the sisters genuinely liked her and that she'd be asked back. Deep down, she knew she *would* see Camille and the sisters of ZZT again.

SORORITY
101

Zeta OR Omega?

KATE HARMON

speak

An Imprint of Penguin Group (USA) Inc.

SPEAK
Published by the Penguin Group
Penguin Group (USA) Inc., 345 Hudson Street, New York, New York 10014, U.S.A.
Penguin Group (Canada), 90 Eglinton Avenue East, Suite 700, Toronto, Ontario,
Canada M4P 2Y3 (a division of Pearson Penguin Canada Inc.)
Penguin Books Ltd, 80 Strand, London WC2R 0RL, England
Penguin Ireland, 25 St Stephen's Green, Dublin 2, Ireland
(a division of Penguin Books Ltd)
Penguin Group (Australia), 250 Camberwell Road, Camberwell, Victoria 3124, Australia
(a division of Pearson Australia Group Pty Ltd)
Penguin Books India Pvt Ltd, 11 Community Centre,
Panchsheel Park, New Delhi - 110 017, India
Penguin Group (NZ), 67 Apollo Drive, Rosedale, North Shore 0632, New Zealand
(a division of Pearson New Zealand Ltd)
Penguin Books (South Africa) (Pty) Ltd, 24 Sturdee Avenue,
Rosebank, Johannesburg 2196, South Africa

Registered Offices: Penguin Books Ltd, 80 Strand, London WC2R 0RL, England

Published by Speak, an imprint of Penguin Group (USA) Inc., 2008

1 3 5 7 9 10 8 6 4 2

Copyright © Marley Gibson, 2008
All rights reserved

LIBRARY OF CONGRESS CATALOGING-IN-PUBLICATION DATA
Harmon, Kate.
Sorority 101: Zeta or Omega? / by Kate Harmon.
p.   cm.
Summary: Three girls from very different backgrounds meet and become friends while
adjusting to their freshman year at a Florida university and making their way through sorority
recruitment together.
ISBN: 978-0-14-241017-2 (pbk. : alk. paper)
[1. Friendship—Fiction. 2. Greek letter societies—Fiction. 3. College freshmen—Fiction.
4. Universities and colleges—Fiction. 5. Florida—Fiction.]
I. Title. II. Title: Sorority one oh one.
PZ7.H22719Sor 2008
[Fic]—dc22   2007036076

Speak ISBN 978-0-14-241017-2

Printed in the United States of America

Except in the United States of America, this book is sold subject to the condition that
it shall not, by way of trade or otherwise, be lent, re-sold, hired out, or otherwise
circulated without the publisher's prior consent in any form of binding or cover
other than that in which it is published and without a similar condition
including this condition being imposed on the subsequent purchaser.

The publisher does not have any control over and does not assume any responsibility for
author or third-party Web sites or their content.

To Mike and the Team . . . you know why

ACKNOWLEDGMENTS

Even though writing is a solitary effort, no one gets to this place without a lot of support, encouragement, and love. All three of which I have in abundance.

First and foremost, thanks to my agent—the most fabulous ever *...you think I'm kidding?*—Deidre Knight for believing in me, my writing, and my ability. Also, thanks to all the wonderful ladies at The Knight Agency and the TKA Sistahs for their support.

Thanks to my editors—fellow southerner, Greek, and lover of SEC football, Angelle Pilkington; and Karen Chaplin, another fellow Greek—for their brilliant input and for loving my heroines as much as I do. And to everyone at Puffin who got behind this series with gusto.

Thanks to my ever-supportive friend, critique partner, and general confidante, Diana Peterfreund, for never letting me give up or quit and always telling me to believe in myself.

Thanks to the WACs, Jessica Andersen and Charlene Glatkowski, for mentoring, teaching, and cheering me along over the years... and every day.

Thanks to Liz Maverick, who said, "Why haven't you tried writing Young Adult? You totally should!" You were right, hon!

Thanks to my sister, Jennifer Keller, who is always a phone call or e-mail away.

Thanks to fellow Greeks Victoria Bendetson and Heather Potter Laskowski for bringing my knowledge of sororities out of the eighties and into this new century.

Thanks to Megan Gleason Bremer, all around best bud, who read the first thing I ever wrote—all 863 (zzzzz) pages of it—and God bless her, she still loves the story.

Thanks to Kirk LeMessurier, one of my favorite Canadians

(and I know plenty!) for being my own personal editor for years and for lending me some priceless Newfoundland phrases.

Thanks to Pamela Claughton for reading all my missives over the years and always being at the other end of the e-mail . . . or the bottle of wine! Foodies Rule!

Thanks to the Sporkies for all of the fun writing talk over meals. Keep those receipts, girls.

Thanks to the ever-sparkly Wendy Toliver, the unique Kwana Minatee-Jackson, the effervescent Elizabeth Mahon, and the phenomenal Roxanne St. Claire . . . just 'cause. Lubs ya all!

Thanks to my boss, Mark Doyle, for getting how much my writing means to me and celebrating my accomplishments through a blast e-mail to the company announcing my sale.

Thanks to the New England Romance Writers and the Chick Lit Writers of the World for all they have taught me about writing.

Thanks so much to my parents, Joe and Lizanne Harbuck, for giving me an overactive imagination and the ability to craft stories. And to my brother, Jeff Harbuck, for being so proud of me. Thanks for loving me and believing I could do this.

Thanks to HomeBistro.com for yummy, scrumptious easy-to-heat meals that my husband, Mike, was able to take care of so I could hole up in the writing room while he "cooked" dinner.

Finally, special thanks to Vicki Lewis Thompson, who gave me the sagest advice of all on April 2, 2005. Words that resonated to my writer's soul and propelled me to keep trying. And thanks to Barbara Delinsky . . . for answering a fan's e-mail.

The publishers would like to extend their thanks to Marley Gibson for her contributions to the Sorority 101 series.

Zeta OR Omega?

CHAPTER 1

She really hoped she wasn't going to gag.

Sure, it was one of *the best* restaurants in Boston—like wicked good and expensive—but her stomach was a conglomeration of nerves over what she had to tell her parents.

"And for the graduate, our Dover sole meuniére with Maine *moules poulettes*," the waiter said, presenting the artfully laid out skillet full of...fish.

Veronica Van Gelderen fidgeted with a blue-and-white tassel, twisting it around her index finger, while the crisply dressed server at Locke-Ober set the chef's handiwork in front of her. She tried not to recoil at the fish and mussels concoction her mother had insisted on ordering for her. Growing up in New England, she'd totally burned out on seafood—shellfish, especially.

Ugh, gahbage men of the sea.

She looked back at her hands. Only a few hours ago, the satiny blue-and-white tassel had swung from her white mortarboard as she was presented with her high school diploma (with honors, *thankyouverymuch*) from *the* Boston Academy. Her diploma was her ticket out. Her passage to a new world. A new life. Her *own* life.

Emily Feason, class valedictorian, had talked in her speech about missing those special bonds of high school and setting off in the world with the trepidation and anxiety of leaving the safety of a loving home.

Emily obviously didn't live in the Van Gelderen house.

"Veronic'er, do sit up," scolded her mother, Cathryn Minson Van Gelderen, from across the table, and adding "the stare" for good measure. Veronica despised that look. Her mother had always disciplined with a stern glare, narrowed eyes, and slightly gritted teeth. Something only Veronica was ever on the receiving end of.

She also hated how the "a" in her name turned into an "er" whenever her very Bostonian, Kennedy-esque parents said it. But she kept quiet by biting her bottom lip.

By reflex, Veronica straightened, nabbed her fork, and started picking at her food. She wished it were a double cheeseburger from Wendy's with everything (except onions) and an order of Biggie fries. Normal food for normal high school graduates. She wished she could be at Emily Feason's postgraduation party instead of here with her parents and their pretentious friends in a posh restaurant, eating an expensive meal that she could barely pronounce, let alone digest.

"I heard your valedictorian got a full scholarship to Brown," her mother said after swallowing a bite of lobster. Turning to their guests, she added, "Most of the children at Boston

Academy go on to the Ivies, Seven Sisters, or other prominent programs in the country. Isn't that Mendelssohn boy going to Stanford?"

"Yes," Veronica said quickly.

"Well, that will give his parents something to brag about at the country club this summer. But we can top that, can't we dear?" Mrs. Van Gelderen said to Veronica's father.

Veronica reached for her water glass and took a deep sip, hoping the cold liquid would dislodge the semipermanent lump in her throat. She was always being talked around. It was never a matter of what she *wanted* to do but what her parents *expected* her to do.

"Linus," her father, Harrison, started, "did we tell you and Barbara that Veronic'er was offered admission to both Cathryn's alma mater, Wellesley, and my Harvard?"

For the money he donated yearly, Veronica thought he honestly *could* call it "his" Harvard.

"Only about a dozen times." Linus Schneider, senior partner at her father's law firm, patted his mouth with the pressed linen napkin. "How will you ever make up your mind, Veronica?"

She placed a small chunk of bread in her mouth to avoid answering. No Van Gelderen would ever talk with their mouth full! Heavens no. But she thought of how much her college selection decision seemed to be about her parents, not her. They didn't know anything about her, so how did they know what she wanted for a career? They'd barely made time for her these past eighteen years, shuffling her off from one au pair or governess to the next and leaving her to be raised by books, television, and the Boston educational system. She wasn't a cherished child, but a prized possession. One with all the "right" friends from the "right" circles—kids from equal wealth and social status.

Thinking about how unloved and unwanted she felt at times was enough to make her cry—particularly now with this circus of a meal going on around her. She swallowed hard and willed her gathering tears just to go away until she was alone in her room.

Besides, her parents didn't show any care or concern about what was best for her future, rather what *they* could boast about to the women of Boston's Junior League and all the other partners at the law firm of Van Gelderen, Schneider, and Fossbaum.

Getting a grip on her brewing emotions, Veronica fingered her long, black hair behind her ears—a fidgeting tactic that always annoyed her mother—and contemplated Mr. Schneider's question about how she would decide between Harvard and Wellesley.

Of course, her mother answered before she could. "We've signed up for summer orientation at both Wellesley and Harvard and put deposits down at each place."

We? Like they were all going off to college together.

"Each place?" Mrs. Schneider asked.

Her mother continued. "You can never be sure these days with how competitive the admissions process is for Veronic'er and her friends."

Friends? Veronica tried not to snort. (Van Gelderens didn't snort, either.) She had never really considered any of the other privileged girls at Boston Academy to be trusted friends. They talked about conquests with boys, their European vacations, and how they didn't need to go to college because they planned on living off their trust funds. Or worse, how they were going to this, that, or the other overpriced pretentious school so their parents could lord it over their peers at cocktail parties.

The only person Veronica considered a *real* friend was her former au pair, Kiersten Douglas. Kiersten had come from the D.C. area to attend Boston's Emerson College and had worked in the Van Gelderen house for extra money. Veronica found Kiersten to be one of the most open, affable, forthright, and trusting people she'd ever met. Different from anyone else in Veronica's life. And it gave her hope that she, too, could be different when she went off to college. Different in a good way. She'd do everything she could to fit in and not be labeled "the rich girl." College would be a fresh start to the next phase of her life.

The Schneiders smiled at Veronica from across the table: shrewd adult smiles, like they knew what was best for her and she couldn't possibly know because she was "only" eighteen. Ah, but eighteen meant she was free to make her own decisions. *Finally!*

"I'm sure you *cahn't* go wrong with either college choice, dear," Mrs. Schneider said, a small dot of lobster stew on her perfectly lipsticked mouth. Veronica found herself hypnotized by the way the liquid just…hung there—judging her, as well.

Mrs. Van Gelderen moved her hand across her Chanel suit and said, "My family has three generations of Wellesley women. So, I'd love for Veronic'er to follow in my footsteps and be the *fahth.*"

Veronica's chest constricted with a morsel of pain as she felt herself vanishing again.

"Mom..."

"Now, Cathryn," her father interrupted sternly. "If she's going to follow in any footsteps, they'll be mine. If the girl wants to be a lawyer, she'll need Harvard University on her résumé."

"Here, here!" Mr. Schneider agreed wholeheartedly. "Hahhh-vahhhd! Hahhh-vahhhd!"

Please don't do any kind of "Yale Sucks" cheer!

Veronica blinked extra hard, feeling like her blue eyes were going to drown in the salty sea brimming on the edge of her lids as the exasperation raged inside. Not that anyone noticed her distress. They were too busy chatting around her, punctuating words with their hands and laughing at what seemed like her expense.

Only seventy-three days until her new life started: 1,752 hours and counting...

The adults chattered on like she wasn't there. Why did they always do that? What ticked her off even more was when they acted like they owned her. Like she wasn't a person with the right to make her own decisions. As much as she appreciated the material things in her life, she'd trade all the Tiffany jewelry, designer clothes, and expensive shoes for just one tangible ounce of their honest love and affection.

Feeling like her lungs might collapse from all the pressure built up inside, she knew she couldn't stay quiet anymore, especially since the Dover sole and *whatever* was gelling before her eyes. Turning to her father, she boldly asked, "What makes you think I want to be a lawyer?"

The graduation keynote speaker—some financial muckety-muck from a downtown Boston firm—spoke to her class about crossing the threshold into adulthood by graduating from high school. Veronica knew from the severe glare on her father's face that she'd just taken one hell of a leap toward it.

"What are you talking about? Of course you'll be an attorney!" he said emphatically. "I've already talked to Christopher O'Leary in the Speaker's office, and you're on the list for an internship next summer in the state capitol. It'll look phenomenal on your résumé."

Veronica set her fork down and wiped her sweaty palms on her napkin. That stupid lump in her throat was still there, threatening to choke her before she could get everything out. Now was the time to reveal her plan, though. The secret she'd kept since March when she'd written a check from her personal account for a deposit on her university of choice. The one she'd chosen quite randomly. But it had been *her* choice.

Due to her extraordinary scores on the SATs, she received e-mails galore from colleges and universities wanting her to join their ranks, or at least to apply. From up and down the East Coast to private universities from the fly-over states and schools on the West Coast, she determined she was going to go anywhere she wanted and break away from the controlling grips of her parents' structured lives and expectations. The world was her proverbial oyster. When a particular e-mail came through promising an electrifying college experience on a beautiful old southern campus, something clicked inside her head and she tapped the mouse to request more information. She knew upon first glance that this quaint university town was where she wanted to spend the next four years—the next phase—of her life. She was an adult, after all, and had made the decision on her own. To do what was best for Veronica Van Gelderen.

I can tell them. I can do this.

Mustering up a substantial, confidence-building breath, she said, "Actually, Dad, I don't plan on becoming a lawyer. That's not what I want from college."

Cathryn Van Gelderen laughed nervously. She turned to her friends. "She's really going for her M-R-S degree."

"It worked for you, Cathryn, dear," Mrs. Schneider cooed.

Veronica resisted the urge to snap that she wasn't going to school merely to look for a rich husband to take care of her. She wanted desperately to scream at the top of her lungs, but that was too childish. She needed to act every bit of her eighteen years right now. And then some.

"What *are* you going to college for then, little lady?" Mr. Schneider asked.

Gross! What was it about older men that they had to talk down to you if you were (1) female, (2) unmarried, (3) under thirty?

He tacked on, "Will it be Wellesley or Harvard?"

She sat tall, thinking *this* little lady was about to take the final step into adulthood.

"Well, I won't be attending either," she announced bravely, her heart banging against her rib cage like she'd just done extra laps in the swimming pool.

Her parents spoke in unison.

"What? You *cahn't*—"

"I've been accepted to Latimer University." She held her head high.

Harrison Van Gelderen seemed to let her news bulletin penetrate his brain. "I've never heard of the place," he said gruffly. "Is it private or public?"

"Public. A state school."

Her father put his hand to his heart, as if shot. "Where is it?"

"In Florida," she said, controlling her own urge to turn the "a" ending into an "er."

"Florid'er?" her mother scoffed. "We're not sending you to school to party."

Veronica leaned forward, hoping she could make her case without crying or losing her cool. Van Gelderens didn't lose their cool...especially in public. "It's not about partying, Mom. It's about finding my place in the world: who I am, what I can do, who I can be."

Her father scowled. "Harvard-educated lawyers know who they are."

"Sure, someone who sits behind a mahogany desk in a two-thousand-dollar Hugo Boss suit!"

"Veronic'er!"

"No, Dad," she said, forging ahead like never before. She'd come this far; there was no turning back now. "I mean, I want to *really* do something that helps people. Something fulfilling and substantial."

"You could be a doctor, then. A physician in the family is respectable," her father said, raising his brow toward his law partner, who was watching the Van Gelderens.

"No, Dad. Thing is, I don't *know* what I want to do."

Her mother gasped. "You what?"

9

"You're giving up Harvard for some backwater school in Florida to go and find yourself?" her father asked with a growl.

Veronica nodded confidently. "Latimer is an excellent school with twelve colleges within it that cover almost any major you can image. I'm going to go there, explore the curriculum, and find out what exactly interests me. Isn't that what college is all about? Discovery?"

And thus started the melee of voices and arguments from the adults at the table, right in the middle of Locke-Ober. Veronica let out the breath she swore she'd been holding, took a mouthful of her baked potato, and sat back as the carnival continued.

No more pretending now. Her secret was out.

"You're not going away for your first year and that's final!"

Lora-Leigh Sorenstein tugged on the bottom one of her six earrings on her left ear and contemplated ripping off her cap and gown and throwing it at her father. But acting like a five-year-old having a temper tantrum wouldn't help matters at all. He'd already sucked the life out of her high school graduation celebration with his stupid decree.

"Why not?" she snapped, hating the way she sounded.

"You're going to Latimer University, and that's that."

"Thomas, Lora-Leigh, not here. Wait until we're at home," Lora-Leigh's mother said in a stage whisper. Louder, she called out, "Smile, you two!" as she clicked away on the digital camera.

Lora-Leigh feigned a smile as her father wrapped his sturdy arm around her shoulder and pulled her to him. Through her fake smile, she said, "I can't believe how frickin' stubborn you're being." Just because he was dean of students at Latimer

University and she could go to school there for free, he thought he could make her decisions for her.

"Stubbornness runs in the family," he said to her.

"I know; I inherited it from you."

Through clenched, still-smiling-for-the-camera teeth, Dean Sorenstein said, "At the end of the first year, we'll sit down, assess where you are, and go from there. But for your first year, you're going to school close to home."

"Yeah, see, I don't get that at all." He was so old-fashioned it wasn't even funny. Her brother never got an edict like this seven years ago when he graduated from high school.

Her father furrowed his brows in that college professor way of his that must have always pulled the shades on his students when he taught. "Lora-Leigh, you're a free spirit and a creative girl, which I admire, but I just don't think you're mature enough to make the right decisions about your future."

"What? I'm eighteen years—"

"And your mother and I feel it would be best for you to stay here for a year so we can watch your development."

"You mean keep an eye on me," she said, feeling her stomach muscles tighten and her future plans slip away.

"Well, yes, dear. Since I work at Latimer and you can go to school tuition-free, it's the best solution for everyone."

Everyone but me.

"Scott got to move away and go to LSU."

Her dad looked her squarely in the eyes. "You aren't your brother."

That was apparent.

Her mother pulled the camera away from her face and

11

looked at the digital image. "I asked you two to behave," she said, eyeballing Lora-Leigh in particular. She looked back down at the camera. "Oh, that was a good one. Look, Thomas, you're smiling nicely."

"Yes, yes," her father said. Shifting back to Lora-Leigh, he asked, "Are we clear on this now? No more talk of other options and fighting your parents? Honestly, Lora-Leigh, it seems that you thrive on rebellion. It's bad enough you've pierced your ears unrecognizable."

Lora-Leigh bit her bottom lip, knowing she was going to act out, not able to stop it. "I'm gonna pierce my lip too. What do you think of that?" That'd show her father, since piercings were apparently the only things she was going to be allowed to do to express herself. "Maybe a tattoo even? A wing-tipped angel from shoulder blade to shoulder blade." She spread her arms wide to demonstrate, laughing at the ridiculousness of it.

"Oh heavens, dear," her mother said, acting like she was going to swoon. "I just won't have that."

"I'm kidding, Mom. Sorry." She hated when her snarkiness upset her mom. "Look, Dad," she attempted one last argument. "You've gotta trust me on this. I want to apply to FIT in New York and—"

"New York?"

"*And* the Fashion Institute in California."

He dismissed her with the wave of a hand.

"You're too young to live alone. Especially all the way out in California. Not knowing anyone. No family. A young girl surrounded by strangers. Who'd take care of you? You need a good, solid education without distractions."

"Why do you sound like a dictator, Dad?"

"Because I love you, and I don't want you to throw your life away on silly pipe dreams."

"Your father's right, Lora-Leigh."

"About being too far from home or not being able to take care of myself?"

"Both." Her mother always agreed with her father...no matter what. She was the diva of the household, making perfect Shabbat dinner every Friday, entertaining his friends from the academic and administrative side of Latimer University, and never going against any of his decisions.

This time, Lora-Leigh took off her red graduation robe and wadded it up under her arm. She was wearing one of her original designs underneath the regalia. Okay, maybe not totally original, since she'd seen the polished denim skirt on Fashion TV and got the idea from the *Project Runway* Season Two DVD to reset a men's suit vest. She thought it looked totally hot and fashionable. Her mother sneered just because it wasn't off the racks of Needless Markup.

"If y'all'd hear me out," Lora-Leigh begged, looking from one parent to the other. "I know you get a deal on the tuition if I go to Latimer, but the fashion design curriculum here is *très* weak. I need to focus and study my craft, really get to know what I'm doing so I'll make it as a fashion designer."

Her father glanced away and took a deep breath. "Lora-Leigh, we've had this discussion a hundred times."

"So make it a hundred and *one*, Dad," she said, with her hand on her hip.

Her mother reached for the wadded up robe and began

smoothing it out. Just like she did at home with Dad's dirty clothes. Lora-Leigh loved her mother, but she couldn't end up like her. A housewife and hostess for a man with a career. Lora-Leigh wanted to make a splash in the world. She wanted to express herself. She didn't see how she could do that stuck in the same town where she was born and raised. New York, L.A.: now those were places where you could really experience life and find yourself.

Her father continued with his speech. "A young woman should be able to take care of herself with the help of loved ones along the way."

"That's exactly what I'm trying to do by starting my own clothing line or maybe even a boutique. You know, Tommy Hilfiger started his design business out of the back of a truck, and now look at him. He's a freakin' fashion icon! The man invented 'Casual Friday.' "

"Tommy Hilfiger isn't my child. Besides, it's different for men," her father said.

"Gee, thanks for the vote of confidence, Dad," Lora-Leigh said with a bit of brashness in her tone, although, quite frankly, she wanted to cry.

"A girl like you needs the fundamentals of education. English literature, history, the sciences, language, mathematics. Those are the things that will get you by day to day, not cutting and sewing. I swear, Hannah, why did you ever give her that sewing machine?"

Mrs. Sorenstein shrugged. "I had one as a girl and thought it would be good for her."

Lora-Leigh rolled her eyes. "There's more to it than that,

Dad. You learn the business. Fashion, design, modeling, retailing, purchasing, what fabrics to use, what the trends are, what's right and wrong. All of it. Don't you understand?"

But he wasn't having any of it. "What kind of income can you earn making dresses for people?"

Lora-Leigh chewed on her lip again and said, "People need clothes. They can't go around *nekkid!*"

Her mother gasped. "Now, Lora-Leigh."

Dr. Sorenstein kept on. "Los Angeles and New York are two of the most expensive cities in America. How would you live in the meantime?"

"I'd get a job."

"Waiting tables?"

"If I have to," Lora-Leigh said a bit too loudly. "Damn right."

"Lora-Leigh . . . shhh," her mother said. "Enough. We'll talk about this later. At home. You don't want the Ledbetter twins and their parents over there to hear you."

God forbid if the Ledbetters—or anyone else for that matter—overhear!

Lora-Leigh sighed. Of course her mother was worried about what people would think, and her dad was concerned about how she'd make a living and support herself. Typical.

"There you are, Lora-Leigh!" someone shouted. It was her best friend, Elizabeth Butler. "Hey, Dr. Sorenstein. Mrs. S."

"Hello, Elizabeth. Congratulations, dear," Lora-Leigh's mother said primly.

"Look, Lora-Leigh, the gang's been talking and we were thinking of road-tripping tomorrow to Molly Ballard's beach house over in Clearwater to celebrate."

Hitching her face into a smirk, Lora-Leigh waited for her father to tell her she couldn't leave the Latimer city limits, but he surprised her. "Sounds like great fun for you kids."

"Yes, sir," Elizabeth said. She pulled her sunglasses from the collar of her robe and secured them over her eyes. "So, I'll pick you up around nine in the morning?"

"You got it, Liz."

Lora-Leigh looked back as Elizabeth hurried off to their group of friends, who were dispersing. The creative bunch from school consisting of Elizabeth, the drama (literally) queen; Frank, the bass player; Bethany, who did the big mural on the side of the Latimer High stadium; and Brian, Lora-Leigh's ex-boyfriend with the shaggy hair, which she knew her mother would love to take a pair of scissors to ASAP. Brian waved over at her and called out, "See you tomorrow!" He was one of those guys who made ridiculously high scores on his SATs, but coasted by in school with a C+ average because he just didn't care. He was laid back and quiet, but he was the one in the gang who could get them beer at the Mini Mart on the corner of Honeysuckle and Fifth.

Mrs. Sorenstein wrapped her arm around Lora-Leigh. "I have a wonderful celebration dinner planned. Several of your father's staff are coming over, and we're having an amazing leg of lamb with mint jelly and roasted baby potatoes just for you."

Lora-Leigh's stomach flipped and groaned at the same time. Not that she didn't love her mother's cooking, it was just that she didn't feel like celebrating. As she watched her friends and their families herding off, she felt stuck. Trapped. In a rut.

Feeling defeated, she shuffled toward the family car. "Can

we just, like, leave now? I want to go home." Back to her room. Back to her sewing machine. Back to the same old routine. She'd have to obey her parents since she had no real savings, and L.A. and NYC were worlds away. Maybe she could play the game for a year. Do as her father wanted and then prove she could make it on her own. At least she'd be able to move into the dorm. Make new friends. Be out from under her parents' always trying to make her conform. She was a creative spirit, indeed, as her father had said. Sure, a lot of kids from Latimer High were also headed to Latimer U, but she wanted to break free from the pack. Thirteenth grade didn't appeal to her.

However, it looked like that was where she was headed.

"All right, Dad," she said with a resigned sigh. "You win... for now. I'll go to Latimer for a year, but after that, we'll talk."

Smiling at her, he reached over and tousled her mortarboard-flattened curls. "That's more like it. And having you at Latimer, I *will* be able to keep an eye on you. Make sure you don't get too wild." At least he winked when he said that.

"Daaaaaaaaaaaad."

Her mother's face lit up. "Oh!! You know what this means, don't you?"

Lora-Leigh slipped into the backseat of her parents' Volvo. "What?"

"This means you can go through formal recruitment! And you can join my sorority!"

The girls of Omega Omega Omega, Lora-Leigh thought contemptuously. She'd seen enough of them at her house over the years in their Burberry and pearls for "alumni teas" and such. Like they'd ever take her. Like she even wanted them to.

17

Her mother forged on. "I'll call Colleen Gagnon, the alumni adviser, and get a recommendation from her. Oh, and Bunny Crenshaw, too. We used to go to mixers together and play Hearts until all hours of the night in the house. You know, the Tri-Omega house is one of the most unique on Latimer's campus. It's shaped like a horseshoe, just like an Omega."

"I know, Mom, I've seen it." Living in Latimer, Lora-Leigh had certainly explored the campus and knew all of its traditions and culture. Like frat parties on Fraternity Row that she and Elizabeth had crashed more than one time.

Her mother took the ball and ran. "Bunny Crenshaw lives just outside of Nashville now, but she'll do a rec for you, no problem. And then we'll get . . . "

While her mother prattled on, Lora-Leigh glanced out the window as her high school football stadium faded out of sight. She looked ahead in the distance as the one for Latimer University drew nearer. Where her future was. But join the Tri-Omegas? Lora-Leigh shook her head at the thought. She'd never fit in with the likes of the campus-ruling Tri-Omegas. She wanted nothing to do with them.

This was going to be the longest summer of her life.

"We did it! We did it! Whooooooooo-hooooooooo!!"

Jenna Driscoll squeezed her classmates as they danced around under the rain of flying mortarboards and tassels. "Pomp and Circumstance" filled the air and made Jenna's skin tingle. Graduation day!

She was suddenly hugged by her friends Casey and Jesey from band; and then Jonathan, Ben, and Sally Ann from student council—people she had spent hordes of time with through the last year. All of her friends were there, celebrating and congratulating one another. It was a perfect day.

"We're totally celebrating tonight, Jenna," Sarah Burlington, her best friend, said. "Nathan and Patrick are having a major party at their house. Swimming, kegs, and tons of food. They're pit-barbecuing a whole hog!"

Jenna sighed hard and waited for the inevitable. The same reaction she'd gotten for the last year, since her diagnosis. Everyone knew. And everyone treated her with kid gloves due to it.

Lily Wilbourne knocked Sarah on the arm with a noogied fist and said, "Dumb shit, you know Jenna can't party with us like that." Jenna watched her friend's eyes widen. "You know . . . the 'betes."

Sarah gasped and put her hand to her mouth. "Oh, I'm totally sorry, Jenna. I wasn't thinking. You know me, I always forget."

"It's okay, Sare," Jenna said.

"It doesn't mean you can't still come to the party," Lily added.

"Yeah, just come and be there. You don't have to drink."

She couldn't really do *anything*, Jenna thought. Even now.

Jenna heaved a sigh and bent to find her mortarboard in the pile. The 'betes had kept Jenna from so much in her senior year of high school. Not her participation in almost every club on campus—Beta Club, Concert Band, Academic Bowl, Environmental Club, French Club, and Future Business Leaders of America, just to name a few—but it had put a damper on her social activities. It kept her from enjoying her friends' eighteenth birthday parties, the class dessert swap at

Easter, and every significant end-of-school party that had booze, music, and boys.

The 'betes (as Jenna's little sister Jayne called it) was diabetes, which she'd been diagnosed with only a year and a half ago. Jenna had been healthy as a horse her whole life until—*bam!*—suddenly she lost a ton of weight, blacked out during a band concert, and had to be rushed to the emergency room, where the doctors gave their verdict.

"Can't you have a couple of beers?" Lily asked. "What's the harm?"

"The harm is, she'd like . . . almost die or something," Sarah said.

Jenna ran her hand down her left side where her insulin pump sat on her hip like a doctor's pager, continuously monitoring her glucose level. She thought about how she could dial in a little more insulin or just eat something as she nursed a beer all night, but where would the fun be in that? Everyone would still look at her as "Sick Jenna."

It was a pain in the butt keeping track of everything she ate or drank and making sure she didn't go "high" or "low" or pass out all together. The worst part about it was that everyone and his brother in the metro Atlanta area knew about the 'betes, thanks to her mother, her teachers, and her friends broadcasting it to anyone who would listen. There was never a day when she was just Jenna, able to enjoy regular teenage things—like Nathan and Patrick's party tonight.

"It's not really smart to drink," Jenna said, although it was exactly what she wanted to do. Belong and fit in again.

Sarah hugged her. "You can be designated driver."

"I'm always the designated driver." Not that she wanted to get sloppy drunk or anything, but she was eighteen, for heaven's sake, and a graduating senior. After all, having a good time was a rite of passage. One she felt was zipping by her on a Jet Ski while she remained in a canoe.

She looked over at a nearby group of classmates yucking it up for the camera. Dead center was hunk-and-a-half Matthew Caldwell, president of the French Club, whom she'd been crushing on all year. They'd had a massive flirtation the end of junior year, and she thought she might be in for a senior year boyfriend. Sadly, when the 'betes news got out, it made people pull away from her and treat her differently. Not in a bad way, just in a you're-too-delicate-now fashion.

Matthew waved at her now and then turned to head off with his friends. Jenna waved to his back, heaved a sigh, and watched him walk away. So much for that crush.

Just wait until I go off to college and no one knows anything about me.

"There you are!" her mom, Olivia Hopkinton, shouted out as she rushed toward Jenna. Jenna's heart expanded seeing the look of überpride on her mom's face. "We're sooooo proud of you, sweetie!"

Enveloped in her mom's arms and showered with kisses, Jenna momentarily forgot her social troubles and hugged back. Soon, she felt more arms join in on the hugfest as her little sisters—Jordan (five), Jayne (seven), and Jessica (nine)—piled around them. Jenna loved her family so much it hurt sometimes. She put her Matthew crush out of her mind and squeezed her eyes shut as she enjoyed the family's smother loving.

21

"Mom, you're not crying, are you?" she asked.

She wiped her face. "Of course I am! It's not every day my baby graduates from high school."

"I thought I was your baby," Jordan cried out.

"You're all my babies," Jenna's mom said.

"But how come Jenna's a baby?" Jordan asked. "She's eighteen."

Jenna watched her mom scoop up the five-year-old—with a grunt—and set her on her hip.

"Yes, Jenna's a big girl, just like you'll be one day."

Jenna reached out and played with one of Jordan's long, blonde ringlets, whose color matched her own hair. *Oh man, this one's gonna be a heartbreaker*, she thought.

"And I can go away to college too?"

"Absolutely! All of my girls are going to be smart and have fun and make lots of friends and get great jobs and have beautiful futures." Jenna's mom was Miss Mary Sunshine, despite all the hurt she'd had in her life, and Jenna totally admired her for that. "Your sister's just paving the way for you."

A smile danced across her face as Jenna pictured her not-too-distant future. She couldn't believe that in only two months, she'd be stepping onto the campus of Latimer University as one of the twenty-five hundred freshmen matriculating to her new central-Florida home. A home that promised academic excellence, a chance to stand out in the marching band—she was one hell of a trumpet player and had received a scholarship—and just enjoy the next step in her life.

I can't wait!

While she loved her passel of Little Js, there was always the added responsibility of being the big sis, watching out for them and making sure they were taken care of. It would be nice to be responsible only for herself. Not getting Jessica to ballet class or picking up Jayne from her play dates. Or making sure Jordan wasn't gorging on too many Barbie DVDs.

Fred Hopkinton, Jenna's stepfather, eased forward and kissed her on the forehead. "You girls will have some big shoes to fill once Jenna leaves home." He winked at her and patted her on the shoulder. "I'm awfully proud of you, sweetie."

"Thanks, Fred," Jenna said, with a lump her throat. Fred had been more of a father to her than her real dad had ever been. She constantly tried blocking out that morning when her father, through a haze of Jack Daniel's, had kissed her on the cheek and said good-bye. He'd apparently decided he loved alcohol more than he loved her and her mother. She hadn't heard from him since.

"Why don't my beautiful girls stand together for a picture," he said, pulling the camera out of his pocket.

"Didn't you get enough pictures already, Dad?" Jessica asked impatiently.

Jenna pinched her lovingly on the shoulder, and her sister straightened up for the photo. Yeah, she was going to miss her family, but stepping away from the semiparental role was going to be good for her. And so what that she couldn't really live it up at Nathan and Patrick's "major" graduation party tonight. So what that Matthew Caldwell's big brown eyes would soon become a distant memory. There'd be plenty of time for boys and parties once she got to Latimer.

"I think I'll go to the graduation party later," Jenna said as they walked to the van.

"But sweetie, we have reservations downtown at Aunt Pittypat's Porch. You know how much Fred loves their amazing peach cobbler with vanilla ice cream."

"I love it, too."

Her mother turned. "Jenna, you know that's not good for your—"

"I'll dial in a little more insulin," she said, looking at the digital readout on her pump. The device supplied the needed medication in a small tube connected to a needle inserted in her hip.

"But, Jenna—"

"Don't, Mom. Not today. Just one day to be normal."

"What can I say? I'm a mother hen."

Jenna smiled again. "I know, Mom. But this chick's about to fly from the nest."

And wing my way south to Florida!

CHAPTER
2

Lora-Leigh squinted at the setting August sun peeking through the slats of the fence in Brian Gregory's backyard. Brian leaned against said fence with a beer in his hand, eyes closed, listening intently to the alternative-rock music playing. The Green Day–esque local band, The Violent Hiccups, had been playing cover songs off and on all afternoon, but they were about to crank it up with some original tunes of their own for the rest of the night.

Lora-Leigh watched Brian tap his foot and mouth the words to the hit song. *He's still a babe*, she thought of her junior-year boyfriend, the guy hosting the college-send-off party for the former seniors of Latimer High School.

Yeah . . . send off down the street for me.

"You're still sulking, aren't you?" Elizabeth Butler interrupted Lora-Leigh's thoughts, shouting over the bass solo. She and Elizabeth had been best friends since seventh grade. They'd gotten their periods the same week, crushed on many of the same guys, and pierced their ears (the second time for Lora-Leigh) together at the pavilion in the mall. Now, Elizabeth was abandoning her and heading north to Pittsburgh to attend Carnegie Mellon. Stupid place was giving her a pretty sweet scholarship.

"I'm not sulking," Lora-Leigh said, knowing damn well she was.

"Like hell you're not."

"Okay . . . so maybe I am a little."

"You've been like this all summer."

"It's just depressing to see everyone one last time before they all head out of the city limits, leaving me here to go to Latimer. Did you know that I can tell you where all one hundred and fifteen people in our senior class are going, what they're doing with their futures?"

"Lora-Leigh, you don't have to—"

She couldn't stop herself. Flashing her right hand five times, she said, "Twenty-five are going into the armed services, including Dan Lefkowitz to West Point, Margarita Escobar to the U.S. Air Force Academy, and the Dunbar twins to the U.S. Naval Academy."

Elizabeth snickered. "Ronald and Donald in the navy? Our country's doomed."

"Twenty-eight kids are going to out-of-state colleges, including Porter Ethridge, who's heading to the University of Hawaii . . . little shit."

"Yeah, he'll probably drown himself in the Banzai Pipeline."

Lora-Leigh kept ticking numbers off on her fingers. "Another twenty are leaving Latimer to either take a job or take a year off to go to Europe, travel to other places, or just find themselves, in general. Ten people are getting married and staying in Latimer, most getting jobs at LU. Eighteen others are headed for other Florida colleges like FSU, Florida, Miami, South Florida, and Stetson."

"I can't believe you're keeping track of this, Sorenstein. You're a loser."

"Listen to me, Elizabeth," she said, taking a deep breath. She was almost done making her point. "That leaves fourteen losers, like *moi*, who are going to Latimer University."

"Okay," Elizabeth noted. "Nine of those people are on athletic scholarships."

"Right... and the five remaining are all girls who are peeing themselves to participate in sorority recruitment. Except me."

"Are you finished?" Elizabeth asked, her brows lowered.

"Yes." She felt like her *life* was finished.

"You've known all summer that this day would come."

"Doesn't mean I like it." Shoulders slumping, Lora-Leigh said, "I guess the reality of it's just hitting me now."

Elizabeth set down her stadium cup of pink liquid—Brian's attempt at a Hurricane—and frowned at Lora-Leigh. "There are people you know from LHS going to LU. Nancy Pickett's going there and Molly Ballard, too. She's cool. You hung out with her sometimes in Drama Club, right?"

Nodding, Lora-Leigh reached for her own plastic stadium cup and took a deep sip of the potent concoction she was trying not to drink too fast. "She's okay. But she's psyched for sorority recruitment. She's been into it since we were in junior high."

"And she's actually excited to go to LU," Elizabeth pointed out. She reached behind her for the bag of Barbecue Lay's Potato Chips that sat open on the picnic table. After cramming a handful of broken chips into her mouth, Elizabeth said, "Remember how we rode our bikes over to Sorority Row each September to watch the new sorority girls running for their houses? Just think... you'll be doing that run yourself soon." She nudged Lora-Leigh with her elbow.

Lora-Leigh's heart sank to her stomach. Was she going to have to participate in that? Would she even get that far in the process? She was, after all, going through the motions only for her mother.

"I really don't want to talk about it."

Elizabeth got quiet for a few minutes, munching the chips and seemingly listening to The Violent Hiccups cranking out an original tune of theirs entitled "Terrell Owens Is My Bitch."

Lora-Leigh took another sip of her drink and nodded in time to the music. "The drummer's pretty hot, isn't he?"

Shrugging, Elizabeth said, "I prefer the lead singer. Those tight jeans do it for me."

They stood there in silence while the band blared on. Lora-Leigh could tell Elizabeth was frustrated with her. It was hard for Elizabeth truly to understand what was going on in Lora-Leigh's head because Elizabeth was escaping the confines of Latimer, Florida.

It wasn't that Lora-Leigh hated her hometown. And she'd traveled plenty with her parents when her father went to educational conferences. Still, it didn't compare to going away to school.

The lead singer of The Violent Hiccups announced, "We'll be back after this break," and the crowd dispersed into Brian's house for more refreshment of an alcoholic nature.

"So, where were you all week?" Elizabeth asked, and then drained her cup. "I left like a kazillion voice mails."

"I was at orientation," Lora-Leigh said, nearly choking on the words. She should have been on Fashion Avenue in NYC rubbing elbows with the teachers at FIT and shopping at Mood Fabric Store for her first class project. But no . . . she was picking out her core curriculum classes for freshman semester at LU.

"What classes did you get?" Elizabeth asked.

"Western Civ, Sociology, English Composition 101, Algebra, and I signed up for Art 110."

"What's that?"

Lora-Leigh smiled. "It's a basic studio course focusing on comprehension of visual concepts and development of skills through exposure to drawing media."

Laughing, Elizabeth said, "You sound like the student catalogue."

"I sort of memorized the course description," Lora-Leigh admitted unashamedly.

"That's great. See, you're not being stymied. After you get your core classes done, then you can start taking more classes in the design program and have a more art-related focus."

"If I'm still there. If my father makes me stay longer than a year," Lora-Leigh said, and then drained her cup. The rum and Kool-Aid mixture was starting to relax her a bit, to the point where she wasn't dwelling on what was ahead for her. Her chest also ached when she thought about Elizabeth getting on a plane and heading north.

She leaned into her friend and laid her head on her shoulder. "When are you leaving me?"

Elizabeth toed the gravel underneath her sandals and stared at the ground. "I was afraid you were gonna ask that."

"So...when?"

"Friday," Elizabeth said, as though she were trying not to sound excited about her own future.

Choking up all of a sudden, Lora-Leigh turned away.

Elizabeth was upon her in a heartbeat. Since she was much taller than Lora-Leigh's five feet six inches, her arms wrapped around Lora-Leigh's shoulders while her head rested next to Lora-Leigh's mass of curls. "You're not losing me, Sorenstein. I don't shake that easily. We're lifers, remember."

Riiiiiight, Lora-Leigh thought. When they were thirteen, they'd declared each other Friends for Life, or lifers, as they referred to themselves.

"Just 'cause I'm in Pennsylvania and you're here in Latimer does *not* mean we'll lose each other. I mean, sure, I'm going to make new friends but so will you. It's going to happen. But it's not a bad thing. If you get over yourself, you might actually enjoy recruitment and meeting new people."

Lora-Leigh shook her head. "I've told you, I'm *so* not joining a sorority. They're all alike. I'd much rather spend time concentrating on my designs and not getting behind the fashion trends." Her stacks of *Vogue, Elle, Jane,* and *Marie Claire* were a testament to that. *Have to remember to have the subscriptions sent to my campus P.O. box!*

"Oh, that reminds me," Elizabeth said. "I'm going out with Judson before I leave for Pittsburgh. Sort of a last-hurrah thing." Judson and Elizabeth had been dating since the beginning of the school year, and he was almost as devastated as Lora-Leigh that Elizabeth was leaving. "I was going to go buy a new outfit, but maybe you can give me some suggestions. Don't want to be too dressy, or too understated."

Closing her eyes, Lora-Leigh concentrated for a moment.

"What are you doing?" her friend asked.

"Shhh... I'm visualizing your closet." After a moment, she opened her eyes. "Wear your tan Banana Republic pants with that thick brown belt, your white button-down stretch blouse, and lots of chunky jewelry—I'm talking bracelets and neck-laces. It'll really set off your thin neck and long limbs."

"Wow. I didn't think of doing that. Damn, Lora-Leigh. Who's going to dress me in college?"

"You're gonna have to start watching the Style Network, *mamacita*," she said, tapping her plastic cup to Elizabeth's.

Just then, someone grabbed Lora-Leigh from behind, spun her around, and started dancing with her to the CD the band had left playing in the background. She craned her neck and saw that it was Brian Gregory. Definitely toasted.

"You like the band, Sorenstein?"

Lora-Leigh returned a smile to the blue-eyed blond in front of her. From a distance, Brian was a hot guy for sure, but up close he was even better. For one amazing month junior year, they'd dated steadily and had even made out in the game room here at his house. He was one of the ones stepping up for duty in the armed services and would be leaving next week for boot camp on

Parris Island. Brian, a responsible Marine? She totally couldn't see it, but she respected the hell out of him for doing it.

"They're not bad," she said, cataloging how cute he still was. "I heard them back in the fall when we went to that Kappa Omega frat party at LU."

"Oh, I remember that," Elizabeth piped up. "The drummer *was* flirting with me. Maybe I should check him out again."

Lora-Leigh shook her head and took another sip.

"What's up with you?" Brian asked Lora-Leigh.

"Ignore her. She's being a party pooper," said Elizabeth.

"Why?" Brian asked, rubbing the back of Lora-Leigh's neck in a way that made her want to start purring.

"Don't go there," Elizabeth warned.

"'Cause all of y'all are leaving, and I'll be stuck at LU." Lora-Leigh stopped for a moment and listened to herself. *Whine, whine, whine!* She slipped her fingers into her hair and let out a guttural growl. "Oh, my God! I bore myself. I say the same thing over and over. Enough!"

"Thatta girl," Elizabeth said, patting her on the back. "I knew the old Lora-Leigh would come around. The Lora-Leigh who doesn't give a shit about what people think. The Lora-Leigh who marches to her own drummer."

"You're so dramatic, Elizabeth."

"So are you," Brian added. With that, his hand slipped around her waist and pulled her tightly to him.

Lora-Leigh tried to act like he was annoying her, but the rum buzz skittering through her system made her get over her hard-to-get instincts. After all, this was Brian. Her ex. Her friend. And he'd be leaving Latimer in five days. The thought of it gave her goose bumps on her arms, which didn't go unnoticed by Brian.

"Are you cold?"

The pressure in her chest was immense and palpable. "No . . . yeah . . . I don't know."

"Come inside with me," Brian said.

Elizabeth raised her drink in a toast and winked. Lora-Leigh's heart expanded, wondering when she'd get to hang with her friend next. Pittsburgh was a hell of a long way from central Florida, as was Parris Island and wherever Brian would get shipped off to after boot camp.

Lora-Leigh followed him into the expansive ranch-style house filled with former Latimer seniors partying it up, saying goodbye, and getting ready for the next stage of their lives. Brian led her through the throngs of people congregating around Captain Morgan in the kitchen, and down into the basement, where she remembered the game room was located, butted up against a storage area, a bathroom, and the laundry room.

He headed straight for the dryer and took out a Latimer Track Team sweatshirt that had obviously been fluffed earlier in the day. "Here you go. That'll help."

She took it from him, layered it over her spaghetti-strap tank-top, and smoothed its length down over her thrift-store jeans. Then she lifted her eyes to his face. "Thanks. Mmm . . . Downy freshness," she said, trying to dance around her brimming emotions.

His grin spread wide, revealing perfectly straight white teeth. "Thank my mom."

Looking at his bronzed skin and flirty smile, Lora-Leigh

forgot all about her Latimer U sentencing and reached forward to hug him again.

The rum buzz was getting the best of her, anesthetizing her to the self-pity she was trying hard to tamp down. "I'd rather thank *you*."

Brian enveloped her in his arms, making her troubles melt away. "I know what's bothering you, and trust me, you're gonna be okay, Lora-Leigh."

"Oh yeah?" she asked, muffled against his chest.

"Sure. I mean, what the hell. You have to stay in Latimer for one year. Big frickin' deal."

But it *was* a big frickin' deal. The biggest. Her dreams of FIT or the Fashion Institute were slipping down the drain. Another year in Latimer. At this pace, she may never break free and be her own person.

Brian lifted her face up with a finger under her chin. "I know it sucks that your dad's making you stay and treating you like you can't take care of yourself, but if anyone can make the best out of this situation, it's Lora-Leigh Sorenstein."

Her heart pounded extra hard at his encouragement. "Why do you say that?"

Brian swallowed, and she watched his Adam's apple dip down. "Because you've always known what you wanted in life. You've never cared what other people think. Don't change."

She shrugged. He did have a point there. She was the one who'd designed her own prom gown instead of spending a fortune at Macy's. She was the one who'd single-handedly designed the costumes for the senior play and then helped sew a good portion of them. She'd written the fashion column for the school newspaper, throwing popular trends into the wind for thrift stores and discount houses. Her mother always called her an original, and Lora-Leigh had prided herself on always staying true to what she believed.

"So you go to LU for a year, you do whatever you want, keep designing clothes and being you. And then next year, you never know what might happen. I mean, I wanted to go to college, and the best way to pay for it was the Marine Corps."

"You're father's an orthodontist," she said, realizing it was none of her business.

"Yeah, but there are three kids behind me who'll all be in college at the same time," he said, speaking of his triplet siblings. "It would be selfish of me to eat up all of my parents' savings when I can go earn the college money as easily myself."

"That's mighty grown up of you."

He shrugged. "That's what my mom said."

Lora-Leigh lowered her eyes. "I wouldn't exactly call toting a gun easy, though."

"You're right. It's a massive commitment, but I know if I put in my time and do my duty, then I can pretty much write my own ticket anywhere."

It was a great comparison. Sure, Lora-Leigh wasn't going to have to learn how to defend herself or the country, for that matter. However, she could take advantage of the fashion design and art classes at Latimer and maybe even get involved in the theater's costume department to enhance her skills. Of course, she'd continue to make and model her own creations.

The ache in her chest began to subside. "Thanks, Brian.

You're right. I've got to find a middle ground and try to make the best of this situation." Glancing at him, she experienced that old familiar volt of attraction. "When did you get so smart?"

"I've always been this smart. I just pretend to be a dumb blond," he said with a jovial laugh.

"I'm gonna miss you, Brian."

"I'm gonna miss you, too, Lora-Leigh," he said, holding her a little closer.

She slipped her hands up over his shoulders, clasping her fingers together behind his head. His blond curls—which would be shaved off soon by Uncle Sam—tickled her hands.

He looked down at her. "Remember hanging out here junior year?"

"Umm-hmm . . ."

A smirk appeared on his lips. "Wanna relive it for old time's sake?"

"Why?" she teased.

"Because I'm, like, going off to war and stuff."

Lora-Leigh giggled and raked her fingers through his thick hair. His head lowered, and Lora-Leigh felt her body shiver as his lips touched hers. Just as soft and warm as they'd been a year ago.

As the kiss deepened, Lora-Leigh relaxed, closed her eyes, and thought that if Brian could go off and join the Marines, then she could handle one year at Latimer University.

Jenna blasted the air conditioner to subzero and steered her mother's Dodge Caravan into the middle lane of Interstate 85.

She was headed north through Atlanta's busy downtown area, which was congested with bumper-to-bumper rush-hour traffic.

"Sweetie, I need you to pick up Jessica in Buckhead at Deliah Fischer's house," her mom said over the cell phone.

Jenna held the device to her ear with her shoulder as she tried to avoid the cab that was cutting her off. She wanted to curse at him, but Jordan was happily strapped in her car seat in the back, watching the latest Disney DVD Fred had bought to entertain her. Instead, Jenna gritted her teeth and counted to five. "I'm taking Jordan to the mall at Lenox to pick up the tights her teacher said she needs for her jazz class."

"Will you have time?"

"I'm making time, Mom."

Exasperated, Jenna blew out of her eyes the wisps of blonde hair that had escaped her messy ponytail. Her mom worked full time as an admin assistant at the Marriott downtown, and often-times she had to work late when they had big groups in. It was Jenna's responsibility to shuttle the Little Js around town, getting them to whatever summer activity was going on. There was dance, of course, but there was also soccer, softball, and swimming classes. Jenna might as well be driving out to Hartsfield International Airport, picking up passengers and charging a fee for it, for as many miles as she added to her mom's minivan.

Someone had to do it, though, and that someone was always Jenna. She didn't mind helping out usually, but today she was at the end of her patience. Sure, there had been a period after she'd first been diagnosed with the 'betes when her mom and Fred had backed off on asking her to do things for her sisters. However, that grace period ended when Fred and her mom's jobs both became more hectic and time-consuming. There hadn't been time this summer for Jenna to prepare for what was ahead of her. College. Being on her own.

"Jenna! I want ice cream!" Jordan shouted from her seat.

"Okay, sweetie. We've got to pick up Jayne from Vacation Bible School, and then we'll stop and get something after we get Jessica." That was if they could ever get through this traffic.

"No! Noooooooooooow!"

The tension started at Jenna's left temple, so she breathed deeply to combat it. "Please, Jordan. Good girls don't scream like that."

Nearly half an hour later, Jenna pulled into the parking lot of the First Methodist Church only to have Jayne and two of her friends noisily climb in covered with enough finger paint to decorate Turner Field. They made the extra stop to get Jessica and then stopped at a corner ice cream place to try to combat the simmering Georgia heat (and get Jayne washed up). Sweat rolled down Jenna's back, even though the air conditioner continued going full blast.

The kids were screaming and bickering with one another, and Jenna could barely concentrate on where they had to go next.

Her cell phone rang again. "Hello?" Jenna asked with a sigh.

"Are you coming to the party tonight?" Sarah asked.

Pulling the van back onto the busy street, Jenna said, "I don't think I can. Fred's flying home from Chicago tonight. Mom's going to get him, so I have to watch the kids."

"I'm no kid," Jessica, nine, piped up.

"Whatever," Jenna said, trying to keep the peace. Into her phone, she said, "Doesn't look good, Sare."

"We've barely seen you this summer, Jenna, and you'll be leaving for Latimer in a week. Can't you get out of it?"

Story of my life.

Even though she loved her siblings, the answer was simple. *No, I can't get out of it.*

One more week and she'd be headed off to her college life. To some peace and quiet. No longer would she be the one responsible for helping the girls with their homework and getting them bathed, in bed, and quiet so her parents could have some alone time. They both worked so hard just to make ends meet that Jenna hated even thinking about complaining. Still, she longed for that time when she wouldn't have to be the big sister in charge of everything. In college, she could mix into the crowd, find friends, and do things that *she* wanted to do.

"Sare, maybe I can stop by for a little bit later... after my parents get back."

Sarah sighed into the phone herself. "What time'll that be?"

"Tenish?"

"We'll definitely still be going by tenish. Unless you can bail earlier."

"Definitely not. I can't just walk away from my responsibilities." It was true. Jenna knew no other way. She volunteered at the church, she helped her mom out with office mailings, she taught Jayne how to play the piano. It had always been second nature to Jenna to ... do. College life, though, promised a whole new opportunity for her. A whole new Jenna. Sure, she'd miss her family, but she wouldn't miss having to be... the parent.

Sarah snickered. "It's time for Jenna Driscoll to run away from home."

I am . . . running away to Latimer.

"I'll try to come, I promise," Jenna said, wanting to believe her words to be true. "I want to see y'all and have some fun." She definitely deserved it.

"Well," Sarah said, "if you can get away, try. I'll save a burger for you."

"Thanks. I appreciate it."

Later that night, Jenna watched the clock and tapped her foot impatiently. Her mother had promised they'd come straight home from the airport so Jenna could get to Sarah's party. As the digital readout on the cable box clicked to 9:48 P.M., Jenna felt the evening completely melting away.

"Great," she said, and flung herself on the couch. She checked the monitor on her left hip and made sure her insulin level was okay, then tugged at her polo shirt to cover the device the best she could. Even though her friends knew about her condition, she still hated to have the thing showing all the time.

Just then a door banged open and in rushed her mother. "We're back! We're back!" She tossed the keys over to Jenna. "I'm sorry we're so late. Go, go, go! Enjoy yourself, but behave."

Without having to think twice about it, Jenna snagged the keys and bolted out the door. She hopped in and backed the van out onto the residential street, and five minutes later, she was at Sarah's house at the end of a cul-de-sac.

Music blared from the backyard, and a dull buzz of voices and laughter mixed together in the late night air. Jenna stopped at Val Bianchi's Beemer—a graduation present from her father—and checked her hair in the window. The windows were majorly tinted to the point you couldn't see in; however, it was the perfect mirror at the moment. Jenna had flat-ironed her hair for an older, more mature look. It looked great, if she said so herself. She leaned in to make sure she didn't have anything in her teeth and wondered if her crush, Matthew Caldwell, and his big, brown eyes would be at the party. Sarah said he'd mentioned that he'd stop by. Maybe he'd finally put a move on Jenna. Or, what the hell . . . maybe she could try putting one on him.

"Jennnnnnnna, you made it!" Sarah called out.

"Hey," Jenna said in return.

"You're here!" Lily Wilbourne shouted.

Lily ran up behind Sarah, and the two of them stumbled over together to where Jenna stood. They wrapped their arms around Jenna and hung off her like a suit. "Ohhhhmuhgod, Jenna. I luuuuv you sooooo much," Lily said in a slur.

"I love y'all, too."

"We've been drinkin' since, like, sundown," Sarah said. "Toooooooooore up, baby!"

"Whooo-hoooo!" Lily echoed.

This is ridiculous.

Not only had Jenna arrived late to the party, everyone was sloshed and way beyond repair. She pursed her lips and sighed, hating that she'd been held back from the fun once again. "Y'all! I can't hold you both up."

Lily doubled over laughing and spilled the beer out of her cup all over Jenna's shoes.

"Can't take you anywhere," Sarah said with a laugh.

All around the yard people danced to the loud music. The food table looked like it had been ravaged by desperately hungry cast members of *Survivor*. She really had missed out on everything.

"Jennnnna," Lily said, "holy shit, you should have seen it!"

"Yeah," Sarah said more sympathetically. "You totally missed it."

"Missed what? Seen what?" Jenna asked, trying to steady both of her trashed friends.

"Matthew and Val."

Jenna raised her brow. "Matthew . . . and Val Bianchi?"

Lily covered her mouth with her hand and giggled like a little kid. "Dude, they were totally going at it. Like he was pe'formin' a tonsillectomy on her!"

"Ewwwww . . . ," Jenna managed to say through her pulse freaking out. *Her* Matthew kissing Val Bianchi? "When?"

"He's been followin' her around all night," Sarah explained, now with a concerned look. Jenna suspected her best friend was sort of clued in on her crush on Matthew. "It happened when they were slow dancin', and they just started kissin'."

Jenna felt the warm tears well up in her eyes. She'd been totally gone on Matthew Caldwell since he'd transferred to their school in tenth grade. With her health problems and the curtailing of her social life, she never had the time to do anything about it. Now she never would. She didn't want her friends to see how upset she was, but Sarah wasn't stupid—even though she was drunk.

"I'm sorry," she said to Jenna as Lily wandered back over to the keg for a refill.

"No biggie," Jenna said, hoping her voice wouldn't crack.

"Don't worry. You won't have to see them," Sarah said. "They left anyway. Said they were going out to her car."

Jenna stood tall and nearly shrieked. "No way! Her car? It's parked out front." She remembered doing the hair-and-teeth check in the glass. Oh God! Had they seen her primping? Were Matthew and Val in there laughing at her? Or worse, occupying themselves in such a manner that they didn't see her at all? *I don't want to know.*

What she did know was she couldn't wait to leave for Latimer. She was counting the days.

Veronica sat at the sidewalk café on Boylston Street with her Prada sunglasses firmly in place as she waited for her friend.

She'd known Kiersten Douglas, her former au pair, since she was eleven and Kiersten was nineteen. Kiersten had been there for her many times when her parents were too busy with their social obligations. She was the one who talked to Veronica before bedtime. She was the one who was there when Veronica might let a tear or two slip out after being mistreated by someone she thought was a friend. And Kiersten was the one who encouraged her to get out into the world and do what *she* wanted to do, not what her parents expected.

She spotted her friend coming down Boylston Street through the throng of late-summer tourists and businesspeople out and about for a quick lunch. Veronica waved as Kiersten, dressed in a smart pantsuit, her sandy hair pulled back, bypassed the line outside of the Parish Café and scooted over to where Veronica was sitting.

Kiersten hugged her and kissed her on the cheek. "I'm so glad you called me," she said, nearly out of breath. "It's been crazy at the office with the launching of our new Web-based products. I had to do a lot of the graphics for it."

Veronica's eyes grew wide in awe of her friend. She'd graduated from Emerson with honors, gotten a stellar Web-design job here in town straight out of school, and was dating a gorgeous Boston College law-school student named Phillip.

"I'm glad you could get away from the office," Veronica said. "I haven't seen you in a few weeks."

"I know. I'm sorry about that. I know this is an important time for you, what with getting ready to go off to school," Kiersten said, reaching across for Veronica's hand. "I'm here for you now, Roni."

Veronica smiled in relief, not wanting to be a burden to her long-time friend. She knew Kiersten worked hard and had her own life now—separate from working for the Van Gelderens— but Veronica still felt that special connection to her.

They signaled the server and ordered two of the restaurant's famed Zuni rolls—turkey, bacon, Havarti cheese, scallions, and cranberry-chipotle sauce—along with an iced tea for Kiersten.

"So," Kiersten started, "how's the preparation going for heading down to Latimer?"

Veronica had already told Kiersten about her decision earlier in the summer when they'd gotten together for dinner one night. "I'm almost all packed. It's going to be weird not needing as many heavy winter clothes."

Kiersten set down her iced tea. "I'm so jealous of you, going to Florida. That's wonderful, Roni. You're going to have a great time and make so many new friends."

"I hope so!" It was all she wanted. To get away from her parents' iron rule and discover a world outside of her Beacon Hill address. Veronica reached into her Hermés bag and pulled out the informational packet she'd received from Latimer University. "I got all of this in the mail the other day."

She spread the information out on the table between them. "There's a lot to do at Latimer. It's a fantastic school with a popular football team, a well-respected liberal arts curriculum, a strong and active Greek community, and plenty of well-rounded extracurricular activities."

Smiling, Kiersten said, "It's obvious you've been reading their marketing materials."

Veronica chuckled, although she was quite serious about this. *"This* is where I belong."

"Have you decided on a major yet?"

Nipping her bottom lip with her teeth, she thought for a minute. "I have orientation right before school starts, but I've been e-mailing with this junior named Beverly Chang, who's been answering questions for me. I can load up on my core classes and liberal arts selections, and, even though they'd like you to declare your major immediately, I don't have to do it definitively until the beginning of junior year."

"Sounds like you've got everything planned." Kiersten smiled heartily and patted Veronica's hand. "So, Roni, have you thought about joining a sorority?"

Now *this* was something she wanted to talk to Kiersten about. Her pulse quickened just thinking about it. "I definitely want to! After all the stories you've told me over the years about how special your sorority sisters were to you and how you still keep in touch with them, it sounds like something I've got to do."

"Did you get anything from Panhellenic?" Kiersten asked. Veronica knew through Kiersten and her own research that the Panhellenic Association was the office that oversaw the Greek organizations on a college campus.

Plundering through her large packet of Latimer information, Veronica withdrew the printed-out Web pages from the university's site. "Here, check this out."

Kiersten took the information and scanned through it. "Oh, it's too bad that they don't have my house, Beta Phi Beta."

"I know," Veronica said, remembering well all the stories Kiersten had told her over the years about her Beta Phi Beta sisters. She even knew a couple of the sorority's songs that she and Kiersten had sung—and harmonized—together when it was just the two of them. "They have ten sororities, though."

Kiersten read through the list and made comments like "I've heard good things about them" or "They're huge nationally."

"This is going to be such an extraordinary experience for you, Roni," she said.

Veronica thought back to last week when she was shopping on Newbury Street with her group of high school friends. They were all going to "designer" schools—ones their parents could gush about—and they had bagged on her choice of college.

"I can't believe you turned down Wellesley *and* Harvard, Veronica. Like, how stupid was *that*?" one friend had said.

"Yeah, to go where?" another asked.

"Latimer University. In Florida," she'd said proudly.

"Whatever."

They didn't understand her. All they comprehended were posh party invitations; hip, trendy restaurants; road-tripping to Manhattan to hit Fifth Avenue; and guys who carried their daddy's Black Card. Veronica knew there must be more to life . . . more to true friendship.

"Here you go, ladies," the server said, setting the warm Zuni rolls and sides of potato salad in front of them.

For a moment, Veronica stared at the cranberry-chipotle sauce with the trail of sour cream through it that sat decoratively to the left of her sandwich. She didn't want to dwell on the negative things in her life—like her former classmates or her parents' expectations. She was taking bold steps to make herself happy. *Truly* happy—perhaps for the first time in her life.

Kiersten interrupted her thoughts. "So, are you excited to leave?"

Veronica didn't have to think twice about it. "Yes, I am."

"You'll love going through sorority recruitment. It's going to be a lot different than when I did it. We used to have a lot of silly sketches and skits and stuff, and we wore these satiny dresses with long white gloves. Now they really focus on the sorority's role in the community, the philanthropy, and how they bond together as one cohesive unit."

Toying with her potato salad, Veronica asked, "How do you know?"

"Oh, I've helped with recruitment at Emerson as an alum. And I read my sorority magazine."

"Sure, that makes sense."

Veronica's fingers itched at the excitement over meeting so

many new people from all over the United States, perhaps even the world. She'd traveled with her parents, but it was always to the most expensive resort locations. Mainly, she wanted to meet some "normal," down-to-earth people who wouldn't judge her by pedigree or her clothing labels.

"Roni, I have faith that you'll find what you need at LU."

What she needed was to know she'd belong. That she'd have lifelong friends she could trust and not simply girls who liked her because of her father's status and bank account.

"And I'm here anytime you need me," Kiersten said, pointing to her cell phone. "I've always been just one call away."

"I know, Kiersten. Thanks so much."

They ate in silence for a while, and then Kiersten asked, "Are your parents going with you to Florida?"

Veronica snickered. "Unfortunately. Can't you just see it?"

"Do you want me to come along? I could probably get a couple days off work."

Veronica's first thought was yes! However, she didn't need to lean on Kiersten as a crutch any longer. Kiersten had groomed and mentored her; now it was time for Veronica Van Gelderen to stand on her own two feet. She was feeling very Jane Austen's Emma Woodhouse to Kiersten's Mrs. Weston. "No, that's okay. I appreciate the offer, but I can handle them by myself."

"You certainly can," Kiersten said with a huge smile.

"Besides," Veronica said with an evil grin, "you don't want to be away from Phillip too long. I know he's going to propose to you any day now!"

Kiersten blushed and then waved the thought away. "He has to finish law school first."

"Which he's about to do."

"Believe me, you'll be one of the first to know if *that ever* happens."

"I better be!"

"You're such a sweetheart. I'm gonna miss you, Roni."

"I'll miss you, too."

When they finished their meal and paid, they hugged each other tightly and said their good-byes. Soon, Veronica would be at Latimer University, moving into her dorm, starting classes, and going through sorority recruitment. Everything was going to fall into place. She just knew it.

CHAPTER
3

"It looks like the Peachtree Road Race!" Jenna exclaimed as she and her family pulled into the line of cars carrying girls moving into Tuthill Hall, the all-girl freshman dorm at Latimer University. There were people everywhere.

Jenna looked up at the towering redbrick building that seemed to touch the blue sky. *I'm finally here!*

The campus was a town all to itself, she had noticed as they headed down University Drive to the heart of Latimer University. She'd rolled down the window to breathe in the almost sweet air, tinged with honeysuckle and the few orange trees scattered here and there. It was just what she had expected of central Florida. The beautiful, lively campus seemed water-colored within a thousand acres of tree-lined pathways and impressive, historic academic buildings that surrounded a grassy quad. It was nothing like the cold concrete-and-glass structures of all the office buildings in downtown Atlanta. The sun highlighted everything here. No wonder the students who were out and about were lounging in the shade of the ancient, twisted oaks with bearded drapes of Spanish moss.

Consulting the map that had been mailed from the Enrollment Office over the summer, Jenna saw that the classroom buildings were within walking distance of one another in the middle and northwest sections. She wondered in which building she'd have her first class, maybe the one with the spiral stairs leading to the top floor? The Strumann Student Union was due north, surrounded by upperclassmen dorms and married student housing. The sports dorms and fraternity houses sat on the eastern side of campus, while the women's dorms and sororities were on the south end. In the middle of it all was the president's house, a pristine white brick dwelling with black wrought-iron railings.

Fred had turned the van down a long, looping one-way street, past the administration buildings. The area was filled with large homes, some with antebellum columns and others with wrap-around porches. Jenna looked at her map. *This must be Sorority Row.*

At the end of the street, her stepfather turned onto Williams Drive and into the parking lot of Tuthill Hall. Her new home. Freshman girls and their families crammed along the sidewalk, jockeying for push carts and access into the twenty-story dorm that would be their residence for the next semester. Jenna watched as Fred tried to slide the family minivan into the small space vacated by a Mini Cooper.

"It's not gonna fit, Daddy!" Jayne cried out from the back seat of the van.

Jenna didn't care whether the car would fit or not. She just wanted to get out of the van because she was finally here! Looking around, she noticed all sorts of girls lugging suitcases, boxes, and garment bags of clothes into the building. Jenna couldn't wait to meet her fellow freshmen. Was one of them her new roommate? She scratched her palms to ease the tingling excitement.

When Fred finally stopped the van, she unbuckled quickly and bolted out the door with her mother right behind her. The August sun blistered down, causing Jenna to overheat immediately. *It's a lot hotter here than in Georgia.* Heat radiated off the pavement as hundreds of people milled about in the parking lot following the directions of the move-in counselors.

The walkway was lined with palmetto bushes leading to the automatic double doors. Little bugs buzzed around in the air, and Mrs. Hopkinton swatted them away. "I hope you girls don't get bitten."

"It's Florida, Mom," Jenna said with a laugh. "Bugs happen."

"Do you need some help?" a nice female voice asked.

Jenna spun around, knowing a ridiculous smile was plastered on her face. "Oh, yes! I just got here from Atlanta and need to move in."

"That's quite a drive." The ponytailed girl lifted an LU visor and squinted at her. "Well, welcome to Latimer! Is this your first time on campus?"

Jenna nodded and swallowed, unable to find the words to describe her enthusiasm. She couldn't stop looking up at the humongous dorm in front of her as she thought about sharing hot buttered popcorn in other people's rooms, gossiping about boys, late-night studying, and ordering (and eating!) greasy, cheesy pizza at 1:00 A.M.—and the friends she'd meet who would last a lifetime. Well, at least that was what she expected it to be like from watching movies. "It's my first time for everything."

"Let's get you settled then. What's your name?"

"Jenna Driscoll," she said proudly. "Jenna Michelle Driscoll."

The girl checked her clipboard and flipped back to the D's. "Yep, here you are. Driscoll. You're on the seventh floor, room 714. Your roommate is Cynthia Amber Ferris."

Right, she'd gotten a card in the mail from Residential Life back in June with the girl's name and e-mail address on it. They'd e-mailed once, nothing too personal or in depth because the other girl was spending her summer traveling abroad with her parents.

Cynthia Amber Ferris. Will we hit it off?

"That's great," Jenna said. "I'm psyched to meet her."

The rest of Jenna's family piled out of the minivan and tugged out her suitcases and boxes. She hadn't been exactly sure what to bring with her—clothes, the mini Care Bears her sisters had given her as going-away-don't-forget-us gifts, her Atlanta Falcons poster, family pictures, her diabetes supplies—because she didn't know what the dorm room would be like. From the pictures on Latimer's Web site, the rooms reminded her of the summer camp she'd gone to in Gatlinburg, Tennessee, two years ago (right before the diagnosis). Hopefully the hot water actually worked here at Tuthill.

After waiting twenty minutes for a push cart—and sweating to death—Jenna and her clan made it inside, where she received a room key and then stood in yet another line to get an elevator up to the seventh floor. Jordan and Jayne fidgeted and wanted to ride on the push cart. She let them since this was the last time she'd see them in a while.

Jenna knew her eyes were big as saucers as she watched the other girls rushing around, saying good-bye to the parents and friends who had dropped them off, and hurrying away to whatever they were doing next.

When Jenna's family reached the seventh floor and found room 714, her hand shook as she placed the key in the door. *This is it!*

As soon as she opened it, she heard a long squeal. "Oh my God! You must be Jenna!"

A girl with fiery red hair and freckles lit up when Jenna walked in. Standing behind her were her parents. Her mother looked like an older clone of the girl. They even had the same haircut.

"You must be Cynthia," Jenna said, her adrenaline racing. Any other time she would have thought she had too much sugar in her system, but right now, she was just unbelievably happy to be here, meeting her new roomie.

"I go by my middle name, Amber. Not Cynthia."

"Oh. Amber. Cool name."

Amber squeezed Jenna's arm. "It's soooo great to meet you! It's going to be fun to have a cute roommate." She leaned in close so neither of their parents could hear. "It'll help us when we go out to meet guys."

Feeling her cheeks flush, Jenna turned back to her family. "Amber, this is my mom, Olivia Hopkinton; my stepdad, Fred; and my little sisters."

The older redhead stepped forward. "So nice to meet you folks. I'm Andrea Ferris. This is my husband, William. William, leave that box alone and come meet Amber's roommate."

"Yes, dear."

Introductions were made, and then everyone pitched in to help unload Jenna's cart. All the while, Jenna noticed that Amber pretty much bossed her parents around, snapping at her father for opening the wrong suitcase and telling her mother what to do every second.

"I told you not to put name tags in my clothes, Mom," she snapped.

"Yes, I know. But they're only in a few," Mrs. Ferris said.

"I'll just pull them out."

"Whatever you think is best, Amber." Her mother reached over and stroked Amber's hair, but the young woman knocked her mom's hand away and grunted in derision.

Right . . . like I'd ever treat my mom like that! Jenna thought.

She looked across the room and noticed her own mother's slight smirk. While Jenna didn't want to judge Amber too quickly, she had learned early on that the way people acted around their parents was a good indication of how they really were as people. She hoped Amber wasn't going to be a nightmare to live with.

"Isn't the room fab?" Amber asked. "There are two desks, cable hookup—I'll let you watch my TV—Internet, a sink, two closets, and we can make the beds go bunk or side by side, whatever you want to do. It's going to be great having someone to do everything with."

Jenna could barely keep up with her roommate, but she admired her energy, albeit leaning a little toward the geeking-out side. She was going to take her cue from Amber, though. She'd be bubbly, exuberant, and ready to face anything. She put herself into everything she did 100 percent and always would. Her band scholarship proved that.

"Jenna, honey," Fred said. "We're going down for the other load."

"Do you need help?" William Ferris asked.

"That would be nice, thanks."

The girls moved to follow their parents. Jenna's mother said, "We'll be right back. You and Amber get to know each other." Then she winked.

Turning back to her roommate, Jenna said, "So . . . here we are. Freshman year."

"It's going to be totally fabulous. Well, once the parentals get out of the way."

Jenna laughed nervously. She was anxious to be on her own, but she was going to miss her family like crazy and would be sad to see them go.

The two of them flitted around the room, claiming dressers and closets and deciding who would get which desk. Jenna looked at Amber's laptop computer, a state-of-the-art blue-and-silver machine. She supposed the used desktop that Fred bought from his work's IT department would suffice for her.

"Do you have a comforter and stuff?" Amber asked.

Jenna glanced over at her box marked "bedding." "Just some sheets and blankets from home."

"We should totally go to Linens 'n Things and get all matching stuff," Amber said. "We'll dress the room up and make it look homey."

"That would be nice," Jenna said with a warm smile.

Fred knocked the door open with his foot and set down a box of Jenna's stuff. Jordan and her mother came in next, carrying one last suitcase, followed by Amber's parents, who were chattering on nonstop about their daughter.

"Amber has her own car and is an excellent driver and is very responsible."

"I'm sure she is," Mrs. Hopkinton said.

"I think that's all, Jenna," Fred said.

"It certainly is roomy in here," Jenna's mom commented. "You girls won't be on top of each other."

Mrs. Ferris took over, once again. "My mother made these curtains for Amber. Don't you just love them? Teal is Amber's favorite color."

"Mom," Amber said, and rolled her eyes. She spun back to Jenna. "Hey, after we go to Linens 'n Things, we should go to Morrison's Cafeteria in the mall. It's delicious . . . real down-home food."

This girl was all over the place. Jenna didn't know if she had the stamina to keep up!

Mrs. Hopkinton chimed in. "That sounds like a wonderful idea, Amber. Jenna needs a few more things to get settled, so let's get unpacked and we can take you girls over to the store."

"Oh, that's okay, Mrs. Hopkinton. Like Mom said, I've got a car."

"Perfect," Jenna said.

Her mother looked around the room and then frowned. "There's only one thing missing."

Jenna glanced about and was afraid of what was coming.

"What's that?" Amber asked.

"There needs to be a refrigerator. For Jenna's—"

Nooooo... don't rat me out! Not when I've got a fresh start. Stepping in front of her mother hastily, Jenna interrupted. "I need a refrigerator for my Diet Coke habit. I drink it all the time and always have to have it around."

"Well, yes, but—" her mother started.

Amber shrugged and pointed out the cabinet between the two beds. "It's right here. Feel free to load it up with whatever. I'm a Fresca addict myself."

Her mother totally wasn't getting the message. "But, Jenna, you'll need to make sure no one bothers your—"

"Juice boxes! Yeah, I just love those, too," she said with a nervous laugh. "Can't get enough of them. You might even see me get up in the middle of the night for one." There, that should prepare Amber for a little taste of her diabetes without revealing too much. She had it all planned out. She'd keep her medication in Tupperware or something, and she'd go into the bathroom stall whenever it was time to replace the insulin and needle. No one would ever know.

"Now Jenna, we need to inform Amber about your situation in case she has to call 911."

Mrs. Ferris stepped forward. "There's not something wrong with your daughter that would cause our Amber any added responsibility? She has to focus on her studies and her social activities."

Mrs. Hopkinton flattened her mouth, and Jenna could tell her mom was perturbed. "I just want Amber—and you—to be aware of Jenna's condition."

Crappity-crap!

"Whoa! What's going on here?" Amber asked with a freaked-out look on her face. "You don't have some weird, infectious disease, do you?"

Here we go . . .

Mrs. Hopkinton stepped forward and wrapped her arm around Jenna. "Jenna is diabetic. It's under control, but she does need insulin to maintain her glucose levels."

"Oh, is *that* all?" Mrs. Ferris said with a dismissive wave.

Amber's eyes grew wide. "Whooooooa! Diabetes? That totally sucks."

"Yeah, it does," Jenna echoed. "But I deal, you know?"

"It's best you're informed, Amber, in case anything should happen to Jenna," her mom said. "She's had only a few diabetic seizures, but when they happen, she can become disoriented and violent, and you'll need to get emergency help here immediately."

"Seizures!" Mrs. Ferris shrieked.

"Amber's not a nurse," Mr. Ferris said. "But she can certainly call for help. Right, Amber?"

"Sure, Dad. Whatever."

Jenna felt her face flame. *I sound like a freak of nature!* "It's actually not that bad, Amber," she pleaded. "We can talk about this later, can't we?"

Mrs. Hopkinton frowned and went back into the hallway

to check on Jayne and Jordan, who were running around like heathens.

Pleading with her eyes, Jenna said, "Please don't tell anyone, okay, Amber? You've got to swear on a stack of Bibles."

Amber shrugged. "Yeah, whatever. No big deal."

"It *is* a big deal to me. I don't want people to look at me like I'm a weirdo."

Sitting on the edge of her bed while her mother unpacked for her, Amber said, "No one's going to think that. Just chill, Jenna. Everything will be fine. You'll totally fit in here at Latimer, especially once we start going out and meeting guys."

"There's more to college than your social life, Jenna," her mom said, stepping back into the room.

"I know, Mom," Jenna said politely, not wanting to sound disrespectful, like Amber.

"I'll take care of Jenna," Amber announced.

"Sounds like you girls have a plan," Jenna's mom said, and then looked at her watch. "Now, we should get out of your hair."

Jenna felt a heavy pain in her chest, like she'd had the wind knocked out of her. "So soon?"

Fred stepped up. "We've got to get back on the road. It's a long drive home."

Her mom enveloped her in her arms, and Jenna gave up trying to hold back her tears. "I love y'all," she said, the words muffled by her mother's blouse.

"And we love you. I'm so proud of you, Jenna."

After hugs, kisses—a few more tears—waves, and good-byes from both sets of parents, Jenna steadied her breathing, dabbed her eyes, and turned to her roommate. Her pulse was a bit jittery under the surface knowing that her secret was out. But she had containment... for now.

"What do you say we unpack later?" Amber asked. "Let's go shopping and really make this a home."

Fifteen minutes later, the two girls stood outside the elevator on the seventh floor. Jenna looked at the bulletin board between the banks of elevators and saw a flyer that read: *SORORITY RECRUITMENT: ONE DAY LEFT TO SIGN UP!*

"What's that?"

"Are you serious?" Amber's mouth dropped open. "It's only *the* most exciting thing you'll *ever* do in your lifetime! It's the formal recruitment time for all of the sororities on campus."

Right... sororities. In all of her college preparation, Jenna had never really considered the fact that Latimer was big on sororities and fraternities. Maybe she should have.

"Everyone goes out for sorority recruitment. It's going to be madness."

"Madness?" Jenna asked, not understanding what Amber meant.

They stepped onto the crowded elevator when the doors slid open. "You'll see."

"Well, not really, 'cause I hadn't planned on doing it. Should I have?" Marching band would provide her with a lot to do, especially during football season when they had road games to attend. She also planned on looking into other campus clubs and organizations, maybe try not to join them all at once like she'd done in high school. Should she consider this sorority thing? Wouldn't joining a sorority take up gargantuan chunks of time?

"You're not going to recruitment?" Amber seemed let down by Jenna's admission. "But you'll meet so many people, and being in a sorority is great! Greek life is the coolest thing to do in college." Amber turned and did a quick survey in the elevator. "Y'all are going to recruitment, aren't you?"

Jenna was surprised by how many girls nodded in agreement and said, "Yes."

Her pulse picked up. "Wow. I had no idea." The serial joiner thing was sort of like a head rush to her, and her adrenaline was whirling at the thought of possibly missing out on something "everyone" did. "Well, sure, I want to meet people and make friends and stuff, but I thought I'd get that through band and just being on campus."

Amber flipped her hair over her shoulder. "You can get it by joining a sorority. There are ten houses, and recruitment is during the first week of school."

"The same time as classes?"

Shaking her head, Amber explained, "Recruitment parties are late in the afternoon and at night so it won't conflict."

"Oh, I see." Jenna was on sensory overload. Why had she never thought about this possibility?

Amber reached for her hand. "You *have* to come to sorority recruitment, Jenna! We'll do it together. It'll be great."

Jenna's eyes grew wide with interest. The elevator reached the lobby, and they stepped out. "You sound like you know a lot about it."

Amber started talking a mile a minute. "Well, my cousin, Tammy, was a Delta Kappa back in the eighties, so they've practically got to take me 'cause I have a connection ... almost a legacy."

Jenna thought for a moment. "Oh. I didn't realize you needed connections to get into a sorority." She didn't know anyone and she certainly wasn't a legacy, whatever that meant.

Her roommate laughed, a high-pitched laugh. "Honey, stick with me, and I'll teach you what you need to know."

"Does it cost anything?" she wondered.

"Only a registration fee."

"It sounds like something I should do."

In the parking lot, Amber bounced up and down, begging her in an almost needful way. "I was kinda dreading doing this alone, but together it'll be so much better."

"It would be fun to do something together."

Taking Jenna's hands, Amber said, "It'll be perfect. And who knows . . . we may join the same sorority!"

"When we get back, we'll go online and look at the Latimer sororities' sites. The kickoff meeting is Sunday night, but everything really starts on Monday."

Jenna lowered herself into the car and latched her seat belt. She let out the breath she'd been holding. "Looks like I'm going out for sorority recruitment."

"I can't believe you drove me here in a *university* van," Lora-Leigh said as she twisted her bottom earring. Her mother pulled into the yellow-curbed loading-zone area and put the van into park. A university cop who was helping direct traffic merely nodded at them.

"Your Jetta's too small to carry all of this, Lora-Leigh," Mrs. Sorenstein said. "Besides, your father works here, and we have every right to use this to move you into your dorm."

"Taking advantage, more like," she muttered.

"What did you say?"

"Nothing, Mom." She heaved a heavy sigh. She shouldn't take her continued frustrations out on her mother, who was simply trying to help, unlike her father, the twenty-four-hour dean, who was tending more to the new freshmen than his own daughter. "I'll still need my car."

"Your father will drive it over for you tomorrow. You do realize how lucky you are to be going to a college that allows freshmen to have cars on campus."

"Yes, Mom."

"If you'd gone to New York, you would've had to ride those nasty subways."

Lora-Leigh rolled her eyes behind her sunglasses. "But I didn't go there. I'm here at good ole Latimer." She pumped her fist for emphasis . . . and mockery.

"Well, Thomas will park the car in the lot next to Tuthill and leave the key in the ashtray."

This was exactly what Lora-Leigh had feared by going to school locally: it was more like thirteenth grade than freshman year at college. Mrs. Sorenstein unfastened her seat belt and started to get out.

"Look, Mom, you can just drop me off. No need to come into the dorm."

"Come on, Lora-Leigh. You won't let me do anything to help with this big step in your life. I tried to take you back-to-school shopping, and you wouldn't even let me do that."

Lora-Leigh smiled weakly. "Shopping at Talbot's over in Tampa wasn't exactly my scene." *Damn . . . I shouldn't have said that. She looks so crushed.* "I'm sorry, Mom. You know I prefer to make my own clothes."

Mrs. Sorenstein looked sad. "I can't help you set up your room?"

"*Mooooom,*" Lora-Leigh said with a sigh, and then stopped herself. "I appreciate it, but I'm not living at home for a reason. Now really, I'm fine. No serial killers, rapists, or terrorists hanging out here or anything. Just a bunch of eighteen-year-old girls like me trying to get away from their parents."

"Now, that's not nice."

"You know I love you, Mom. But this is *my* time."

Lora-Leigh got out, her Marc Jacobs knockoff sandals landing firmly on the pavement, and yanked out two suitcases, one large box, two milk crates full of books, and her portable Singer sewing machine, setting everything on the sidewalk. She didn't really want all of the girls to see her getting out of a university van. Lora-Leigh merely wanted to blend in, as much as possible—crazy-curly hair, self-designed clothes, and all.

"Don't pout, Mom. I appreciate the ride. You're the best," Lora-Leigh said.

"I know, dear. There's just so much to go over."

Lora-Leigh lifted her brow. "Go over?"

"Monday. It's the big day. The start of sorority recruitment."

This was getting to be her bat mitzvah all over again. Lora-Leigh had wanted to make her dress; her mother special-ordered one from a boutique in New York. Lora-Leigh had thought simple sandwiches would suffice; her mother had full catering brought in. Lora-Leigh had been busy studying, while her mother had been busy with orchestrating everything else. Just like now.

Mrs. Sorenstein reached for "The Notebook" and passed it over the seat to Lora-Leigh.

Oh no... The Notebook. All of the inside scoop on Omega Omega Omega.

"Mom, I've been studying that all summer." She grabbed onto her hair to exemplify her frustration. Why should she care what the president of the sorority was majoring in? Or what the colors and mascot were, or that the founders were from Indiana? That was all stuff that new members had to learn. Since she wasn't planning on being one, why did she have to fill her brain cells with info that didn't matter? "You don't honestly think it's going to help me get in, do you?"

"All I know is that the more prepared you are going in to recruitment, the more successful you'll be. First impressions are everything. Besides, you're a legacy."

"Legacy-schmegacy." Lora-Leigh knew that a legacy was the daughter, sister, niece, or granddaughter of a member of a particular sorority. Since her mother had been an $\Omega\Omega\Omega$ (at Latimer, no less), Lora-Leigh was a legacy to the sorority. Which really didn't mean that much to her because chapters weren't required to admit every legacy. They were, however, obligated to give a legacy "special attention and careful consideration" (according to The Notebook).

"Don't back-talk me, Lora-Leigh," her mom scolded. "It's important that you stand out from the other girls."

"I'm sorry, Mom." Lora-Leigh pointed at her double tank top, the khaki skirt she'd whipped together, and her black high-heeled sandals. "I don't exactly fade into the scenery, you know?"

Her mother would have none of that. "You're perfect." She ticked off points on her thin fingers: "There are approximately twelve hundred girls who will be going through recruitment, including freshmen, transfer students, and a handful of sophomores who didn't make it last year and want another chance. Each house has a quota."

"A quota?" Lora-Leigh asked, not sure she liked the term.

"Well, certainly. Haven't you been listening to me? The houses will have anywhere from twenty to forty spots available. That's their quota of how many new members they can accept. Each house's quota is different. What that means, though, is that only about four hundred girls will get spots."

Lora-Leigh sighed again and shifted her weight from one foot to the other. "Right... I've heard this mathematical equation nine times over the course of the summer." At her cousin Lucy's (also a Tri-Omega) wedding up in Pensacola, over Fourth of July, when most of the faculty had been at their house for a backyard barbecue, and again just last week when the infamous Bunny Crenshaw, Tri-Omega sister from Nashville, called to tell her the same thing.

"One more time doesn't hurt, dear."

"I know, Mom. I know. Remember, you want this more than I do. I'm just doing it to please you." It would be the most painful week of her life. No doubt about it.

"Do it for yourself, Lora-Leigh. Your days as a Tri-Omega will be some of the most fulfilling of your life. Friendships you'll have forever. Trust me. I know what's best for you."

You seem to think you do.

The idea of forming lasting friendships was certainly

intriguing, but Lora-Leigh didn't have to join a group of plastic Barbies to get that, did she?

"You've told me all of that, Mom. Don't worry. I'll try to have fun with it." She looked at her watch. Move in ended in three hours, and she desperately wanted to get into her room and set up before her roommate swooped up the best spot. While most students were probably gunning for the best computer space, Lora-Leigh wanted to make sure there was room for her Singer and supplies. "Look, I gotta go."

"I'll see you Monday at the Tri-Omega house. I've volunteered to help out."

"I wish you wouldn't do that, Mom. Recruitment is going to be stressful enough without your being there making me more nervous."

Mrs. Sorenstein paused for a moment. "I never thought my presence would make you nervous. Maybe I'll just help out on Preference Night. That's the most special night of all. You'll see."

Lora-Leigh knew that seeing her mom at any point during recruitment would simply make her feel guiltier for not enjoying the process more. "Whatever you think is best."

When Lora-Leigh hefted her purse onto her shoulder, she glanced back inside the van. Mrs. Sorenstein's eyes filled with tears. "My baby really has grown up."

"Awww . . . Mom." Lora-Leigh choked back her own surprising emotional bubble. She tried to laugh it off, though. "It was bound to happen, you know?"

"I just never thought it would be this soon."

"Love ya, Mom."

As the van pulled off and her mother waved, Lora-Leigh looked down at the gold-seal embossed notebook, full of recommendations, notes, and the history of Tri-Omega. She appreciated her mom's fervor, but Lora-Leigh completely dreaded what was ahead for her. Recruitment would waste time she could be sewing or getting used to freshman life.

She glanced over the finely manicured lawn of Tuthill Hall and across Williams Drive to where Sorority Row started. Sure, she was familiar with the street. It was a one-way bending road filled with oversize houses, each with well-kept lawns. Cheerful girls flitted around, taking things into the various houses and welcoming their sisters back with hugs and kisses. She'd admitted that the majority of them looked charged to see one another, like they really got along and stuff. Was it all just an act, though?

Lora-Leigh gathered her things and started toward the freshman dorm. Expelling a deep, pent-up sigh, she mentally resorted to dealing with recruitment when she had to: Monday morning.

"I really wish you hadn't come with me, you guys," Veronica said as she pushed open the door to her private room on the seventh floor at Tuthill Hall, which smelled of Pine-Sol and Pledge. It was bad enough her parents had flown to Tampa with her, but then they'd rented a limo to drive them to Latimer. God, she hoped no one had seen her getting out of it. She'd immediately be labeled a snob, and no one would want to have anything to do with her.

Instead of thinking on that, she peered around the room, taking in the pale peach painted walls made of cinder blocks, the corkboard including a smattering of tacks, and the single bed at the far end. One entire wall of her railroad car–type room was nothing but windows, allowing the bright, yellow sun to fill the space. She'd read on the LU Web site that these rooms used to be balconies back in the seventies, but had been closed off in the eighties to make private rooms.

Something her parents insisted she have.

A private room. How unsociable.

But it was a compromise she'd made to get her way and come to Latimer. And to get them to pay the out-of-state tuition. (Which was a drop in the bucket compared to Harvard!)

While her father occupied himself on his BlackBerry, her mother wiped her perfectly manicured finger across the top of the desk on the far left wall and sneered as she blew away imaginary dust. "Well, we had to check out this cesspool of a university here in the swamps of Florida, which you chose over my Wellesley."

"And my Harvard," Mr. Van Gelderen added disdainfully.

Veronica wasn't listening to either of them. She was in heaven. Her heart pounded like the techno dance beats she'd listened to on her iPod on the flight down here. "I think it's wicked cool," she said, dropping her Louis Vuitton bag on the unmade bed. "The windows are fabulous, and check out all this space. I'll get a rug for over here, and I can set up my computer over there and—"

"Do they have maid service here?" her mother asked.

"Why, do they have it at Wellesley?" Roni caught herself. It was so not like her to snap like that.

"No, I'm just thinking this place needs a good cleaning. I could arrange for a maid to come here for you once a week or so."

"Mother!"

"I'm just saying... It's not like you to live in such filth, Veronic'er."

"You know, not everything is Beacon Hill, Mother." Veronica looked around and laughed. "This is the most beautiful room in the world to me. It's... *home*."

Her mother folded her arms across her chest. "You've apparently lost all good sense that your father and I taught you."

All Veronica could think of was how absent her parents had been and how she'd literally been raised by a string of governesses who took care of her and saw to all of her needs. And Kiersten, of course. None of that mattered now, though. Veronica was starting her collegiate career.

She tucked her hair behind her ears and stood tall. "Look, I'm pleased with my decision. I wish you could be happy for me, as well. This is a great school, and I'm going to take advantage of every opportunity here."

Cathryn Van Gelderen reached over to move Veronica's hair back into place. Her mouth flattened. "I always said I wouldn't treat my children the way I was treated by my parents. I was told not to stifle your creativity, punish you, or tell you no, so I didn't and I haven't. But Veronic'er, you've made a very poor decision, and I only hope some time here in this... *redneck town*... will help you to come to your senses."

Latimer was hardly a redneck town. Aside from the university, there was a distinguished, respected medical center known for advanced sports medicine. The population of Latimer was about a hundred thousand on a good day, and the campus was like its own little town within a town. It seemed everyone in the surrounding area was connected to the university in some way. Banners for the football games were in the windows of local stores, and even the city limits sign read: WELCOME TO LATIMER—HOME OF THE RED RAIDERS. It was *not* a bad place at all.

Veronica impatiently gathered her long hair off her neck and twisted it into a knot on the top of her head, securing it with an elastic. "Thanks for your support, Mother," she said with an air of sarcasm. Changing the subject, she said, "What time is your flight back to Boston?"

"Trying to get rid of us?" her father asked, while continuing to look at his BlackBerry.

She smiled sweetly. "Actually, yes. I want to meet people and make friends and unpack my clothes and... and..." She looked toward the telephone. "And order a pizza. A big, gooey, fattening, cheesy pizza. I'll eat it with my hands, and I won't use a napkin."

Her mother cringed outwardly and then stepped forward. "With a diet like that you'll gain the freshman fifteen and then some. Don't go losing your manners, Veronic'er. You're still a Van Gelderen."

Veronica wasn't worried. She knew Latimer University had an impressive, state-of-the-art natatorium, and she planned on swimming daily. Swimming laps had always been a stress reliever for her.

"Don't worry, Mother." *I won't do anything to embarrass you.*

"Cathryn, we should go," her father announced. "Veronic'er, take care of yourself." He glanced away from his handheld long enough to kiss her lightly on the cheek and hug her for only a second.

Come on, Dad, tell me you're proud of me.... Tell me you support me.

She held her breath, but... nothing.

As she said her good-byes and watched her parents walk down the long hallway, she felt, for the first time in her life, a sense of relief and adventure. She was here. She was settling in, and, dammit, she'd make things happen.

Flipping onto her unmade bed, she pulled out the schedule of Recruitment Week activities. She scanned down the list and saw that orientation started tomorrow afternoon with the Recruitment Counselors—Rho Gammas—in the university's Strumann Student Center grand ballroom. The Rho Gammas were girls from each of the sororities who acted as counselors for the recruitment process and would help guide the potential new members. Veronica hoped they wouldn't steer her in the wrong direction.

After all, she was in search of a new family. Of a new Veronica.

And I will *find her!*

CHAPTER
4

"Come on, Jenna," Amber called out on Sunday evening. "We're going to be late for the recruitment kickoff."

"Just a sec," she answered, fumbling with the keys to Amber's Mazda. Jenna had just stood in line for an *hour* at the Campus Supply Store—Supe Store, in campus vernacular—getting books for her classes that started tomorrow morning. She couldn't believe how much the textbooks had cost her! Three books alone for her Western Civ class. "I'm stashing my stuff so I don't have to haul it to the orientation."

She'd been overwhelmed inside the Supe Store, running around gathering her textbooks, workbooks, and readings, so much so that she ran smack into this amazingly cute guy. She was mortified, flushing from head to toe. But he'd been nice enough to gather her spilled books while she took a moment to check him out. He had shaggy brown hair and muscled arms, and he wore a yellow-and-red T-shirt that read PHI OMICRON

CHI ARABIAN NIGHTS. Hmmm . . . must be some kind of fraternity party. She'd shyly taken her stuff from him—not before drowning for a sec in his blue eyes—and then she'd dashed to the checkout counter with a quick thanks to him so she wouldn't keep Amber waiting any longer.

"Well, come on. We want to get good seats," Amber said, impatiently crossing her arms over her chest.

Jenna didn't get what the importance of getting a good seat had to do with the sorority orientation. In fact, she was a little discombobulated over the whole day in general. It had started with a quick breakfast of nuked Quaker Oats in her room and then an early band orientation. She was fitted with her Marching Red Raiders uniform, which was made of the scratchiest polyester ever—even worse than her high school outfit. Then, after a lunch of microwave popcorn, she went online and got the course description and syllabus for each of her classes and then made a list of all the books she needed. Amber had wanted to eat dinner together in the dining hall, so they spent a good hour there eating some pretty decent dorm food. They got to the Supe Store and barely checked out before it was time to report for the sorority recruitment orientation at nine P.M.

Jenna felt a zigzag of energy bolt through her as she and Amber climbed the Strumann Student Center's large staircase, which led up to the second floor. In the grand ballroom, girls were everywhere, congregating around the door, talking together, hugging, laughing, and smiling. Excitement tickled the air, and Jenna sensed an invigoration dancing over her that she hadn't experienced since before her 'betes diagnosis. *Surely I'm not the only girl here with such a challenge.* She resolved to stop thinking about it—stop dwelling on it—and just get into the spirit of everything around her.

"Let's go up front," Amber said, pulling Jenna along.

"Sure thing."

Amber had convinced Jenna that joining a sorority would be "muchas fun." Since Jenna wanted to get as much out of her time at Latimer as possible, she went online; researched properly (like any good straight-A student); read all the disclaimers, rules, and regulations; and clicked the registration form. Worse thing that could happen would be getting "cut" or "dropped" (as Amber had explained was what happened when none of the sororities invited you back) from recruitment, but it wouldn't be a big deal because Jenna had band to keep her busy. Best-case scenario was she'd be invited into one of the campus sororities.

Once in their seats, Jenna tucked a leg up underneath her as she settled in. Amber sat next to her, and girls were packed tightly on either side of them. The room buzzed with overlapping conversations. Jenna looked around, marveling in the fact that *all* these girls were hoping to join a sorority.

"So, when will we be put into our recruitment group?" Jenna asked, holding up the card indicating she would be in Group 7. Her roommate was in Group 11. Too bad they weren't together.

"We'll break into groups right after the orientation," Amber said. "The Rho Gammas will explain everything."

"Why didn't you bring a notebook?" Jenna asked her roommate. "There's going to be a lot of information to remember."

Amber snapped her gum and played with a split end on her long red hair. "I've got it covered. I know everything there is to know about LU sororities, remember. I'm just doing this 'cause I have to. I can't wait until tomorrow night when the real fun begins."

Glancing around the room again, Jenna scrutinized the girls sitting in her vicinity and wondered if any of these myriad faces might soon be her sorority sisters, if she were lucky enough to get picked to join one of them. One girl looked like one of the fresh faces from *Seventeen* magazine. The girl sitting at the end of the row in front of her, sort of away from the rest. The one with the long, black hair.

She's so pretty that she'll get in automatically.

The lights in the ballroom flickered, and about fifty girls crossed the stage to the center. Everyone began to clap and cheer, so Jenna joined in. She felt her heartbeat pick up in rhythm with the rowdiness around her. The cluster of girls on the stage were dressed alike in khaki shorts, tennis shoes, and light-blue-and-yellow jersey-type shirts that had two Greek letters on them—PΓ.

"What do those letters stand for?" Jenna asked Amber.

"Duh . . . it's means Rho Gamma. You've totally got to learn the Greek alphabet if you want to do well."

"Really? Why?"

"It makes you look smarter," Amber said with the wave of a hand. "Like you really want to belong."

Jenna screwed up her nose and wondered if Amber was merely making some of this up to seem more knowledgeable. It was great that Amber knew so much about the process, but why did she have to make Jenna feel stupid?

One of the Rho Gammas stepped from the pack and moved

to the microphone. "Goooooooood evening, ladies! Welcome to the opening of Latimer University's Sorority Recruitment Week!"

The room broke into applause again, and Jenna and Amber cheered along. Music blared from the speakers, and the Rho Gammas clapped to it, really pumping the ballroom up. Jenna's foot tapped in time with the funky beat, and her body swayed in the chair.

How exciting! It's like a pep rally!

"Just think, Jenna," Amber said over the melee, "we'll be in a sorority by the end of the week."

Jenna simply smiled. She'd agreed to go through recruitment, but had never agreed to join. What if she didn't like any of them? What if they didn't like her? Would she still be able to fit in socially on the campus?

But there was no time to think about that, or anything really—especially not with her eight A.M. class tomorrow. She sat up in her seat and listened intently as the head Rho Gamma started reciting many of the rules Jenna had read on the Latimer Web site.

"As you know, ladies, we have ten fantastic houses here on campus: Alpha Sigma Gamma, Beta Xi, Delta Kappa, Eta Lambda Nu, Omega Omega Omega, Omicron Chi Omega, Pi Epsilon Chi, Psi Kappa Upsilon, Theta Beta Gamma, and Zeta Zeta Tau. Recruitment is a process of mutual selection between potential new members and the individual houses. You will attend an open house and then a series of invitational party rounds. Each round, you will attend fewer parties, to help narrow your decision."

Jenna furiously wrote in her notebook, making sure she understood all of the instructions and directions.

The Rho Gamma continued: "Round One parties will start tomorrow, Monday, September 14, from six until ten P.M. Round Two will be on Tuesday, and you'll be able to go to six houses maximum. Round Three will be on Wednesday, and you'll be able to accept four invitations maximum. Preference Parties will be on Thursday night, from seven until ten-thirty P.M. You may accept two invitations maximum and will then immediately come back here to Strumann to fill out your preference cards."

"Preference cards?" Jenna asked Amber.

"Yeah, our Rho Gammas will tell us more about it."

Jenna nodded and listened to the rest of the directions. "Attendance at each party is mandatory. Throughout the process, each potential new member will be assigned to a neutral Rho Gamma—or Recruitment Counselor, as seen up here behind me—to consult with you."

"Oh, that's great!" Jenna said to Amber. She was relieved that she wouldn't be going through the week in a vacuum.

"At the completion of each round," the head Rho Gamma continued, "you will be asked to establish your preference of sorority to return to. Potential new members and sorority preferences will be matched up by computer to determine invitations for the next round of parties. At the end, you will be asked to decide your preference of sorority chapters visited and will subsequently receive an invitation to membership from the sorority you are matched with."

Jenna put down her pen and sighed hard. "I think my head is going to explode."

"It's a lot to take in," Amber muttered.

Whispered conversations scuttled around the room, and the Rho Gamma held up her hands. "I know this is a lot of information, but your individual Rho Gamma will explain more to you if this isn't clear." She adjusted her stance and held the microphone closer while she kept going. "Remember, potential new members aren't allowed to have contact with sorority members outside of the formal activities. Name tags should be worn at all times. That's how the sorority members will identify you."

Jenna kept scribbling notes, trying to keep up with everything being said to the assemblage.

Finally, the Rho Gamma instructed them, "Okay, girls, now we'll break into your individual recruitment groups. Your recruitment group will attend the first-round parties together, and, after that, you will meet every evening after your visits so you can follow up on the day's activities. Then you'll meet before the next round of parties to find out what invitations you've received." She smiled at the room. "Again, any questions at this point should be addressed to your individual Rho Gamma. Now, please go join your group, and remember to have fun!"

"Catch ya later, roomie," Amber said, and headed off to find Group 11.

Jenna followed the sea of girls moving about the room in waves of enthusiasm. She saw large signs being held high, indicating the different recruitment groups. Toward the back of the room, she spotted the sign that read GROUP 7. Jenna noticed the gorgeous black-haired girl, dressed in a black T-shirt and really nice jeans, so she walked over to her.

"Hey, there! You're in Group Seven?" she asked, knowing good and well the girl was.

The tension in the girl's face eased, and she smiled. "Yeah, I am."

"I'm Jenna Driscoll. My roommate's in another group." Why that information was important to say, she didn't know. *What a goober!*

The girl wet her lips and swallowed, as if nervous. "Great to meet you. I'm Veronica Van Gelderen."

"Great meetin' you, too. This is really weird, huh?"

"It's a little overwhelming. There are a lot of girls here, more than I expected."

"I know." Jenna was intrigued. "So, did you plan all along on going out for a sorority?"

"Sure. I've been looking forward to it all summer. What about you?"

Confessing, Jenna said, "I don't really know much about it, other than what my roommate told me, and what I've read on the LU Web site. I'm sort of winging it, you know?"

Veronica nodded as their group began to move, following the large sign out into a lounge area on the right.

A girl dressed in a pink sweater and low-riding black pants hurried up to Jenna, tapped her on the arm, and asked, "Group Seven, right?"

"Yeah, it is," Jenna said as the girl caught her breath. "Are you okay?"

"S-s-sorry," she said between huffs and puffs. "I'm running late. Couldn't find a frickin' parking place. Did I miss anything?"

Veronica turned and said, "You've missed an awful lot of information."

The curly-headed girl shrugged. "Whatever." She stopped, frowned, and then said, "Dude, I'm sorry. It's not you. My mom's been hassling me all summer about recruitment."

"Oh, that's okay," Veronica said with a shy smile.

"Holy shit!" the girl exclaimed, looking at Veronica. "Are those Chip and Pepper jeans?"

Jenna noticed Veronica cringe a little at the blatant attention. Veronica forced a smile, though, and said, "I, uhh, got them at a consignment place back home."

"What idiot would put their Chip and Pepper jeans into consignment? I mean, they totally took off as a big name in fashion when Naomi Campbell smacked the crap out of her maid when she thought the maid had stolen the jeans from her. They're like a hundred seventy-five dollars a pair."

Veronica darted her eyes nervously. "Oh, well, umm . . . not mine, like I said."

"Whatever you say," the girl said with a wink and a smile, as if she knew a secret. "So, hopefully they won't keep us long. I've got a dress I'm working on back in my room."

"A dress?" Jenna asked the new girl.

"Yeah, I love to sew. It's the one I'm wearing on Preference Night, and I need to finish it so I won't be walking around nekkid."

Veronica stifled a laugh.

Jenna wondered about the attitude of the newcomer. Like this girl would rather be anywhere than right here in the Strumann Student Union. Wasn't sorority recruitment supposed to be fun and exciting? This girl looked like she'd rather

have needles stuck in her eyes. "We're getting our group information right now," Jenna explained.

"Cool," the girl said, taking a seat. "I'm Lora-Leigh, by the
way. Lora-Leigh Sorenstein."

Jenna made the introductions right as the Rho Gamma
spoke up and said, "Y'all have a seat and make yourselves comfortable. This is where we'll meet every day for Group Seven,
so remember it."

"This will be a piece of cake," Jenna overheard a girl behind
her say.

Leaning close to Veronica, Jenna confessed, "Boy, some of
these girls are pretty confident about this, not nervous as all
get-out like me."

Veronica laughed, and her eyes lit up. "Thank *Gahd*. I was
terrified everyone here knew all the ins and outs and I would
look like a fool. All I know is what my friend, Kiersten, told me.
She went to school in the Northeast, though."

Jenna sensed a slight aristocratic air in Veronica's accent.
"You're not from the South, are you?"

"No, I'm from Boston," she said. "Does it show that much?"

Lora-Leigh lit up. "I've always wanted to go to Boston. The
farthest north I've been is Baltimore, on a trip with my parents."

"Does it snow all the time?" Jenna asked.

Veronica giggled. "Only in the winter."

Lora-Leigh laughed and said, "Good one, Boston."

"Sorry...that was a dumb question," Jenna said, rolling her
eyes. She turned to Lora-Leigh. "I'm from Marietta, Georgia."

"First time away from home?" Lora-Leigh asked with a grin.

Lora-Leigh certainly was outgoing, Jenna thought. Jenna looked at Veronica, who seemed to be sizing up this Lora-Leigh Sorenstein girl. They certainly were night and day. Quiet vs. Boisterous. Demure vs. Flashy. Maybe Jenna should keep the convo flowing. "Yeah, sort of. Although I went to Boston once in eighth grade. Walked the Freedom Trail."

Veronica simply nodded.

"Where are you from, Lora-Leigh?" Jenna asked.

"Homegrown, I'm afraid."

"I beg your pardon?" Veronica asked.

"You know . . . a product of Latimer, Florida."

"Oh, I understand."

"Cool! You're from here?" Jenna asked. "You can show us all the hot spots and fun things to do."

Lora-Leigh fiddled with the hem of her sweater and shrugged again. "Not much to do, really, but I'm happy to show y'all around. I grew up sneaking into Latimer fraternity parties and going to football games. Not much of a change for me."

"Change isn't always good," Jenna said.

"Change is necessary," Veronica added.

"Apparently not for me, Veronica," Lora-Leigh said.

Jenna wasn't sure what to say next, so she blurted out, "My best friend back home had a cat named Veronica."

"A Christian name for a cat?" Lora-Leigh asked with a teasing smile.

Jenna thought for a minute. "Well, sure, the cat was a member of the family."

It took a minute, but Veronica eventually broke out into a wide grin. "You know, I've always wanted to go by 'Roni.' My friend Kiersten calls me Roni. I'd like to go by that mainly because New Englanders always turn the 'a' in Veronica into an 'er' sound."

"That won't happen here," Jenna said, noting southern accents were more the norm than the exception here in Latimer, although there were girls from all over. Over her shoulder, she heard a girl say she was from way out in California.

"Where do y'all live here on campus?" Jenna asked.

"Tuthill . . . seventh floor." Veronica said.

"Get out of town! Me, too." She turned to Lora-Leigh. "You?"

"I'm in Tuthill on eight."

"You're right near us. Isn't it amazing that we ended up in the same recruitment group?"

Lora-Leigh looked at her and said, "You're so cute, Jenna. I've never met anyone with such a bubbly personality."

"Thanks, Lora-Leigh," Jenna said, feeling herself blush. "So, do you think the dorm will be a lot more fun than living at home?"

Lora-Leigh rolled her eyes. "Anything would be better than being eighteen and living with the parentals."

"No kidding," Veronica said, loosening up some, it seemed. She pulled her name tag out of her recruitment packet and held it up. "Maybe I'll put 'Roni' on this."

Lora-Leigh sat up. "You can use your name tag to say something about yourself. See?" She held hers up, showing that it was already decorated with a gorgeous sketch of a woman in jeans, a black top, and a cartoon face to sort of match Lora-Leigh's.

"That's amazing," Roni noted. "Did you do that?"

"Yeah, well... you know..."

"You should be a designer," Jenna said.

Lora-Leigh's smile danced across her face. "That's the plan."

"Okay, ladies. We're going to get started," the friendly Rho Gamma announced.

Jenna and Roni took a seat on the couch next to Lora-Leigh. The buzz in the lounge area died down and everyone settled in. Jenna laced her hands together to keep from twitching nervously.

A tall, thin brunette addressed them. "I'm Darcy, and this is Tricia. We're the Recruitment Counselors, or Rho Gammas, for Group Seven. We're all so happy that you decided to go through sorority recruitment. I'm sure you're going to remember this as one of the most exciting times in your life. Fraternities and sororities have been an integral part of student life at Latimer University for a long time. Fraternities started here in 1877, and as women began to enroll here, the first sorority chapter was started in 1914. Today, the Greek organizations make important contributions to university life with over forty percent of the undergraduate student population in the thirteen fraternity and ten sorority chapters."

Tricia explained further. "Rho Gammas are fundamental for the formal sorority recruitment process. Darcy and I are assigned to this specific group for the duration of your recruitment time. It's our responsibility to guide you through and provide you with information and counseling whenever necessary."

"Counseling?" one girl asked.

Darcy grinned a gorgeous white smile that made Jenna's nerves calm slightly. There was something about her—an aura, almost—that made Jenna think she was probably a kind, caring, and overall kick-butt friend. After all, she was here being a Rho Gamma instead of working recruitment from the inside with her own sorority. "There are over twelve hundred girls going out for about six hundred or so spots in houses. It's a crazy, fun time, and we're here to help however we can."

"I think I'm going to be sick, I'm so nervous," Roni whispered.

Jenna looked over at her. "It's okay," she said to her new friend. "You're sure to get into a great house."

Lora-Leigh lowered her brows. "If that's what she wants."

Jenna didn't know how to respond, so she sat back and kept quiet.

Roni raised her hand and asked, "How will we know which sorority is right for us?"

Darcy spoke up. "From my own personal experience, believe me, you'll just know."

"Which sororities are y'all in?" a girl shouted from behind Jenna at the Rho Gammas.

"We can't tell you," Darcy said. "See, an important aspect of the Rho Gamma's function during recruitment is disaffiliation. We sever all connections with our own sorority during this time."

"Exactly," Tricia added. "The purpose of our roles is to provide you with unbiased help and support in making the difficult decision of choosing a chapter."

"That makes sense," Roni said to Jenna. She seemed relieved to know there were people who could help her through this week.

Jenna wished it were starting right now!

"I bet you're a Tri-Omega, Tricia," a girl to Jenna's left said.

"Nuh-uh, she's not wearing Elsa Peretti," Lora-Leigh added, as a few girls laughed.

"Elsa who?" Jenna asked in a whisper.

"Tiffany and Company," Roni clarified.

Ahhh...

Tricia waggled her finger and said, "Don't worry, we'll reveal our affiliations at the end of recruitment. Now, Darcy's going to pass around an information sheet to help with final preparations for tomorrow."

"We need you all to write down your class schedules and pass them up to us when you're done," Darcy said. "If you've got a phone in your room or a cell number, please put it down. We need to know how to get in contact with you during the recruitment process."

Jenna watched Darcy move about the room, so friendly, kind, and helpful to everyone. She seemed trustworthy. Maybe Jenna could check with her about her diabetes and whether anyone really needed to know about it while she was going through recruitment.

Raising her hand, Jenna waited for Darcy to come over. "Hi ... Jenna, is it?" Darcy said, noting the name tag.

"Right ... Jenna Driscoll."

"And you're from Marietta, Georgia. My roommate freshman year went to Sprayberry High School."

"Oh, yeah! Home of the Yellow Jackets," Jenna said with a laugh. "I went to Marietta High."

"Cool." Darcy smiled. "So, can I help you with something?"

"Yeah, I need to ask, like, a private question."

"Sure, come over here," Darcy said, stepping them away from the group.

Jenna ground her teeth together for a second while she gathered her thoughts. "Are there first-aid stations and stuff set up around Sorority Row...you know, in case anyone gets sick and needs help?"

Darcy's face showed concern. "Are you okay? Anything I need to know?"

She wanted to tell Darcy, but she'd be branded as different. "Yeah, I was just asking."

"We have volunteers who can attend to anyone who isn't feeling well."

Not wanting to completely reveal why she was asking, Jenna carefully continued. "So they'll have water and juice and stuff if you get too hot . . . or whatever?"

The brunette nodded her head. "Absolutely. I have to tell you, Jenna, that it's very important to stay hydrated during this process. It gets awfully hot out there, so you want to make sure you get plenty of fluids. The first set of parties is called Ice Water Teas, so be sure to drink water at every house. You won't think of it with everything going on, but you really need to take care of yourself. Of course, I'll be watching out for you, too."

"Great... thanks... for all of it." Knowing she could get an emergency juice or water if needed really set Jenna's nerves at ease. There was something about Darcy's genuine smile and kind eyes that almost made her want to come clean. It wasn't necessary, though. Not right now.

"You'll do great, Jenna. Just be yourself and meet as many

girls as possible at the Ice Water Teas. You're sure to make a great impression on them."

"I'm a little nervous, but excited."

Darcy laid her hand on Jenna's shoulder. "That's perfectly natural. When I was in your shoes, I had no clue about sororities. But it has been the best thing I've ever done. This is a great time to really discover yourself and meet some wonderful girls who you'll see every day on campus."

Breathing out, Jenna said, "Thanks, Darcy. That's good to hear."

Moving back to the group, Darcy turned and winked at Jenna and then went to help a couple of other girls.

She's so cool. I wonder what sorority she's in.

Tricia continued the orientation. "Just to let y'all know a little more about your recruitment group. We'll meet here every day in the lounge before and after the parties. These meetings are your opportunity to ask questions and share any thoughts. You'll receive your invitations for that day's parties, decide which ones to accept, and then go to the parties. The meeting after the parties is designated for you to choose the houses you're more interested in and drop others, eventually coming to your top choice."

"We have to drop sororities? How will I know if I'm choosing the right one?" Roni asked as Darcy neared.

"After visiting the houses, learning how they're all special and different, and getting to know the sisters... you'll know," she said.

"I hope so," Roni said.

Tricia continued. "Okay, girls. A few tips for you to remember. Listen up."

Jenna poised her pen to write again.

"Talk to your Rho Gammas and get to know us. We don't bite," Tricia said with a laugh. "Travel light when you go to the parties. No need for purses or cameras."

"Be sure to wear sensible clothes and comfortable shoes," Darcy said. "It's Florida, ladies . . . it's hotter 'n hell out there."

Everyone laughed, especially Roni.

"Here are the important things to remember," Tricia instructed. "This time is about you. Make your own decisions about each house that you visit. Don't let others influence you."

Jenna's eyes shifted to Lora-Leigh and her last comment. Lora-Leigh was playing with a curl on the right side of her head and biting her bottom lip with her teeth, seemingly uninterested.

"You're absolutely right, Tricia." Darcy stepped through the crowd, and Jenna could see her better now. "You really have to approach recruitment with an open mind. I can't stress that enough."

Jenna merely had to take everything in, relax, and be herself, like Darcy had told her. She was going to face sorority recruitment with a smile on her face and a bounce in her step.

"Here's a quick rundown of how Recruitment Week is going to work," Tricia said as she looked at her clipboard. Round One parties are called 'Ice Water Teas.' You'll spend fifteen minutes at each house, with the opportunity to meet as many actives—the initiated members of the sorority—as possible. It's crazed and fast-paced. It's also a lot of fun. Wear comfortable shoes, casual shorts, and nice tops. You'll see all ten houses the first day."

"For only fifteen minutes?!" one girl screamed out.

"You're kidding!" another said.

"That's insane," Roni echoed. "How are we supposed to get to know people like that?"

"It's a tradition that's worked for years," Tricia explained.

Again, Jenna felt exhilarated over the chance of meeting *sooooooo* many people in the next few days. What better way to get acclimated to college life than being thrown into the deep end.

Tricia then went on to explain the other rounds, like the Rho Gamma in the ballroom had told them. The event that sounded the most exciting was Preference Night, when they would spend an hour each at their top two houses, depending on the invitations they received.

"Invitations?" a girl from the table asked. "I thought the choices were ours?"

"Well, they are," Tricia explained. "But you still have to get invited back. And you choose throughout recruitment which invitations you accept. Everything still needs to match up. Right up to the final two houses."

Only two houses to choose from?!

"And for those of you who make it all the way through, Friday afternoon"—Darcy said, with a look of excitement—"will be Bid Day! Bid Day is a time for fun, entertainment, pictures, and seeing the new friends you made during recruitment. The day is the exciting beginning of your life as a sorority woman at Latimer, and your entrance into a sisterhood that will continue throughout your lifetime. You'll gather at the Strumann Student Union in the ballroom, where bids will be handed out. Then, you'll run home to your new sisters, and it'll be like nothing else you'll ever experience."

The girls in the room started whispering, laughing, and giggling. Jenna was glad Amber had encouraged her to come, and she was psyched to have met Roni and Lora-Leigh. Hopefully they'd get to know one another more as this week progressed.

Jenna wasn't sure she'd get an invitation to join a house, but she did know that her pulse had kicked into overdrive at the thought of the excitement to come. Although she knew very little about what was ahead of her, she'd put herself into recruitment 100 percent and show all of these houses what Jenna Michelle Driscoll was made of.

Roni placed her shower kit on the floor underneath the sink and then gathered her hair into a high ponytail. The seventh-floor communal bathroom was packed early this Monday morning, and all eight of the showers were going full blast. Since Latimer's new school year started in about an hour and a half, everyone was hustling to make their eight A.M. classes on time.

"Did you hear Nancy-Jean in 712 backed out of recruitment?" someone shouted out from a shower stall. "Broke out in nervous hives—like welts all over her body—and she had to be taken to the Health Center."

"Shut *up*! She was a legacy to Beta Xi," another responded.

Trying to ignore the banter around her, Roni squeezed some whitening paste onto the end of her toothbrush and quickly scrubbed away at her teeth. Her heart slammed against her rib cage due to the feverish combination of classes starting in a little while and sorority recruitment starting tonight at six P.M. Some of these girls were bordering on frantic over the anticipation of Ice Water Teas.

"Hey, Roni," Jenna said, sliding up to the sink next to her. "I could barely sleep last night from all the excitement. Starting classes, band practice, and this whole sorority thing."

Roni smiled through a mouthful of white foam and then did her best to spit daintily into the basin. "I couldn't sleep either," she said. She rinsed and then dried her mouth with her towel. "All I could think about was getting to my first class on time and not getting poked fun at about my Boston accent later tonight during recruitment."

Jenna, tiny and cute, with her flowing blonde hair piled in a messy bun on top of her head, talked through her striped gel toothpaste. "No one's gonna do that to you."

Roni hoped not. She so much wanted to belong, to be another one of the girls and really make a difference in whichever sorority she joined. If she was one of the lucky ones to get in.

"Did you hear about the girl in 712?" Jenna asked as she rinsed her mouth.

"Right, that Nancy-Jean girl. Dropped out from nerves or something."

"Get out of town," a random girl said on her way out of a shower.

A tall African American girl at the mirror plucked at her eyebrows and commented, "Dropping out yourself is much better than hearing The Knock at your door, I'm told."

Once again, Roni's pulse sped up. "What's The Knock?"

"The Knock is when your Rho Gamma comes to your door with bad news," the girl explained. "It's the worst. No one has invited you back for any more parties. You've got nowhere to go;

therefore, you're dropped—or cut—from recruitment."

Dropped. Cut. The words themselves seemed so . . . dreadful. Why had Kiersten never told her that part? Roni sent up a quick prayer, hoping she could hang in until Thursday night.

"I'd be paralyzed if I got The Knock," Roni said, picking up her kit and moving to the short line for the showers.

"I promise you don't have to worry about it," Jenna assured her. Sweet, nice, bubbly Jenna, who was going through recruitment for the sheer fun of it. Roni wished she could relax and enjoy it, but so much was riding on it. Finding bona fide, true-blue friends who would love her like family.

Suddenly there was a scream out in the hallway, followed by, "Man on the hall!"

Roni popped her head out and saw someone's father carrying what appeared to be grocery bags.

"Holy shit!" someone yelled from shower one. Then the door burst open, and a dripping wet girl in a towel exited with blood running down her leg.

"Ewww . . . ," Jenna said.

Roni gasped. "Are you all right?"

The girl frowned. "Yeah, I'll live. Triple-action blade, my butt."

Roni nudged Jenna forward to the shower that was open. "You go ahead," she said.

"Thanks. I desperately need to exfoliate. Check out this humongoid zit on my cheek. Hello!"

"It's not that bad," Roni assured her.

"Not that bad? No cute boy is going to want to ask me out with *this* on my face."

"It'll be okay."

"Easy for you to say; it's not on your face!"

Digging in her kit, Roni pulled out one of her secret weapons—Acne Solution Cleansing Foam—and tossed it to Jenna. "Here, try this. It'll do the trick."

"Thanks, Roni!"

Roni stood patiently waiting for her turn, thinking how horrified her mother would be if she could see her standing here in a discount towel and two-dollar flip-flops to take a shower in a stall other people had used. Cathryn Minson Van Gelderen had never bathed in anything less than pure marble and would certainly be appalled at having to wear shower shoes to avoid foot fungus.

"Hell, yeah! I can actually get a shower down here," said a familiar, boisterous voice behind her.

Roni turned and saw the cute, short girl from last night. The one with a head full of crazed curls who was now wearing a pink moon-and-stars bathrobe. Lora-Leigh.

Lora-Leigh smiled at her. "It's just whack up there on eight. This one chick from Memphis is totally homesick, and she's locked herself into a bathroom stall. She won't come out. The RA is trying to talk her off the metaphorical ledge, and, in the meantime, I can't get clean."

Roni giggled at Lora-Leigh's scratchy voice, like she'd been cheering at a pep rally all night. Very Demi Moore–ish. She could see beneath the jumble of unruly curls that the girl was a true, natural beauty, with clear green eyes and flawless skin. Although Roni was a little taken aback by her extroverted nature, she found Lora-Leigh to be one of the most interesting people she'd met so far. However, she wasn't sure the native of Latimer returned the sentiment.

"We just had a shaving injury down here," she explained, trying to make small talk.

"Was there blood?"

"Yeah, a lot."

Nodding, Lora-Leigh said, "*Excellllllllllllllent.* No one said college would be easy."

Roni covered her mouth as she laughed at Lora-Leigh's sense of humor. "Well, welcome to the seventh floor. We live on the edge down here."

Lora-Leigh looked at her for a moment, as if studying her, scrutinizing her, and then she cracked up laughing.

They stood in silence until an odiferous stench wafted throughout the bathroom.

"Gross! What is that?"

Roni lowered her voice and whispered, "That's Taylor Britt. She's got irritable bowel syndrome that's exacerbated by stress."

"That's nasty. We definitely need a mercy flush."

"Shhhh!"

When the toilet flushed a second later, Roni covered her mouth to hold in her guffaw. The door to shower two opened, and a toweled girl walked out with her cell phone, rolling her eyes. She covered the receiver part. "Gotta keep my parents informed at every stage of the game."

Raising an eyebrow, Roni muttered, "A cell phone in the shower?"

Lora-Leigh leaned toward Roni and said, "If my mom had her way, she'd put GPS on me twenty-four/seven."

"She can't be that bad, can she?"

Lora-Leigh shrugged her shoulders.

Roni shook her head. Her parents could care less where she was and what she was doing, as long as it didn't reflect negatively on them. "Why don't you take the open shower?"

"That's okay, Boston, you were here first."

"Okay... but don't say I didn't offer." Roni stepped into the vacant shower stall, undressed, and then squealed when the lukewarm water hit her.

"That first spray is a killer, Roni!" Jenna called from her shower.

Roni heard Lora-Leigh call out from the other stall. "Who's that over there?"

"Who's *that*?" Jenna called out over the splashing sounds.

"It's me, from Recruitment Group Seven. Lora-Leigh Sorenstein. Native of Latimer, Florida. Doomed to spend my whole life here. Remember?"

As their mutual showers commenced, the girls talked over the tiled booths. "This one girl on my floor said last year her sister totally puked at the Tri-Omega house when they served the shrimp rolls at one of their parties," Lora-Leigh reported. "Seems she was allergic to shellfish or something."

"Bet she didn't get asked back," Jenna quipped.

Lora-Leigh added, "She threatened to sue."

Roni shampooed her long tresses and tried not to laugh. She'd be mortified if that happened to her. Might as well pack up everything and go back to Beantown and admit defeat. Of course, had her father been around when that occurred last year, he would've handed the girl a business card for representation in her lawsuit against the whole organization—as long as he got his proper cut of the settlement.

She rolled her eyes at the thought and stepped back under the water. She'd heard around the halls that the Tri-Omegas were a great house, where the girls tended to be more upscale, fashionable, and popular. Sounded like they were similar to the circle of high school friends she'd left back in Boston. She wasn't sure if she should be excited about meeting them and thinking she'd feel at home, or whether she should run screaming because it might represent all she was trying to get away from.

"Hey, you guys—" she started to the other girls.

"Wait a minute!" Lora-Leigh burst out laughing in her stall. "It's 'y'all,' Boston, not 'you guys.' Are you a guy, Jenna?"

There was a pause. "Umm... not that I can tell from this angle."

"I like you, Jenna," Lora-Leigh shouted out.

Roni frowned into the steamy water. She wished Lora-Leigh liked her, too. "As I was saying before I was so rudely interrupted," she said with a giggle, "what class do *y'all* have first today?"

Jenna piped up. "English Composition 101 in Billado Hall."

"Better watch out, Jenna," Lora-Leigh warned. "Billado has two sections. The new construction 'round back is Billado New Hall, and the colonial design out on the front part is Billado Old Hall. Which one is your class meeting in?"

Roni noticed a palpable pause while she scrubbed at her skin. "Jenna?"

"Y'all, I have no flippin' *clue* which part I'm supposed to go to! I better get my butt in gear."

"Didn't mean to freak you out," Lora-Leigh said. "That's not something they tell you in your orientation class. It's been tripping up new students for years."

Roni heard Jenna's shower stop and realized she couldn't luxuriate in the hot stream either. Especially when there were other girls waiting and she had no idea what she was going to wear to her first class: Geography 101. It looked interesting from the course description.

"What's your first class, Lora-Leigh?" Roni asked, still trying to get the girl to warm up to her.

"I've got Western Civ over in Palmer Auditorium."

"In an auditorium?" Roni's prep school in Boston had an auditorium, but it certainly hadn't been used for classes.

"Yeah, it's a freshman weed-out class," Lora-Leigh explained as her shower went silent. "You know, to see who's serious about studying, who's here to party, who can move on to the higher-level, tougher classes next semester."

She and Lora-Leigh exited their showers at the same time. "I'm here for the long haul," Roni said, smiling at the girl's wet ringlets. "How about you?"

There was a distant look in Lora-Leigh's eyes, and she zoned out for a moment. Roni feared she may have said the wrong thing.

"Long haul? We'll see . . . ," she trailed off.

Roni nervously reached up and twisted at her left earring; a two-carat brilliant cut from Tiffany's in New York. The action caught Lora-Leigh's eyes, and she stared.

"Nice rocks. Are they real?"

Coming from any other girl, Roni might have considered the

question rude. However, Lora-Leigh didn't seem to be one who played games, and Roni didn't want to lie to her. "They were a graduation present from my parents."

Lora-Leigh nodded and scrunched up her face. "I see."

Feeling tension bouncing between them, Roni felt it was best to get back on her schedule. "Well, I better run. See you tonight, Lora-Leigh."

"Sure." She turned away, then stopped and spun around. "Oh, and Boston?"

"Yeah?"

"I bet you'll love the Tri-Omegas." And with that, she exited the bathroom.

I wonder what that means?

CHAPTER
5

Lora-Leigh felt like a complete shit.

She shouldn't have been rude to Roni. She probably had no clue why she irked Lora-Leigh so much. It wasn't Boston's fault she was the textbook case of what Lora-Leigh knew Omega Omega Omega would be looking for in their new members: thin, gorgeous, fashionable... from money. That was another reason Lora-Leigh knew she wouldn't fit in there. She knew she'd be that legacy they *had* to take.

Sort of like how Latimer University *had* to let her in because of her father.

She thought she could slink into Professor Romero's Western Civilization class unnoticed this morning. Wrong! The older man with the funky handlebar mustache—that her mother thought was the most charming thing in the world—saw her the minute her Steve Maddens hit the auditorium carpet.

He took six long strides toward her with his hand stretched out to her. "Well, if it isn't Thomas and Hannah's little girl."

"Hello, Professor Romero," she said through a forced smile. She half expected him to ruffle her curls like he used to do whenever he came over for faculty dinners at the house.

The professor released his grip on her and then dangled his hand in the air between them for a moment.

Don't do it, Doc. Resist. The. Urge.

She must have been a strong sender because he reached to stroke the length of his salt-and-pepper mustache instead of going for her scalp. "I never expected to see little Lora-Leigh Sorenstein in my class. It seems like only yesterday you were riding your bike all over Latimer. Now look at you."

She looked down at her feet and wished the auditorium floor would open up and swallow her whole. She heard a small snicker to her left and quickly shifted her eyes to see some beef-cake athlete sitting at the end of the row, listening intently.

Great, make me look like a dork in front of my new classmates.

"How are your parents?" the professor asked.

"Fine," Lora-Leigh responded, trying not to look at her fellow students, who were sitting at rapt attention. "They're just fine. You know Dad, works twenty-four/seven."

"And your brother? How's he doing?"

Lora-Leigh's brother was twelve years older and had left Latimer when Lora-Leigh was only six years old. "Scott's in Germany, working for a computer company," she reported. "He'll be home for Thanksgiving."

"Good...good," he said with a nod. "Well, it's very nice to have you here at Latimer with us. Don't expect any special treatment, though." He knocked her on the shoulder and winked.

"Of course not, Professor." She glanced around the room and saw that it was jam-packed with eager freshman. Maybe not eager, but here, at least. She knew from the LHS grads who'd come to school here that the first few weeks of class were always highly populated. That was until everyone got bored, slept too late, were hung over, or begged others to take notes for them. "I should probably find a seat," she said, wanting to end this convo.

"You do that, dear." Professor Romero ambled back down the aisle and began shuffling papers at the podium.

She looked over at the cute athletic guy sitting there in his jeans and white T-shirt. He looked vaguely familiar, but she couldn't put a name with the face to save her life. She slipped into the seat two down from him and quickly opened her notebook. His eyes were on her, she knew it from the shiver that skipped up her back. Trying to be coy—not one of her better traits—she craned her neck to see the guy and noticed his brilliant green eyes staring back at her from his dark face. She smiled weakly and turned back to her notebook, pulling her curls around her chin to hide her embarrassment at being caught gawking.

"Okay, class. Welcome to Western Civilization 101," Professor Romero said, breaking into her awkward moment. "Let's get started."

The professor dove right into the lecture, not giving the students a chance to acclimate to their surroundings. Lora-Leigh listened carefully. History had been her favorite subject in high school, so this class should be a breeze for her.

It obviously wasn't going to be a breeze for the cute athlete, though. Halfway through the class, Lora-Leigh stole a glance at him and saw that he was asleep. Not an obvious nap in his seat, rather his arm was propped on the armrest and his left hand cradled his head while his right hand was poised to take notes. In a class this full, he wouldn't get in trouble, though he needed to watch napping in smaller classes.

Typical jock.

As the professor droned on about Mesopotamia or the Ottoman Empire or something they'd be covering during the semester, Lora-Leigh thought about how much her father disliked the athletes on campus, feeling they were given special treatment because of the popularity of sports at Latimer. Lora-Leigh didn't care . . . as long as the guy didn't fall asleep on her and drool.

When Professor Romero dismissed the class, Lora-Leigh shoved her notebook into her backpack, tossed it over her shoulder, and bolted out of the auditorium before the professor could corner her again. Besides, her art class—which she was looking forward to most of all—started in ten minutes, and she had to walk from the auditorium, behind the library, and to the Art Department complex.

Outside the air was thick with humidity, and it made Lora-Leigh wish she'd brought a ponytail holder so she could get her curls up off her neck. She walked through the hordes of students shuffling from one building to the next in the time between classes. Some ran while others took their time, as if they didn't care. Her pace was solid since she wanted to get a good seat in Art 110.

The Art Department sat between the looming campus library and the Strumann Student Center, and consisted of three brick buildings facing into a courtyard. The area included a small park enclosed by a black wrought-iron fence that looked very New Orleans–ish to Lora-Leigh. She moved through the open gate and took in the scent of oil paint in the air, combined with the sweetness of begonias and Shasta daisies. Monkey grass surrounded a small fishpond, where a couple of students sat with their sketch pads. The tranquil setting made Lora-Leigh smile, no longer feeling so out of place here at LU all of a sudden.

She headed straight to the back building and took the steps two at a time to get to room 242. Once inside, she gasped when she saw a familiar face.

"You," she said.

The sleepy athlete from Western Civ answered, "Yeah, me."

She looked at the empty desk and easel next to him. "Anyone sitting here?" she asked boldly.

"Looks like you are, Curly," he said with a killer sharp smile.

Lora-Leigh's knees literally went weak from his overt flirtation. Fortunately, the hard, wooden seat solved the stability problem. *Attitude, girl.* "Name's Lora-Leigh, not Curly. Who do you think I am... one of the Three Stooges?"

"Curly was bald," he noted, and then laughed. The guy peered at her with those amazingly clear green eyes she'd noticed earlier. The kind you see only in the advertising pages of *Vogue* or *Elle* or *GQ*. Oh yeah, he could be in *GQ* all right. He stretched out a large hand to her in offering. "I'm DeShawn."

She couldn't contain a gasp. She may not have wanted to attend Latimer University, but she was certainly a gigantic fan of the Red Raider football program. Anyone with half a brain in the city limits knew who DeShawn was. From the looks of his marble-toned and muscularly shaped body, he had to be the one and same. "You're DeShawn Pritchard, right?" Star running back of the football team.

"In the flesh," he said, followed by a dazzling smile.

Oh. My. God. He really did go to school here and wasn't just some sports celebrity they flew into town for football games. Sure enough, DeShawn Pritchard, sophomore, number 33, was a genuine student.

She had to be cool. He was just a guy.

Yeah, a drop-dead gorgeous, hot guy.

He pulled out a metal tray of Caran d'Ache Pablo Colored Pencils. Wow, she thought, Swiss precision wasn't just for watches and army knives. These pencils were expensive and professional. Much better than the Prismacolor Colored Pencils she used for her clothing designs.

"You surprise me, DeShawn Pritchard," she said with a slight smirk.

"How so, Curly?"

"Lora-Leigh . . . Sorenstein," she corrected.

He rubbed a large hand across his chin. "Yo, we've got a Dean Sorenstein here."

"Funny, I have a father named Dean Sorenstein here."

They laughed together at the vague *Animal House* reference.

"Before we start talking about sensual vegetables," he said, "why don't you tell me how I surprise you?"

She loved quoting movies and was glad to see DeShawn hadn't missed a beat in the conversation. "You surprise me because you're this big, superstar jock. And you're in Art 110?"

He shrugged and fingered his pencils. "I want to be an architect, and I figured the art classes would help. Besides, I love to draw."

"That's pretty smart," she said, genuinely impressed. Most athletes she'd known relied on their physical prowess instead of brains to get them through life, hoping for big contracts in the NFL, NBA, and other acronyms. Nice to see that DeShawn had other plans.

DeShawn's right leg was stretched out and his jeans bunched up at the ankles, like he was wearing them low on his waist. New Nikes adorned his enormous feet, and she wondered if those were gratis from the LU Athletic Department. He smelled lightly citrusy, like he was wearing Tommy Hilfiger or—she sniffed—Happy for Men.

He looked up at her, and she silently prayed he hadn't heard her sniff at him. To cover it, she tried to make conversation.

"So, what was with the catnap last class?"

He rubbed his eyes and straightened in the seat. "Coach had us running the stadium stairs last night and we're doing two-a-days. I'm wiped."

"Two-a-days. Practice in the morning and the afternoon, right?"

"Right."

"It'll pay off next week when y'all play your first game."

"If I live to see it," he said with a sigh. "That's why sitting here and drawing for an hour is good. Helps me relax."

"Me, too," she said with a smile. What were the chances that an offensive powerhouse like number 33, sophomore DeShawn Pritchard, relaxed by drawing? All she knew was that she loved it, and now she had a major reason to look forward to every Monday, Wednesday, and Friday.

"Where is it?" Jenna pleaded to no one as she wandered the halls aimlessly. Class started in *five* minutes! This was ridiculous.

Lora-Leigh had warned her about Billado Hall being New and Old. Her class schedule said nothing about New or Old. How hard was it to find one stupid English composition class?

A shaggy-haired guy bounded down the stairs to her left.

"Excuse me," she said, feeling incredibly idiotic. "Can you tell me where room 227 is?"

The cute guy turned around, looked her up and down, and smiled. "Hey, you're that girl I knocked into at the Supe Store yesterday. How random is that?"

It *was* him! "Yeah, that was me. Just call me Grace."

"Nice to meet you, Grace," he said with the sweetest grin.

"No, sorry, I was poking fun at myself. My name's not Grace. I meant I wasn't very graceful, you know?" She really needed to shut up.

"So, what were you looking for?"

She held out her class schedule. "Room 227."

"In Billado Old or New?"

She wanted to scream and pull out her hair. Or his. "That's the problem," she said, exasperated. "See, I have no idea."

"Freshman, huh?"

Dropping her eyes, she said, "Does it show?"

He smiled. "Nah. Well . . . sort of. Everyone has this problem at first. I did last year when I was a freshman. What's the section number for your class?"

Jenna peered at the card in her hand. "Section four."

The guy scratched his chin and thought for a moment. She took the opportunity to check him out more. Tanned skin, probably from hanging outside all summer, deep blue eyes (which she remembered from the Supe Store run-in), and quite a nice build. He wore Gap-looking khaki shorts and a red T-shirt with yellow writing that read GOING ON A FOX HUNT with the Greek letters ΦΟΧ underneath. Phi Omicron Chi. Right. (She'd been studying her Greek letters.) They were known on campus as "The Foxes."

After thinking for a sec, he said, "You probably want Billado Old because of the section number. They tend to put the higher section numbers in Billado New."

"Wow, thanks," she said a little too breathily. "How'd you know that?"

"David Harrison, sophomore extraordinaire, knows the lay of the land," he said with a smile.

"Thanks . . . David." She held her hand out. "I'm Jenna, not Grace. Jenna Driscoll."

"Well, nice to meet you, Jenna. You can call me Tiger."

"Tiger?" she asked, with a puzzled look. How could someone this incredibly adorable be called Tiger? It sounded so fierce, so predatory, so . . . not him.

"My fraternity brothers call me that. I'm on the Latimer golf team. Tiger, like Tiger Woods . . . get it?"

She laughed like an eighth grader. *Geez... get a grip.* "I get it. Cute."

After a moment of smiling at her and—*dare I think?!*—checking her out, he asked out of nowhere, "So, if you're a freshman, are you going through sorority recruitment?"

"I am. I'm starting to get excited about it." She certainly was glad she'd signed up so she had something to talk to Tiger about.

"I'm sure you'll have a lot of fun," he said. Then he cocked his head to the side and added, "All the really cute girls get into sororities."

He thinks I'm cute? Jenna felt herself blush from the top of her ponytailed head to the bottom of her sandaled feet. Her tongue seemed as if it weighed ninety pounds all of a sudden, and she was at a loss for words. A garble sound a little bit like an "uh" and a "whuuuh" came out, and she covered her slip with a bright smile.

Tiger smiled back, apparently pleased at himself for making a newbie to campus swoon like a southern belle of old. "Well, Jenna Driscoll. You should get going if you're going to make it to class on time."

She panicked and her pulse sped up. "You're right! Thanks, David! I mean, Tiger."

As she began heading up the stairs, he called out to her. "Hey, Jenna, good luck with recruitment."

"Thanks."

"I live over at the Phi Omicron Chi house. Maybe I'll see you around."

"Maybe so," she said.

David turned and continued down the stairs to the ground level.

Jenna leaned over the banister and watched him walk away. *I better move it!*

She spun around fast to head up the stairs, but missed the next step altogether. Her books went flying out of her hand and she tumbled down to the bottom, landing *hard* on her tailbone and smacking her forehead against the metal railing. That was gonna leave a mark.

"Crap!"

Dizzy from the spill, Jenna sat there for a moment to get her equilibrium back. Had her 'betes caused that? Nope. A cute boy had caused it. Plain and simple.

An older woman in sensible shoes hurried out of a nearby office and asked, "Are you okay, sweetie?"

"Yeah," Jenna managed to answer while getting back to her feet. "I was in too big of a hurry."

The woman put her hand under Jenna's elbow and ushered her toward the office. "You come in here with me, and I'll get you something from the first-aid kit."

"No really, I'm okay. I have to get to class. Thanks."

"Are you sure?"

"Yes, ma'am. Can you tell me where room 227 is?"

"Right up the stairs, third classroom on the left," she said. Then she added, "You be careful now, you hear?"

Jenna smiled and tried the stairs one more time. That was what she got for paying too much attention to David "Tiger" Harrison. A bruise on her butt and—she lifted her hand to her forehead—an impressive welt on her head.

Great... she'd get to meet all of Sorority Row looking like she'd gone three rounds with Oscar de la Hoya.

"You did that exactly how?" Roni asked Jenna as they were standing in the bathroom looking at the bluish bump on Jenna's head Monday afternoon.

"I don't want to talk about it."

"Come on, Jenna. Tell her the story," Lora-Leigh said.

Roni frowned slightly at the thought of Jenna telling Lora-Leigh before she'd told her. "You don't have to tell me if you don't want to."

Jenna grabbed Roni's arm and held on. "No, Roni! I'm just embarrassed. I mean, first the zit this morning and now this. I'm a klutz and a half."

Roni hugged Jenna to her and smiled at her in the mirror. Even with the large, pink Barbie Band-Aid—care of Lora-Leigh, she'd been told—placed at a jaunty angle on the side of Jenna's forehead to cover the purple bruise, she was still adorable. Jenna regaled her with the details from this morning, including meeting a cute Phi Omicron Chi and then taking a header down the stairs. I'm glad you didn't break anything! Could you imagine going through recruitment with a broken arm or leg?

"I don't think the Band-Aid is going to work, though," Roni offered. "I have this really terrific makeup that can cover up your bruise, and it won't draw attention like a Band-Aid."

"Kind of like that magical makeup on television that Jessica Simpson uses?" Lora-Leigh asked with a wink.

"No, that's acne stuff," Jenna corrected.

Roni swallowed and then surged ahead. She knew these two were just kidding with her, but she honestly wanted to help Jenna. Opening her large Hermés bag, she drew out some foundation from her makeup bag and dabbed it on her fingers. "I'll try to be gentle," she said to Jenna.

As Roni spread the base around, Lora-Leigh reached for the bottle. "La Prairie? Holy shit, Boston! That stuff's over two hundred dollars."

Pulling back, Jenna's eyes grew large. "Oh, Roni, I can't use your expensive makeup."

Roni pursed her lips, ready to defend her products, but she wanted to do everything she could for Jenna—and to show Lora-Leigh she wasn't some sort of snob. "It's really okay. I got it at a discount store . . . on closeout." She hated lying about her material things, and it amazed her how easily the half truths were slipping out of her mouth. "This is really good stuff, Jenna, and it'll help cover up your bump, I promise."

"Thanks, Roni, you're the best."

"Yeah, Boston. Good move," Lora-Leigh said, and then gave her a thumbs-up.

They chattered and laughed while Jenna had the makeup and powder applied. Roni hadn't chatted this naturally with people for as long as she could remember. All of her friends back home cut up only when it was at the expense of someone else. She'd never participated in such bad karma, always making sure she smiled at whoever was being ridiculed by her pack. They always thought she was simply going with the flow and doing what they were doing, but she knew the truth.

Trying to help, Roni said, "You know, Jenna, we can play

with your hair a little bit so your bangs cover up the bump for the most part."

"Oh, but she'll have a story to tell at each house," Lora-Leigh said in contradiction. "No one will ever forget the cute chick who literally fell for a hot guy."

Roni sighed. It seemed that no matter what she offered, Lora-Leigh had some commentary. Roni was starting to think that Ms. Latimer had something against her. Maybe she was just being paranoid.

"Where have you been, Boston, that your hair's all wet?" Lora-Leigh asked. This time, Roni knew Lora-Leigh's inquiry was genuine and not messing with her in any way.

"I just got back from the natatorium."

"The nata-whatty?" Jenna asked, screwing up her face.

Roni laughed hard. "Natatorium. Indoor swimming facility, over by the tennis courts and near the Athletic Department offices. I like to do laps every day to stay in shape and also to clear my mind."

"That's cool," Lora-Leigh said, as if surprised. "I like to sketch when I need to clear my mind. It's a good way to focus and to relieve tension or stress."

Roni nodded. The chlorinated water always seemed refreshing to her, every time she dove in. One of the things that sealed the deal with Latimer University for her was the fact that they had a state-of-the-art natatorium. Sure, her parents had paid for an expensive swimming coach—none other than U.S. Olympic double-bronze medalist in the 100 and 200 meter relays, Haley Dieterle—but it was the escape into the water and the movement through the pool that kept her body and mind exercised.

"There, Jenna. All set," Roni said. She put the makeup bottles back into her purse and zipped it up, not going unnoticed by Lora-Leigh, who seemed to be able to zero in on designer labels. "Now I need a quick shower."

"So, what are y'all wearing tonight?" Jenna asked, turning away from the mirror.

"I have a black miniskirt, a pink tank, and a black lace overtop to go with it," Roni reported. She left out the detail of paying two hundred dollars for said lace overtop.

Lora-Leigh perked up, though. "Does it have a plunging neckline and a tiny elastic notch at the waist?"

Roni nodded her head. "It does. How did you know?"

With a proud smile, Lora-Leigh said, "Last year's Club Monaco collection."

"Good call. Wow. You're good, Lora-Leigh."

Lora-Leigh winked. "That's what I've been told."

Roni sensed a flush on her neck. "What about you, Lora-Leigh?"

"Well, tonight I'm wearing this fuchsia outfit that's got spaghetti straps, a deep neckline, and pleats around the waist, along with hot pants," Lora-Leigh announced.

"Hot pants?" Jenna asked.

"Yeah, I made the whole outfit myself."

Roni's mouth dropped. "That sounds daring."

"If I have to do this, I want to be remembered."

How will I be remembered? Roni asked herself.

As if reading her mind, Lora-Leigh said, "Wear your hair down, Boston." She held her hand up to stop what Roni was about to say. "I know it's going to be majorly hot, but you've got hair other girls would kill for. It'll really bring out your eyes."

Okay, so maybe Lora-Leigh didn't dislike her if she was making fashion suggestions. "Thanks, I'll do that."

"I gots to go get ready," Jenna announced in an exaggerated southern accent. "I should take a couple of Tylenol for this headache, too."

"You poor thing," Roni said. "You guys want to walk over to Sorority Row together?"

"Y'all, Boston . . . *y'all.*" Lora-Leigh teased, with the nudge of her elbow.

Half an hour later, Roni met Lora-Leigh and Jenna in the lounge on the seventh floor. A bump on the head certainly did *not* slow down Jenna Driscoll in her jean skirt and striped green-and-blue shirt, which hung on her in a slightly baggy way. She had such a cute figure; she should show it off instead of hiding it. Lora-Leigh looked like a million dollars in her flaming pink hot pants and chiffon sleeveless shirt. Thin tanned arms led to her trim wrists covered in bangle bracelets. The three girls couldn't be more different than morning, noon, and night, yet there was something pulling them together.

"Ready to go?" Lora-Leigh asked.

"As ready as I'll ever be." Roni's palms were damp, and she wanted to wipe them down the sides of her skirt. That would be too obvious, though.

"Aren't y'all a nervous wreck?" Jenna asked as the elevator doors slid open, full of girls from higher floors dressed and ready for the recruitment festivities to begin.

Lora-Leigh placed her hands on both Jenna's and Roni's shoulders and said, "It's showtime."

When they reached the first floor, the girls poured out into the Tuthill dormitory's main lobby and out onto the front walk. Much like marching ants, they followed the line of the sidewalk to the crosswalk. Local traffic respectfully stopped for the flow of girls dashing across Williams Drive over to Sorority Row. The sun was still shining bright even at six in the evening, and Roni could hear what she'd been told were cicadas in the trees. It was as if they were watching the festivities and providing their own sound track.

Up ahead, she saw the sign for Group 7 and looked down at her informational card to verify they were headed to the right house. Ten visits between now and ten P.M. How were they ever going to do it? How would she ever remember anyone's name or face? How would they remember her?

"You're really into this, aren't you, Boston?"

Roni shifted her gaze to Lora-Leigh and gave a half smile, as if apologizing. "I admit it. I am. This is the most exciting thing ever. The tradition, the process, the thought of a house full of new friends. How can it be bad?" When Lora-Leigh opened her mouth, Roni halted her. "Nope. You're going to go into this with an open mind and to have fun."

"Yeah, Lora-Leigh," Jenna echoed. "What she said."

"All right! All right! I can't fight both of you," she said, with a slight crack in her voice.

It was at that point—right then—that Roni saw a tiny fissure in Lora-Leigh Sorenstein's tough veneer. There was a shyness under the surface and a plea in her eyes to belong... just like every other girl here tonight.

"Don't you ladies look nice," Darcy said as she approached. Roni noticed a quick wink to Jenna. "Are you ready to start?"

"I'm wicked psyched," Roni said with exuberance. "We have to watch out for Jenna tonight. She banged her head today over at Billado."

Darcy was at Jenna's side instantly to hear the whole story.

"Well, kids . . . this is it," Lora-Leigh announced.

Roni took a deep breath, mentally outfitted herself in bungee attire, and said, "Let's go!"

Lora-Leigh thought she was going to sweat to death or melt into a puddle on the ground from the frickin' heat as she and the rest of Group 7 stood in front of the Alpha Sigma Gamma house on Sorority Row. They were awaiting the official start of recruitment with the traditional southern Ice Water Teas.

She thought of the contradiction of ice water and hot tea. Apparently, back in the olden days, they actually served tea, but nowadays, they served water in a tea cup or something like that. Hopefully someone would offer finger sandwiches or a chicken wing or something. Her stomach was growling fiercely.

A sigh escaped from deep within her chest. She honestly didn't want to be here. But she knew it was easier to do what her mother wanted than to have to hear about it the rest of her life. *"If you'd just gone out for a sorority, Lora-Leigh . . ."*

Roni and Jenna were cut out for this, she thought. Typical teens, fresh-faced girls, neither from here. Lora-Leigh sensed she'd run into way too many former Latimer High people who would skip over her in favor of girls from other places.

She'd already run into Justine Thornton from LHS, who'd joined Eta Lambda Nu last year. Now, she was a Rho Gamma, and Lora-Leigh had to act like she didn't know her... or her sorority affiliation. Again, the trappings of a university town.

"Are you nervous?" Roni asked for the third time.

Lora-Leigh shrugged. She supposed she should be, but honestly, she couldn't care less. This was more of a formality than anything. Besides, once all of the WASPish Buffys in these houses took one look at her eclectic designs and nine hoop earrings, they were likely to drop back five yards and punt her. Which would be fine with her. It would give her time to finish a couple of outfits before the first football game.

"No, I'm not nervous."

"How can you not be?"

Lora-Leigh knew she shouldn't be such a pessimist—or bust Boston's chops too much—but she couldn't help herself. After all the buildup and talk and pretending she could enjoy this, she snapped. "Because, Boston, they're just trying to make you think they like you when really they're all cardboard cutouts of one another."

Roni stared at her in horrified shock. "Then what are you doing here?"

"Same thing as about half of these girls, I bet," Lora-Leigh snarked. "Doing it because my mother is making me."

"Mine, too," another girl chimed in.

Other girls around them snickered. Apparently, Lora-Leigh was absolutely right.

Roni's bottom lip quivered, and Lora-Leigh felt like a royal shit. "Look, I'm sorry, Boston. You'll have fun, and you'll do great. We're just here for different reasons, that's all. Nothing wrong with that."

For a moment, Lora-Leigh wished her new roommate was here with her. Virginia—from Virginia, no less—was a Goth chick. Virginia had no interest in joining the Greek system, thinking it was nothing but a bunch of clones that made you conform to their rules and ways.

That would be Mom's Tri-Omegas.

Jenna was obviously trying to ease the tension and couldn't stop chattering. "Amber tells me the Alpha Sigs are a real party house."

"They all enjoy a good party," a blonde girl said. "It's a rite of passage."

An Asian American girl spoke up. "I'm ready to get through here and get to the Zeta Zeta Tau house."

Lora-Leigh glanced down the street to where she knew the ZZT house to be. Then she looked up at the Greek letters over the door of the huge house before her: Alpha Sigma Gamma. The houses here had to be massive to hold so many girls, usually more than a hundred. The antebellum, Tara-like design in front of her certainly stood out on the street, where there were a couple of modern-day mansions and one house that even looked like a New Orleans French Quarter home, with wrought-iron balconies. And, of course, there was the uniquely shaped Tri-Omega house.

"I heard the Alpha Sigs do a credit check on your parents," one girl said.

"No," another piped up. "That's the Tri-Omegas who do that."

Lora-Leigh liked the Tri-Omegas less and less the more she heard about them.

"That's not true, is it?" Roni asked with wide eyes.

"Don't worry, Boston. You'll pass." Crap, there she went again, taking a swipe at Roni. She didn't mean to do it. It was simply that Roni reeked of what Tri-Omega was looking for. Maybe in a small way, Lora-Leigh was jealous she didn't have the same thing to offer. If she did, her mother wouldn't be as disappointed in her.

"Why is this taking so long?" Jenna asked impatiently. She glanced at her watch and said, "I have that it's after six."

"They go by the official Rho Gamma clock," another girl said.

So they stood there on the porch of the Alpha Sigma Gamma house, waiting to see what would happen next. Summer gnats swarmed around in the Florida heat, aggravating the waiting Rushees. Lora-Leigh desperately hoped her deodorant and body spray held up in this weather.

Quite frankly, she wanted to be done with all of this nonsense so she could go back to the dorm and take a long, cold shower. And order a grilled chicken salad from the dive Bash Riprock's on The Strip—they delivered! Oh yeah, and finish the boyfriend pants she'd started last night.

Unexpectedly, there was a flurry up and down the street.

"What's going on?" Jenna and Roni asked together.

Another Recruitment Group stood behind them at the Pi Epsilon Chi house and one more next door at Beta Xi. All around Sorority Row, fellow potential sorority girls gathered around . . . waiting for *something* to happen. No one knew what. Lora-Leigh had an idea, based on what her mother had told her, but it had sounded so brainless. Surely they'd updated recruitment in the gazillion years since her mom was in college.

Looking around, Lora-Leigh saw the Rho Gammas were strategically placed by the front doors of the houses up and down the street. For some reason, Lora-Leigh's heartbeat sped up, and she was suddenly very aware of everything going on around her.

"Something's about to happen," Roni muttered. Then she reached for Lora-Leigh's hand and squeezed tight. Lora-Leigh expected to want to pull back; instead, she held on.

A loud police whistle cracked through the air—scaring the shit out of her.

Darcy knocked hard on the double door and then got out of the way.

Lora-Leigh, Roni, and Jenna jumped back when the door of the Alpha Sigma Gamma house flew open, revealing tons of girls in matching yellow dresses piled up together in the doorway. They started clapping, screaming, and . . . singing.

Singing? You've got to be kidding me.

Then the same loud noise came from behind them and next door and down the street and over on the other side of the street. Voices, some shouting, some singing, sounded out over Sorority Row, blending together and trying to outdo one another.

It was chaos! It was madness!

Jenna was smiling like a goofball. Roni looked totally jazzed. Lora-Leigh tried hard not to laugh.

The girls in front of her stopped singing and began chanting out their welcome in a cheer worthy of any rowdy Red Raiders football game: "Alpha Sigma Gamma, it's the place to be! Alpha Sigma Gamma, it's the place for me! Ain't nobody finer than the sisters here. Join us if you wanna, you will be a dear.

Those Alpha Sigs are the best! The best of all the rest! Alpha Sigma Gamma, it's second to none. Alpha Sigma Gamma, we think you're the one!"

"Oh my God," Lora-Leigh exclaimed.

"I think I'm going to pass out," Jenna whispered.

Roni said, "Here we go. Everyone ready?"

Lora-Leigh grimaced, supposing she had no other choice. "Whatever."

The Rho Gammas guided them into the opening of the house as the Alpha Sigs crowded around. Lora-Leigh felt an extremely welcome gush of air-conditioning from inside. The girls moved into the tiled foyer and, one by one, were paired up with a sorority sister and guided deeper into the house. Quickly, she lost sight of Roni and Jenna in the sea of brunettes, blondes, and a few redheads.

"Hi! What's your name?" a bubbly brown-haired Alpha Sig asked.

"I'm Lora-Leigh."

"I'm Astor! Welcome to my house."

"Thanks for having me," Lora-Leigh said with a smile, not knowing what else to say.

"Do you mind if I guide you through the party?"

Lora-Leigh furrowed her brows. Oh right, some people preferred not to be touched. "Sure."

Astor beamed a smile at her. "I can't wait to introduce you to all of my sisters! We're going to meet them all!"

"Okay," she said. Did she really have a choice? This Astor chick could use a dose of Ritalin to calm her the hell down.

And with that, Astor tugged Lora-Leigh into what appeared

to be a large dining room that was completely bare of furniture except for an expansive table in the back with a punch bowl. It was so loud in the room that Lora-Leigh thought her ears were going to burst. Nothing her mother had told her could have prepared her for the actual frenzied pace of this event. Sisters of Alpha Sigma Gamma had each paired with a potential new member and were hastily steering her around the room.

This is nuts! This is no way to meet people.

"Let's get you some ice water," Astor said, pushing Lora-Leigh through the crowd.

At the punch bowl an older woman—probably an alum—ladled ice water into a cup and passed it over. Lora-Leigh downed it like it was a Red Bull, giving her energy and quenching her thirst all at once. Another older woman zipped by and took the cup from her, and then she and Astor were on their way to the middle of the room.

Lora-Leigh got the feeling she was in a computerized video game, with people coming at her from all directions, smiling and shouting. There was Jenna over in the corner and Roni in the middle of a group. The room was full of nothing but hands and arms, hair and smiles. *And those butt-ugly yellow dresses.* There was no way on God's green earth she'd ever remember anyone's name or face. But Astor powered her through the room, circling and pushing and introducing her, moving in and out, dashing over there to catch a new face.

People yelled out their name as Astor shouted Lora-Leigh's. There was no time really to answer or even start a conversation because she was herked and jerked to the next person. So much for the gentle guiding from Astor.

Lora-Leigh's head was abuzz. Ice Water Tea made her feel exactly the same way she felt when she hung out with her friends and got a good beer buzz, only with her blood NASCARing underneath her skin. And around again they went, twisting and turning in and out among the bodies as the air conditioning tickled her bare arms.

The lights in the dining room flickered, and there was a collective "awwww..." as the Alpha Sig sisters began corralling them back through the front hall and out the door.

Was that really only fifteen minutes?

"It's over? That was quick."

Lora-Leigh was belched out of the house with the rest of the girls as the sisters inside waved good-bye and thanked them for coming. Like that, it was over.

"That was crazy!'" an exasperated Jenna said as they walked down the path and followed their Rho Gammas to the next house. Jenna ran ahead and caught up to Darcy to walk with her.

Roni flipped her hair and fanned her face. "That was a complete high! I've never experienced anything like that before. So, come on Lora-Leigh, what did you *really* think?"

Lora-Leigh shrugged, unimpressed. "Bring on the other nine houses."

Three hours later, Lora-Leigh thought this night would *never* end. They were nearing their last house, though. *The home stretch.*

"It's amazing how different houses try to get you to remember them," she said to Roni while they walked.

"What do you mean?"

Lora-Leigh ticked off points on her fingers. "The Delta

Kappas served slices of lime in their water; the O Chi Os served sparkling water. The Alpha Sigma Gammas chilled their house so much that you could hang meat in there, while the Beta Xis had no air-conditioning on at all."

Jenna rejoined them. "You're right. I'll never forget the Beta Xis because they smelled!"

"You guys!" Roni giggled.

As their group rounded the bend of Sorority Row, Lora-Leigh looked up at the last house on their card. The warm yellowy stucco design and red tile roof made the Zeta Zeta Tau house look quite homey and inviting. Like they weren't trying too hard to be different... just doing it in an elegant, Old World way.

"I don't think I can smile anymore," Jenna said.

"Only one more house, Jenna," Darcy said, and then patted her on the back.

"I'm superjuiced for this," Roni said. She was as fresh as she'd been at the first house hours ago. Hair in place, makeup perfect. Lora-Leigh wanted to hate her.

When the whistle blew and the door flew open, the ZZTs silly door song—which sang out of "everyone belonging... the home you've been longing"—actually made Lora-Leigh *feel* welcomed. Maybe she was merely exhausted and hallucinating.

A cute, thin black girl latched on to her the minute she stepped into the house. "Hi, Lora-Leigh!" she said, looking at the name tag. "I'm Camille."

"Hey, there!" Lora-Leigh dashed her eyes over the girl in front of her. Camille had a sense of style about her with a flowing summer skirt and navy blue tank top that showed off her caramel-colored skin. Lora-Leigh was relieved to see the girls in this house dressed their own way instead of wearing matching outfits like some of the other houses. Okay, so they were sort of color-coordinated, but she wouldn't hold that against them.

"I see you're from Latimer. That's great!"

"Where are you from?" Lora-Leigh said, playing the same game she'd played nine other times tonight.

"Miami." Camille leaned close and shouted above the noise, "I have to tell you, I just *looooooooove* your whole outfit. So hot! Where did you get it?"

Lora-Leigh beamed up at her over the compliment of her chiffon layered top paired with hot pants. "I made it. I design my own clothes."

"Shut up! You do not?"

Lora-Leigh's chest filled with pride. "I do!"

Camille's mouth dropped. "Honey, you can design my clothes any day. That's fantastic."

"Thanks," she said, although her natural instinct was to wonder at Camille's sincerity. Lora-Leigh had seen the looks she'd gotten at a couple of houses over her fashion sense.

"You have the perfect figure to wear hot pants."

"Thanks, Camille. What can I say? I'm a junkie for anything to do with fashion."

"One of our philanthropy projects last year was donating clothes to a battered women's shelter and then going in to help the women with makeover tips. It was such a satisfying experience."

Lora-Leigh cocked her head a little, letting Camille's words sink in. She was moved by their charitable efforts, but they—all of the sororities—had a lot of convincing to do.

Camille whizzed her into the living room, cleared of furniture so everyone could move about. While there was still the normal "hello my name is" and quick pace, Lora-Leigh noticed these girls more. The one with the long red hair had a cool set of dangle earrings like ones Lora-Leigh had seen at a downtown thrift store a couple of weekends ago. Another girl had a small diamond stud in her nose. They didn't seem pretentious or judgmental.

Being steered around by Camille, Lora-Leigh met a Megan, a Sarah, an Amy, an Erin, and two Nicoles. Girls were all over the room, weaving in and out, shouting louder and louder. Lora-Leigh's heart pounded to the cadence of the room and the kinetic energy being generated. Out of the corner of her eye, she caught glimpses of Jenna and Roni, both seemingly enjoying themselves.

All right, I admit it . . . this is a bit of a rush!

The lights started flickering, just like they had in the previous houses. Only this time, Lora-Leigh wasn't as eager to leave. She wanted to stay longer. Hang out with Camille and get to know her better.

Camille leaned in. "You did a great job, Lora-Leigh! I think we met everyone twice. I *really* hope to see you again!"

"Thanks, Camille. Great meeting you!"

And then Lora-Leigh did the last thing she expected herself to do. She turned and squeezed Camille's hand.

"Good luck," the ZZT whispered.

Lora-Leigh was surprised to find herself hoping that the

sisters genuinely liked her and that she'd be asked back. Deep down, she knew she *would* see Camille and the sisters of ZZT again.

CHAPTER
6

Roni smoothed her hand down over her green silk shirt while she looked at her recruitment party invitation card.

She'd had a beast of a time steaming the shirt before the party, trying to get all the wrinkles out from its being packed. Because her family's maid had always done her laundry, Roni had taken for granted being able to step into her walk-in closet—no problem—and pick whatever outfit she wanted to wear for the day. Now that she was here on her own, she was finding mastering the steamer a bit of a task. Sure, she'd scored high on her SATs, but she hadn't known how close to hold the device to the garment without damaging it. She was determined to learn such domestic tasks, though. Normal human beings on Planet Earth didn't have a maid to take care of them at every turn.

Recruitment Group 7 had met with Darcy and Tricia in the Strumann Student Center right before the parties started—

Jenna had assured her the steaming job was "just fine"—to see what invitations they'd received and which parties they would attend. Roni was floored when her computer printout indicated that all ten houses asked her back for Round Two—Skit Night. It had been an extremely hard decision—one she had to make without consulting Jenna—but she'd gone with the following six choices:

Party One	Omega Omega Omega
Party Two	Theta Beta Gamma
Party Three	Delta Kappa
Party Four	Zeta Zeta Tau
Party Five	Omicron Chi Omega
Party Six	Alpha Sigma Gamma

Waiting to go into the first party, Roni had a hollow feeling in her stomach, wishing that Jenna was with her right now. Since the second round was an invitation party, girls in the Recruitmment Group went to different parties at different times. But she figured the odds that both Jenna and Lora-Leigh had some of the same houses on their invite list were pretty good. Maybe they'd end up at another party at the same time. Roni saw Jenna in front of Beta Xi, and Lora-Leigh was across the street at Omicron Chi Omega.

Roni looked at her card again and up at the three matching Greek letters on the house: ΩΩΩ.

From what she'd overheard in the hall and in the bathroom, Tri-Omega was one of *the most* elite houses on campus. Lora-Leigh was a legacy to Tri-Omega, but from the snide comments she'd made, Roni got the distinct impression she wanted nothing to do with these girls.

Lora-Leigh probably thought Roni was a snobby rich girl and belonged with the same type of people. Sighing, Roni realized she'd been tagged with that label her whole life. The "right" friends, the "right" private school, the "right" connections. That had all gone out the window when she'd announced she was coming to Latimer University. So why would she gravitate toward the same kind of people—the Tri-Omegas—now?

Don't judge them until you go inside.

Just then, the Rho Gammas blew their whistles, and the doors to the houses opened all around Sorority Row. Roni and the rest of her group started laughing when they realized the girls of Tri-Omega were dressed as flight attendants, each wearing black suits, sensible shoes, white blouses, and scarves around their necks. They wore wings on their breast pockets, which she'd learned were a symbol of the sorority. The girls sang their door song and proceeded to welcome them inside.

Roni and her group began moving into the horseshoe-shaped house. The blonde Tri-Omega with the blunt haircut—who had taken Roni around yesterday—saw her, waved, and hooked her arm through Roni's.

"I'm sooooooooo glad to see you again, Roni!"

What's her name? Oh, no . . . I can't remember!

Biting her lip, Roni improvised. "It's good to see you again, too."

Blunt Haircut Girl pulled her in through the main foyer, then the dining area, down the back steps, and into the open courtyard that was in the middle of the horseshoe. The house wrapped around the courtyard and was filled with sisters gathered on the balconies of the three stories, where it appeared the sleeping rooms were located. Roni looked around at the finely tended southern garden full of gardenias, hydrangeas, and rose bushes. The sweet smell of the flowers wafted around in the night air and tickled Roni's nose. *This place isn't so bad.*

Just past the garden in a large rec room in the back, a stage was set up. Roni was amazed at the pageantry they put on to make the room look like an honest-to-God airplane. The seats were arranged in rows of two, three, and two across, and were made of blue leather. She was escorted to the first-class section up front. This staging must have cost a small fortune, what with the authentic-looking airline seats with $\Omega\Omega\Omega$ embroidered into the back of the headrests.

"May I get you something to drink, Roni?" Blunt Haircut Girl asked expectantly. "We have excellent service for our first-class passengers today."

"Sure," Roni said, her eyes taking everything in. "Whatever you've got."

A moment later, the young woman returned with a tray containing a lemonade, a bowl of peanuts, and a small plate of cucumber sandwiches (with the crusts off). Roni was afraid of eating anything that might stick in her teeth or cause smelly breath, so she simply smiled at the small bounty before her.

"We're happy to have you flying Tri-Omega Airlines with us today. We hope your experience will be pleasant."

A taller girl dressed in a captain's uniform stopped at Roni's set of seats. "Mignon, is this Roni Van Gelderen, whom you were telling me about?" the girl asked.

Right... the blonde's name is Mignon... as in filet. How could she forget that?

"Yes, Captain Cornelia! This is Roni from Boston. Her father's a senior partner at the law firm of Van Gelderen, Schneider, and Fossbaum."

Roni's mouth almost fell open. How did Mignon know that?

Equally impressed, "Captain" Cornelia reached out for Roni's hand and shook it. "You're the one whose mother went to Wellesley, right?"

"Ummm... that's right. How did you know?" Roni took a quick sip of her lemonade to ease her parched throat. Who were these girls... Homeland Security?

Cornelia continued. "We try to learn everything we can about the girls going through recruitment, especially the ones of such top caliber, as yourself."

"Cornelia is the president of the chapter. She's from Connecticut."

"That's right," Cornelia said. "A fellow New Englandah."

Roni laughed at her put-on accent, but it made her feel more at ease in this opulent setting.

"You had really good grades in high school," Mignon commented. "What are you going to major in here at LU?"

"I'm not sure yet," Roni said. "Right now, I'm loading up on core classes and then deciding what really speaks to me."

Mignon frowned; Cornelia lowered her brows at her sister and said, "I did the same thing when I first started. Now I'm in broadcast journalism."

"Oh wow, that's ambitious," Roni said, and then sipped her lemonade again.

"I've been doing the pageant circuit," Mignon piped up. "Journalism is a really good career to get into after doing pageants."

Roni's eyes widened. "Have you won any?"

Mignon shook her head. "Not since high school. I'm only a sophomore, so there's plenty of time. You should totally think of entering the Cressida Beauty Pageant."

"What's that?" Roni had to remember how big beauty pageants were in the South. Certainly not anything she'd ever been exposed to in Boston.

"*The Cressida* is our yearbook, and they hold a yearly pageant. It's a prelim for the Miss Florida, United States, contest."

"That's big." At least the way Mignon said it made it sound like a huge deal.

For some reason, she could just hear Lora-Leigh laughing at how this tête-à-tête with Mignon was going. Talk of beauty pageants and popularity. No wonder Lora-Leigh dreaded having to come here. It definitely was not her scene. But Roni wondered if it was the place for her.

Mignon and Cornelia chatted away, asking her about everything from what kind of car she drove to whether she wanted to date fraternity guys. Roni's brain hurt from having to come up with clever (or vague enough) answers. She nearly rejoiced when the show started.

The houselights went down and the United Airlines music — George Gershwin's "Rhapsody in Blue" — started playing. Roni watched as the stage cockpit lit up in the symbol of an Omega. Several Tri-O's acted as if they were going through recruitment, entering the plane and being looked over by the flight attendants. They were trying to decide which girl was worthy of joining Tri-Omega Airlines. They cracked some jokes and made everyone laugh, but the message was clear: Tri-Omega was the best sorority on campus, and they expected their new members to live up to that reputation.

At one point, Mignon leaned over to Roni and said, "You'd totally pass our in-flight test."

Roni was flattered that these outgoing, popular, and pretty girls would take to her. However, there was something... not right. These girls seemed so much like the flock of friends she'd just escaped. She didn't necessarily need to surround herself with people who looked exactly like her, or the image she once portrayed.

The skit ended with confetti flying out from where the oxygen masks would be, out onto the seated girls. The thirty minutes were coming to a close. Mignon escorted Roni to the front door.

"I know Cornelia can talk your ear off, but since she's on the board of the house, she really wants to get to know the special girls."

I'm special? "Oh, that's nice."

"I really think you'll fit in here, Roni. You're exactly the type of girl we're looking for. I hope to see you again." Mignon gave her a quick hug, and said, "Thanks for flying with us today at Tri-Omega. Have a safe trip, and whenever you're making your sorority selection, we hope you'll consider the sisters of Omega Omega Omega."

That was cute.

Roni didn't want to judge the Tri-Omegas simply by

Cornelia's inquisition. Mignon was friendly and outgoing. Someone Roni would be comfortable hanging out with. Maybe the Tri-Omegas weren't merely about looks, money, and social status. Maybe they liked her for who she was.

She'd give them one more try... if they asked her back.

Amber waved at Jenna from across the room at the Delta Kappa house Round Two party. Jenna started to lift her hand but didn't want to make a big scene. Amber leaned toward the Delta Kappa sitting with her, pointed, and waved again. The Delta Kappa craned her neck at Jenna and smiled. Jenna smiled politely. Amber nodded again.

Jenna sipped her diet soda and looked around the room at all of the Delta Kappas running around, getting girls seated and welcoming them.

Too bad Jenna couldn't be as confident about this whole process as Amber. Nothing bothered her roommate. Not the group meetings, not the thought of getting cut, and certainly not the idea of having to choose which sorority, if any, to join from all these really nice girls. Her Rho Gamma, Darcy, had been really attentive to her when they picked up their recruitment invitations and when they were going from house to house. Jenna wished she could figure out what sorority Darcy was in. It would be supercool to be in Darcy's house.

"Are you having fun, Jenna?" the freckle-faced Delta Kappa named Roxanne said to her. Roxanne had taken her through Ice Water Teas and had been there waiting for Jenna tonight when her group entered the house. "I'm so glad to see you back."

"This is great, Roxanne," Jenna said, and then took another sip of the soda Roxanne had brought her.

Roxanne's strawberry-blonde hair was pulled into two high ponytails, one on either side of her head, and her costume was a pink-and-purple-checked dress, à la the 1960s. Their party theme was "The Delta Bunch," and several of the girls looked like they were trying to channel Cindy, Jan, and Marcia Brady.

"It's really far out here with the Delta Bunch, Jenna," Roxanne said, staying in character. "We're really into campus activities. We have sisters involved in all of the campus political organizations, including the SGA. Dana Hanover over there is on the Latimer tennis team—they won the regional championship last year—and Katy McGill is on the gymnastic team."

Jenna listened carefully, and her heartbeat accelerated. "Anyone in the marching band?"

"Oh yeah… see the girl with curly black hair? That's Raven—aptly named, eh?—who's one of the Raiderettes."

Looking at the raven-haired beauty, Jenna nodded. Not really a trumpet-playing geek like herself, but she was in the band, so that counted. The Raiderettes were the high-stepping dancers who entertained in their sequins and satin as the band played for them. Raiderettes were all tall, thin and gorgeous, and had legs that went on for years. In other words, the total opposite of Jenna.

"There are a lot of girls coming through the house who are doing band," Roxanne reassured. "Are you?"

"I'm a third trumpet."

"Cool! Do you have any questions about the Delta Bunch that I can answer for you?"

Jenna shook her head. "I can't think of anything right now. Y'all are great. Everyone's so friendly and nice." A lot of smiles and giggles, and the girls in the house actually seemed to like one another.

"We're a family here, Jenna. We support one another and always look out for our Delta Bunch sisters."

Jenna was finding a common theme with the sorority houses she'd visited: everyone seemed to be an important motor in the overall machine, and everyone's contributions and assets blended in to make the group better. She had her band participation to offer, and she also had her tremendous organizational skills. Maybe joining a sorority wouldn't be too taxing on her. And she'd have this new family.

"Thanks for having me here, Roxanne," Jenna said politely. "I'm glad I came today."

"Me, too. Wait 'til you see our skit. That'll win you over," Roxanne said with a laugh. "I'll be back after the sketch."

Roxanne wasn't kidding about the fun skit, Jenna thought, as the entertainment began. The Delta Kappas used their front staircase as the stage, looking very *Brady Bunch*. The girls in the sketch lined up in height order from top to bottom, all dressed in the pink-and-purple-(the official colors of Delta Kappa, Jenna had learned)-checked dresses. The sixties seemed a million years ago to Jenna, but she enjoyed the tribute to one of her favorite TV reruns.

Jenna clapped along as the girls sang *The Brady Bunch* theme song with Delta Kappa lyrics. The skit was about a girl who met the Delta Bunch and was invited to join their family. Jenna found the skit heartwarming and funny. She actually felt a lump in her throat when the lights flickered and the party came to an end. She had three more parties to go to, but could any of them really live up to this amazingly warm feeling she had going right now?

It was at that moment that Jenna realized what had hit her. Whether it was within the Delta Bunch or not, she *wanted* to be a sorority girl more than anything else.

Last party of the night, and Lora-Leigh's ass was dragging. Just now, the Theta Beta Gammas had girls in their house act as potential new members in an *American Idol* skit. The girls sang along with the ΘΒΓ songs as if auditioning to join the sorority. Lora-Leigh had never enjoyed singing, and certainly wasn't thrilled to have to sit through a Theta-ized version of some Faith Hill song. The Delta Kappas had been more imaginative with their *Brady Bunch* tribute, and the Pi Epsilon Chis had had an amazing *Willameena Wonka and the Pi Ep Chi Factory* skit, in which sisters acted out the role of orphans touring the Pi Ep Chi house, but only one was offered membership. It was a bit on the cheesy goofy side, but Lora-Leigh appreciated their set design, intricate costumes, and, most of all, the massive amounts of chocolate they'd fed her.

She didn't even want to *think* about the Fly Omega Airlines skit. *Lame, lame, lame.*

If any of these sororities really wanted to make an impression on her, they needed to crank it up a notch and get the room alive. She longed for something fresh and hip and active.

As she walked into her last party, she noticed that the sisters of ZZT were dressed in the smartest fashions. Some wore suits;

others had on cocktail dresses. Some looked like they were going to a backyard picnic in the Hamptons, and others were dressed in crazy, outlandish formal dresses. Like something Lora-Leigh would make. The foyer of the house was decorated in black, gray, and white cutouts of buildings and skyscrapers. *Ahhh... it's New York*, she thought, making out the silhouette of the Chrysler Building. Once deeper into the house, music poured from the room they were headed into, and Lora-Leigh could feel her pulse betray her by speeding up in anticipation. At the darkened doorway, a ZZT stood with a clipboard at the velvet rope, checking girls' names off and allowing them access into "Club ZZT." Overhead, House and Dance music shuffled together, and the entire atmosphere was hot and hip.

I totally dig this.

Inside, the sisters met them, pulling them into the club, sparkling with lights of all colors. A cute, chubby brunette came up to her. "Welcome to Club ZZT, Lora-Leigh!" the girl said, and smiled brightly. "We're so happy to have you back for our ZZT and the City party."

"Oh wow, that's cool," she said in response. "Thanks for having me." She spun around, taking in the club atmosphere, complete with a small stage, dance floor, and a DJ's booth. She didn't see Camille anywhere. She sighed and choked down her disappointment when her new escort said, "I'm Megan, and I want to introduce you to more of my sisters."

Megan led her deeper into the dining space, which had been redecorated into a club atmosphere. A bar was set up in the back. They offered her a ZZT Cosmopolitan (cranberry juice and soda water) and introduced her around. One girl was a Web-design major, another was in nursing school, and a third was in hospitality. They all commented on Lora-Leigh's swanky print dress that was a bit of a rip-off of a Just Cavalli design she'd seen in *Vogue* last month.

As much as Lora-Leigh appreciated the attention of these girls, she couldn't help but continue to look around for Camille. Did she have another (better) potential new member to attend to? Was that quick bond they'd had at the Ice Water Teas just part of the act?

"We have a table reserved for you at the front," Megan said.

Lora-Leigh tossed her curls away from her face and put on her best smile. She might as well enjoy the rest of the party. Jenna was in the back of the room with another sister, and Lora-Leigh nodded at her. It was apparent Jenna was having the time of her life. Lora-Leigh sat at the small cocktail table near the front of the stage.

"We'll have two more people sit with us," Megan explained.

Then Roni, of all people, sat down at the table with her.

"Hey, Lora-Leigh!"

"Fancy meeting you here, Boston." She wasn't sure Roni would appreciate the *Sex and the City* tribute, most of all the costuming. It was really eclectic and paid homage to another one of Lora-Leigh's favorites, Patricia Field, the TV show's costume director.

"Y'all know each other?" Megan asked.

"We're in the same Recruitment Group," Roni explained.

The girl with Roni stretched her hand out. "So nice to meet you, Lora-Leigh. I'm Beverly Chang."

"Get this," Roni started. "You know how after you accept admission to Latimer, they have current students e-mail you?"

Lora-Leigh had ignored most correspondence from Latimer, other than her dorm assignment letter. "Yeah, right."

Roni was literally beaming with enthusiasm. "Beverly's the one who e-mailed me! How wicked exciting is that to meet her like this?"

"Small world," Lora-Leigh said, and smiled. She wished she could drum up some of the enthusiasm both Boston and Jenna had going. Maybe she should get the hell over herself, relax, and enjoy this last party. Let it be fun instead of work. She sipped the ZZT Cosmopolitan and tried to loosen up.

Before Lora-Leigh could even settle into any kind of conversation, the houselights flickered, the music faded, and the stage lit up.

"The show's starting," Megan said. She leaned closer. "I hope you like this, Lora-Leigh. Camille told me you were quite the fashion designer and wanted you to know we made all of the costumes."

"Where is—?"

But she was cut off by the hooting and clapping when the theme song to the show *Sex and the City*—of which she owned the full DVD collection—cranked up. Four sisters crossed the stage together and took a seat at the mock-Manhattan streetside café. The snazzy dresser in the red suit and plunging neckline was playing Samantha Jones. The girl named Erin, whom she'd met yesterday, was playing the prim and proper Charlotte York. A red-headed girl in a business pantsuit was in the role of Miranda Hobbes. And Lora-Leigh nearly choked on her ZZT Cosmopolitan when she saw that none other than Camille, with her curly hair spread over her shoulders, was acting the part of Carrie Bradshaw.

Camille winked at Lora-Leigh but went straight into character.

The skit was hilarious... very true to the classic TV show. The girls talked about how, when they came to Latimer, they didn't know anyone, but when they'd found one another and ZZT, they knew they'd come home to a wonderful family... and that family was oftentimes what you made it.

Lora-Leigh could see Roni was totally buying into the whole presentation, and Lora-Leigh had to admit this was one of the freshest and most creative sorority sketches she'd seen. At least it was something fairly current and relatable. Who didn't want to be like the fabulous women of *Sex and the City*?

Camille was doing a great job as Carrie, too, whining about Mr. Big (who was a frat guy) and how she'd chosen her family: Zeta Zeta Tau.

Okay... I'll buy that.

At the end, other sisters joined the fun onstage, and they all danced together with the music cranking up again. The room lit up with excitement, everyone clapping to the House rhythms beating out from the speakers. These ZZTs sure knew how to put on a show.

Lora-Leigh stole another glance at Roni sitting next to her. The Bostonian's face shone in the stage lights reflecting on the audience, and she sat there engrossed in her surroundings. Lora-Leigh couldn't believe such craziness and pop culture was Roni's scene, but she was pleased to see her enjoying it. Maybe she'd judged her wrong.

Shrugging at the thought, Lora-Leigh swayed to the music, clapped her hands, and elbowed Megan to let her know that this was *waaaay cool* in her book.

Lora-Leigh felt herself getting caught up in the moment— like Roni, sitting next to her. When Camille pointed a finger toward her from the stage, continuing to sing, Lora-Leigh felt the insatiable urge to jump up, start dancing, and singing along with them.

Uh-oh... I'm in deep shit.

CHAPTER
7

After Geography 101 on Wednesday morning, Roni's head was pounding right at the temples. Not a migraine like her mother constantly got and treated with days in bed, ample meds, and all of the shades pulled. The throbbing was enough to annoy Roni, though. It was probably due to the droning, monotone lecture. Or maybe it was the overambitious cologne from her neighbor in class. It could have been the grueling fifty minutes of Calculus that followed Geography. No matter, she needed to clear her thoughts with a strenuous workout. Right after calculus, she'd made her way to the natatorium, quickly got into the pool, and began her laps.

Stroke, stroke, stroke ... breeeeeeeeathe.

Stroke, stroke, stroke ... breeeeeeeeeathe.

Stroke, stroke, stroke ... breeeeeeeeeathe.

Roni held her breath and executed a perfect flip underwater to touch the side wall of the pool, push off, and swim to the opposite end.

Roni loved swimming. Loved how it made her feel. It was the one time she was completely . . . free.

She stopped in the shallow end, tugged off her goggles, and dunked them in the water to clear off the fog from her workout. Before slipping them back into place, she squeezed water out of the ends of her ponytail and cocked her head to the right to rid her ear of some gathered water.

That was when she noticed him.

How could she not? He was two lanes over from her and one of the only other people in the pool. Cutting through the blue water, he created very little wake behind him as his long strokes carried him the length of the pool. His muscled back rippled with each movement, and his chiseled calves powered him forward.

Suddenly, her competitive gene kicked in.

Feeling up to a challenge, Roni wondered if she could match his pace. When he made the return trip to her end of the pool, she readied herself to race him. He executed a flip underwater, and she took off.

Stroke, stroke, stroke . . . breeeeeeeeeathe.

Stroke, stroke, stroke . . . breeeeeeeeeathe.

Stroke, stroke, stroke . . . breeeeeeeeeathe.

She didn't stop to see if she was staying with him. Her coach, Haley, had taught her to concentrate on her strokes alone. Focus on breathing, never losing the rhythm.

Roni kicked her legs harder, pushing herself more than she ever had. At the end she flipped and turned around, catching his physique in her peripheral vision. He was right there, swimming with more force, it seemed. Had he noticed what she was doing?

Roni didn't care, tucking her head down and concentrating on making it to the other end of the pool. Surprisingly, she wasn't winded at all. Rather, she was energized by the impromptu competition. Her arms stretched around and around, slicing through the water and zooming her toward the other end. One more flip and another trip to the other end.

Her heart slammed away under her black one-piece bathing suit, her chest tightening with the excitement and adrenaline rushing through her.

This time, when she reached the end, she stopped, grabbed the side of the pool, and whipped off her googles. Smiling broadly, she turned to her left to see if the guy was still there. He was! Looking at her with wide, sparkling hazel eyes.

"I give! You beat me." A deep chuckle bubbled from him, and she couldn't help giggling. She didn't want to admit she was racing him, but he was no dummy.

"I was just trying to keep up," she said.

"You're an awesome swimmer," he admitted.

He looked vaguely familiar to her. Where did she know him from? "Thanks," she said politely.

He ran his hand through his wet, thick brown hair and smiled at her again, a dazzling show of straight white teeth that almost made her legs turn to Jell-O under the water. "You should try out for the swim team."

Her face heated from the compliment, and she went under the water for a moment to douse the flames. When she surfaced, she wiped her face and said, "No . . . I just do it for exercise and stress relief."

"What's a girl like you got to be stressed about?"

She had no idea what to say to this gorgeous guy. "Ummm . . . you know, school and stuff."

Speaking of which, she glanced at the natatorium clock. Round Three of recruitment parties started in two hours. She needed to get home, get a shower, and get ready to put her best foot forward again.

Roni pulled herself out of the pool and reached for her towel. She could feel his eyes on her as she dried off, and it nearly made her shiver.

"What . . . no rematch?" he asked from the water.

She laughed and faced him again. "Sorry, I've got to run. Maybe another time."

"I'm always here," he said.

Roni wrapped the towel around her waist and released her hair from the ponytail holder. "Yeah, me too. See you around."

And with that, she dashed off to the women's locker room. She couldn't wait to get back to the dorm and fill Jenna in on *this* development!

Lora-Leigh walked into her dorm room, ready to plop down on the bed and get some rest. "What is that smell?" she asked, looking around.

Virginia was standing in the corner, her bed pulled away from the wall, with a paintbrush in her hand. "It's a class assignment. I'm painting my half of the room black."

"You're what? Dude, are you kidding me?"

Virginia adjusted one of her nose rings and frowned at Lora-Leigh. "The professor in my Interpersonal Communication class said we needed to do something to express ourselves, even if it might make another person uncomfortable. I'm to do the action, observe, and take notes."

Lora-Leigh shook her head and tried not to laugh. "Couldn't you have stood too close to someone in an elevator? You know, invading their personal space or whatever?"

"This is much more fun," Virginia said, stroking the large brush with black paint on the nice, soft industrial yellow walls. "I can't wait to see what the RA says when she sees this. Maybe it'll get me on probation. That would make an excellent paper for my class."

"Whatever," Lora-Leigh said with a laugh. "I don't give a rat's ass what you do on your side of the room." She knew her father *did* give a rat's ass. If the dean of students found out freshmen were going Goth in their dorm rooms and taking it upon themselves to change the university's decor, Virginia would be yanked into his office, or taken to the Student Health Center for a full suicide watch or something. In any case, Lora-Leigh had other things to worry about.

She tossed her stuff on her bed, changed into a zip-up hoodie and a pair of sleep pants, which were her favorite non-Lora-Leigh-made wardrobe items, and grabbed her laptop.

"I'll be in the lounge if anyone is looking for me."

Lora-Leigh knew she would have at least enough time to check her e-mail, see if there were any posts on the message boards of any of her classes, and do a little surfing. L.A. was having Fashion Week in a few weeks, and she wanted to read up on who was showing and whether or not they were doing any sneak peeks on their Web sites.

Once in the common area, Lora-Leigh settled into the corner of a couch, booted up her laptop, and enjoyed the wireless connection available throughout the dorm. Having Internet was one thing; being able to escape the confines of her dorm room (and the Eau de Sherwin-Williams) was priceless.

The minute her computer booted up, her instant messenger software chord sounded out and a new IM screen appeared from The_Butler_Did_It. *It's Elizabeth!*

The_Butler_Did_It: what up Sorenstein?

Designs_on_you: Yo, Butler. How's Pennsylvania treating you?

The_Butler_Did_It: brutal. studying until all hours. i love it. hows lu?

Designs_on_you: Cool so far, I guess.

The_Butler_Did_It: see any1 i no?

Lora-Leigh typed for a minute about seeing Molly Ballard from Drama Club when she was outside of the Omicron Chi Omega house yesterday. Molly was really into sorority recruitment and was so glad to see a familiar face. She'd also asked about Elizabeth, so Lora-Leigh passed that on. Typing fast, she told Elizabeth about seeing people she remembered from the hallways of Latimer High School, like Justine, the Rho Gamma.

The_Butler_Did_It: hows recruitment going?

Designs_on_you: It's okay. Not as stupid as I thought it'd be.

The_Butler_Did_It: hows that?

Designs_on_you: If you must ask . . .

The_Butler_Did_It: i must

Designs_on_you: It hasn't been as fake as I expected. Well, except for the Tri-Omegas. They're nice enough girls, but they're all so rich and pretty and . . . cookie-cutter. I just don't fit there as much as my mother would like to pound my square peg into that round hole.

The_Butler_Did_It: makes sense.

Designs_on_you: I'm just ready for this to be over with.

The_Butler_Did_It: maybe its a good idea 2 join a sorority. youre cute and fun and hip. every1 needs 2 have good social experiences in college.

Designs_on_you: And I need to be Greek for that? Besides, I'm only here one year. I mean, I have met some cool chicks and I see where maybe I could lend some of me to a house or two. If I'm leaving, though, I don't want to get too attached.

The_Butler_Did_It: r u trying 2 convince yourself or me?

Lora-Leigh looked at the words on the screen for a moment. She thought about the night at ZZT and their *Sex and the City* party. Sure, she'd had fun and they'd gotten to her a little, but was it worth giving up her plans for fashion design school to have that "normal" college experience other girls have? Would she lag too far behind fashion trends by not getting the concentrated training she so wanted? She admitted hanging out with a fun bunch of girls was a good enough idea. Would she be able to walk away, though, at the end of the year?

The_Butler_Did_It: u still there?

Designs_on_you: Yeah, sorry. People walking through the lounge.

The_Butler_Did_It: so what r u going to do?

Designs_on_you: About what? Recruitment?

The_Butler_Did_It: durr

Designs_on_you: Finish it up and see what happens. But I tell you, Elizabeth, I'm gonna need one hell of a sign to change my mind about staying here past a year and committing myself to a sorority.

The_Butler_Did_It: isnt the fact that u r enjoying it a sign?

Designs_on_you: I need a BIGGER sign. Otherwise, I'm leaving my card blank.

The_Butler_Did_It: What does that mean?

Designs_on_you: That I'll leave my preference card blank. I won't choose anyone.

The_Butler_Did_It: i hope u get ur sign, Lora-Leigh.

The_Butler_Did_It: look, my roommate wants to head over to the caf. there's this junior engineering student she's got her eyes on and she knows when he eats, so i gotta bolt. i just wanted to say "hi," honey.

Designs_on_you: Thanks, Lizzy. Miss ya.

The_Butler_Did_It: miss ya 2. l8r.

Lora-Leigh closed the window and then powered down her computer. She didn't feel like surfing or anything now. What she needed was an extra hot shower to soothe her thoughts. She *was* enjoying sorority recruitment and meeting all these girls. And that knocked her world slightly off its axis.

Would she get her sign?

"Where are you headed?" Amber asked Jenna as they exited Tuthill Hall and carefully made their way across the traffic of Williams Drive to Sorority Row.

Jenna looked at her card of party invitations and read it to her roommate:

Party One	Beta Xi
Party Two	Alpha Sigma Gamma
Party Three	Delta Kappa
Party Four	Zeta Zeta Tau

"Those sound great for you," Amber said, glancing at her own card. "I've got only three party invitations, but I'm not worried 'cause they're all good houses. First up, Theta Beta Gamma."

"Yeah, I don't have them." The Theta Beta Gammas had invited Jenna back, but that was one of the invitations she hadn't accepted. She hoped she hadn't screwed things up.

"I'm just going to go," Amber said. "The important party is Delta Kappa."

"Okay, I'll see you back at the dorm then," Jenna said.

"No, we're at Delta Kappa at the same time. You know, with

my connection there, it's pretty much a formality. And how cool would it be if we both joined Delta Kappa?"

"That might be fun, Amber," she said. Truth be told, she thought her roommate's overconfidence might hurt her if she went into these houses with her devil-may-care attitude. Secretly, if Jenna was going to go through with all this, she wanted to join Darcy's sorority, not Amber's.

Sweat rolled down Jenna's neck, moistening her back. This September weather was certainly making her wilt, so much so that she wished she could chop her hair off. What was that thing Roni did with hers? She'd take it, twirl it around into a bun, and then tuck the ends in. Jenna tried, contorting into this psycho hairdresser position, but it didn't stay.

"Crap."

"Do you need some help, Jenna?"

It was Darcy who was always there to rescue her.

Jenna frowned. "Do you have a rubber band I can borrow?"

Darcy smiled at her. "Sure! Long hair's a bit much in this heat, isn't it?"

"Thanks! You're the best, Darcy."

"Gotta take care of my girl." She winked and then shooed Jenna away toward the girls gathering outside the Beta Xi house.

Forty-five minutes later, Jenna exited the Beta Xi house— where she'd just helped paint some pottery the Beta Xis were going to take to a nursing home—and turned up the street for her next party at the Alpha Sigma Gamma house. The heat reached out and wrapped its sticky fingers around her again, but she was much more comfortable with her hair up. She fanned herself briefly, plucking at her loose blouse over her hips. Then she remembered it was covering her insulin monitor, and she stopped picking at it. Since they served sweet punch and cook-ies at a lot of these parties (alcohol was strictly forbidden!), she ratcheted up her insulin just a squidge to compensate. *I'd be soooooo embarrassed if anything happened during a party.*

The other girls inched up the front path of the Alpha Sig house, but Jenna couldn't help glancing over at the Delta Kappa red-brick estate on the corner. Jenna wasn't sure, but everyone else in Group 7 was convinced Darcy was a Delta Kappa and that Trisha was an O Chi O. That was why Jenna had accepted the Delta Kappa's invite back for Four Party. Well, that and she really enjoyed their *Brady Bunch* skit.

Something caught her eye around back of the Delta Kappa house. The rear door opened, and she gasped when she saw someone slip out—a Rho Gamma (she could tell from the uniform). The girl didn't have on a visor and—

"Oh, my God! It's Darcy," she said in total shock.

"What was that, Jenna?" a fellow freshman asked.

"What?"

"Sorry, I thought you were talking to me," she said, looking at Jenna like she was crazy.

Jenna wondered if she should "out" Darcy. Tell her group they'd been right all along? She watched Darcy stop, wave at someone still in the house, and then head around the corner, disappearing back into the Four Party hubbub.

No, she'd keep this to herself. But deep down inside, her heart was freaking out and her feet wanted to jump up and down because she knew. She knew!

Darcy's a Delta Kappa!

Then the whistle blew, there was the knock on the door, and the Alpha Sigs burst forth, welcoming the Rushees. Jenna could hardly wait until her third party with the Delta Bunch.

"Yo, Boston, wait up," Lora-Leigh called out to the familiar girl ahead of her. It was a little after ten P.M. and Four Party Day was finally over. It was time for them to take the escorted walk across campus to make selections for Preference Night, the last night of recruitment where they visited two houses for the "hard sell," as her mother put it.

"Hey Lora-Leigh," Roni said, and tossed her hair over her shoulder.

Lora-Leigh wished she weren't so unnerved by the Bostonian's drop-dead gorgeousness and her perfect white teeth and her expensive designer clothes.

"How'd it go for ya tonight?" Lora-Leigh asked.

"I had a great time with the Omicron Chi Omegas . . ."

"O Chi O's," Lora-Leigh corrected, and then rolled her eyes at herself. Perfect, she'd studied The Notebook *way* too much this summer and was now turning into her mother after all. *God forbid!*

Roni frowned, but kept going. "Right, right. I *hahve* to remember that."

Lora-Leigh frickin' *loved* Roni's accent and wished she had something so distinctive. She was doing well if she could get enough mousse in her hair to tame the curls out of her eyes. Her accent was southern—not country—and certainly blended into the Latimer scene.

As they crossed the street back to the quad, Roni told Lora-Leigh all about the party at the O Chi O house. "They had us help out with a philanthropy project for a battered women's shelter over in Tampa. We took these old soup cans and decorated them with wallpaper and other pretty stuff and then made flower arrangements in them. It was so much fun. I was glad to participate in something that might bring some happiness and joy to someone else."

"That's cool. I can totally respect that," Lora-Leigh said.

"Where were you?"

"The Pi Epsilon Chis put on a slide show with pictures of the sisters doing all sorts of things, like decorating their Christmas tree and doing a puppet theater at the children's hospital." Before that night, Lora-Leigh hadn't really thought of the charitable aspect of sororities. They were actually making a difference. There was nothing lame about that.

Roni nodded. "There's so much going on here. It's hard to be labeled a 'do-gooder' when everyone is doing such helpful things. You know, like the Tri-Omegas. They raised over three hundred thousand dollars last year in a breast cancer walk. Don't you think that's amazing?"

"Yeah, amazing," Lora-Leigh said blandly. She had seen the same slide show at her third party at the Tri-Omega house tonight. And while there, she had helped make pink charm bracelets that the house was going to send in to the Breast Cancer Foundation to hand out to cancer survivors. But she was still wary of the genuineness of the Tri-Omegas.

Roni didn't seem to think twice about it.

"Do you like them?" Lora-Leigh inquired, really hoping Roni

wasn't going to get sucked into that cult. Lora-Leigh continued going back there and accepting the invitations only because, otherwise, her mother would totally have a cow.

"The Tri-Omegas are nice," Roni started. "I really liked their slide show and looking at all the fun they have at their parties and events."

"But?" *Please let there be a but . . .*

"But they're sort of too much like the people I've tried to move away from."

Lora-Leigh was intrigued. "How so?"

Roni took a deep breath. "While there have been all these great things about the Tri-Omegas, I still feel like I'm hanging around with the privileged kids from my high school. The sisters have all commented on my jewelry and know my dad's a lawyer and my mom's in the Junior League. It's like they know my *parents'* résumés better than mine. I mean, do they want *me* or my parents?"

So there was hope for Boston, after all, Lora-Leigh thought. To show Roni she understood, Lora-Leigh uncharacteristically wrapped her arm around the taller girl.

"I know *exactly* what you mean."

"You do?"

"You want to break away from your past and do something on your own."

"Exactly!" Roni said, beaming.

"I can relate."

"You can?"

Lora-Leigh nodded. "I think I've been rebelling for as long as I can remember."

"I think it's time I start," Roni said.

With a sidelong glance, Lora-Leigh took a careful look at Roni. Past the perfect teeth and shiny hair and designer... everything. Underneath, Roni was just a girl.

A companionable silence settled over them as they walked around the library and headed toward the Strumann Center.

"So, what are you breaking free of, Lora-Leigh?" Roni asked.

"Being seen as a contrarian or not being able to make up my own mind. My mom's been pushing the Tri-Omegas at me since May. They have a good reputation on campus, but do I really fit in there?" She stopped and swallowed, thinking about the possibility. "At the party today, Mignon—that's the girl who was escorting me—"

"I know! I had her, too!"

Another connection, Lora-Leigh thought.

"Well, Mignon got to me a little bit today with all the talk of how Mom and I could have this other bond, more than just mother and daughter."

"Wow . . . I hadn't thought of that. That's really deep," Roni said, nodding.

"I don't know. The feelings from Tri-Omega were nothing compared to how I felt today at the ZZT house."

Roni took Lora-Leigh's hand, obviously seeing that the wall between them was now gone. "I know exactly what you mean. I love them!"

Lora-Leigh didn't want to admit that... just yet. "This cool ZZT, Camille, escorted me around again today, and we totally connected." She'd had such fun conversations with Camille. And actually with all the ZZTs she'd met. They seemed to love... *her.* Despite her wild head of hair and the many dangling earrings she wore this evening.

Lora-Leigh suddenly felt she could confide in Roni, so she continued. "When the ZZTs showed their slide show, I had this total connection with them, their house, their way of life. I hate to say it, but they seemed to reach out and be talking only to me tonight."

Roni continued to nod her agreement. "I had the same thought!"

Lora-Leigh nodded. Studying Roni, she noticed a distant sadness in her deep blue eyes. Roni hadn't mentioned her mother being involved in her recruitment process. Maybe Roni really was going at this all on her own? Hell, Lora-Leigh's own mom might be a total pain in the ass, but at least she knew her mother was just trying to help, even if it was a bit smothering at times. Lora-Leigh felt like she was gaining strength through the act of recruitment, though, and it empowered her to want to really do this for herself. Not like she'd admit that to her mom. *No way, no how!*

She wrapped her arm around Roni's shoulder again, even though the girl was about four inches taller in her heels—*Wow! Are those Christian Louboutins?* "Come on, Boston. Let's get to Group Seven and make our choices."

They shuffled into Strumann along with the rest of the hot, tired, and exhausted girls. To think, they had one more day of this.

As if on cue, Darcy and Tricia cut the chatter short and began the group meeting.

"Okay," Tricia said. "We need for you to listen up. We're

going to talk about your parties today and then tell you a little bit about Preference Night, the most special night of recruitment. You'll go to a maximum of two houses and will then come straight over here to fill out your preference card. You'll be choosing the sorority you most want to belong to. This might be one of the most important nights of your college life."

Lora-Leigh looked at Roni and Jenna, who were simply glowing. Sorority recruitment was good for them. And it was good for her, too. She was loosening up. What was one more night?

Wanting to make up to Roni for being kind of cold to her from the start, Lora-Leigh leaned over and said to her, "When this is done, let's go back to the dorm, change clothes, and meet Jenna and Amber. We can order pizza and hang out."

"I'd like that, Lora-Leigh."

"Me, too, Roni." Lora-Leigh hip-checked her. "You're a'ight."

Jenna gnawed on the top of her gel pen while she stared at the sorority names on her card. She'd had four exhausting and exhilarating parties tonight and had met so many awesome girls. Ice Water Teas had been a head rush. Six Party had gone by in a flash. Now, this Wednesday night, after Four Party, she had to wheedle her choices down to just *two* houses?

Sliding her eyes to her roommate's card, she queried, "Which two are you choosing?"

Amber sighed hard, flipped her red hair around her index finger, and said, "Well, Delta Kappa's a no-brainer, since I'm almost a legacy there. In fact, I dropped that bit of information at the other houses I was at today."

Jenna sat straight up. "You did what? That could be, like, bad for you, Amber. Don't cut off your choices yet."

Amber waived her off. "It's no biggie. Gretchen in the Delta Kappa house was giving me the hard sell. I know they're going to give me a bid. And probably you, too. They were totally fawning over you during the party."

And Jenna was fawning over them, too, ever since she'd seen Darcy coming out of the house. It was *her* house and maybe it could be Jenna's, too. Still, Amber shouldn't have been so pushy.

"I'll mark down the Theta Betas, too," Amber said, moving the pen to color in the bubble on her card. "You know, just in case something weird happens at Delta Kappa."

Jenna stared at her card to the point where the letters blended together in one big blurry mess. Decisions, decisions, decisions. An eerie tickle crawled up Jenna's throat. Everything had gone pretty smoothly so far this week, and Jenna didn't want to do anything that would jeopardize her chance of getting into Darcy's house.

Stepping over the girls sprawled out on the floor chatting about their invitations, Jenna made her way toward the table where Tricia and Darcy were hanging out.

"Hey, Jenna! Did you have fun today?" Tricia asked.

"You looked like you were having a great time," Darcy said, her pretty smile settling Jenna's nerves a touch.

"Yeah, it was awesome, but I don't know how in the world I can ever decide on just two houses to go to tomorrow."

Tricia shrugged. "We've all been there."

"I wish someone could just tell me the answer."

"It's not that simple," Tricia said.

Darcy pulled Jenna over to her and wrapped her arm around her shoulders. "You have to pick the houses that speak to you the most. The ones where you feel you'll be able to contribute to the overall sorority and where you'll meet the friends of a lifetime. The best friends and *family* for your college time and years to come."

At the mention of the word *family*, Jenna thought of her own sisters and how much she missed them. Joining a sorority would mean a whole house of *new* sisters. Girls she could depend on, hang out with, study with, and everything else. Maybe Darcy could be a sister.

Jenna pointed to her card. "What do you think about these houses?"

Darcy's dark brown eyes scanned the paper and she nodded appreciatively. "Can't go wrong with any of those, Jenna."

"But which ones would *you* pick?" Jenna knew she was pushing, but maybe she could read a confirmation in Darcy's eyes. "The Delta Kappas were amazing to me. Really made me feel like I belonged. Do you like them?"

"They're a great sorority."

Time to lay my cards on the table.

"I want to be in your house, Darcy."

The smile returned, and Darcy lowered her voice. "I'd love that, too, Jenna. Your decision has to be yours, though."

"Yeah, I know." *But I know you're a Delta Kappa!*

Darcy said, "Any house would be lucky to have you. Just remember that."

Jenna sighed hard, knowing her Rho Gamma wouldn't do anything dishonest, like letting her know what sorority she was actually in. Without another thought, Jenna returned to her seat and filled in the dot next to Delta Kappa, feeling super-stoked that she might actually get to join the house.

A wall of black hair passed in front of her, followed by a squeeze on her upper arm. "Which two did you choose?" Roni asked.

"Hey, kids," Lora-Leigh said, plopping down on the couch and waving her completed card in the air. "So who are we hoping for tomorrow, Jenna?"

Needing a second house, Jenna glanced at Lora-Leigh's card and saw that she had ZZT marked, as did Roni. Well, sure, there were cool girls there, too, and they'd been soooo nice to her. So as far as sorority choices went, Jenna couldn't go wrong putting down Zeta Zeta Tau. "Here's my card," she said to Roni at last.

Roni's eyes sparkled. "I have ZZT, too. And O Chi O."

"You didn't go with Tri-Omega?" Lora-Leigh asked, her eyes wide.

"Nope. That's for *you* to explore."

Lora-Leigh laughed. "Good for you, Boston. I have Tri-Omega and ZZT."

Jenna looked down at her card with the selections of Delta Kappa and Zeta Zeta Tau, and she took a deep, confident breath. She couldn't go wrong with either house.

CHAPTER
8

At the crack of dawn Thursday morning, Jenna lay in her bed staring up at the swirled plaster ceiling pattern in her room, visible by the sliver of light under the door. She hadn't had a bad dream, but something wasn't right. Her heart slammed away underneath the oversize Wynton Marsalis T-shirt she slept in almost every night.

Her first class wasn't for another two and a half hours, yet she couldn't sleep. She peeled back the covers and crept over to the fridge for a Diet Coke. The cool liquid would sooth her nerves. When she popped the top, she woke up the snoring Amber (*Hello . . . get some Breathe Right nasal strips*) from under her mound of comforters and pillows.

"Huh? Wh-ut?" Amber asked, revealing her auburn head.

"Sorry. I needed something to drink."

"You're not sick, are you?"

"No, I'm fine." It wasn't the 'betes that was troubling her; it was sorority recruitment.

Amber squinted at her. "What time is it?"

Jenna glanced at the green digital readout on her clock. "Five thirty-five."

Her roommate rolled over and grunted, balling the chunky yellow comforter around her in the chilled air conditioning. "Ugh, Jenna. Go back to sleep."

"Today's a big day for recruitment."

Groaning, Amber pulled the covers over her head further and said in a muffled tone, "The parties aren't until tonight. Go back to sleep."

Taking a quick sip of her soda, Jenna swallowed hard and then said, "Yeah, but The Knock goes from eight A.M. to three P.M. The Rho Gammas have our schedules; there's no escaping them."

"It's a piece of piss, Jenna. Go back to bed. We're fine."

"How can you be so sure?"

"Because I... like... *am.* Now *shuuuud uuuup* and let me go back to sleep."

Jenna couldn't be as self-assured as Amber. Recruitment was a numbers game, Darcy and Tricia had told Group 7. Matching and selecting, computers taking data and finding the compatibility. If neither the potential new members first- nor second-choice sorority invited her back, she'd be cut. And she'd get a knock on her door, a visit from her Rho Gamma delivering the news that she'd been cut. It was all out of Jenna's control.

She slipped on her shower shoes and grabbed her bathroom kit. At this hour, she'd have her pick of shower stalls. If she was going to get The Knock, at least she'd have scrubbed skin, clean hair, and fresh breath. As she padded to the bathroom and began brushing her teeth, she replayed the many parties in her head. The Delta Bunch, Club ZZT, the slide shows, the philanthropy projects, the girls, their smiles... everything. All of the stories and messages meshed in her head, sounding out one vibrant message: *We want you to join us.*

In the privacy of the shower stall, she took the blue serter — the stamp-like device that allowed her to insert the insulin-feeding tube — and quickly punched it into a fresh spot on her right hip. She removed the serter and assured herself that the tube was secured a good nine millimeters under her skin, just like she'd done many times before. Her Preference Night dress was the one she'd worn to prom, a black two-piece lacy top and skirt that showed off her tan, but not her medical device. She showered, dried off, dressed, and returned to her room, deciding whether she needed to read the chapters of Western Civ for her morning class (too bad she and Lora-Leigh weren't in the same section)... or could be unproductive and take a crack at the expert-level Sudoku puzzle. Something — anything — to keep her mind off not getting selected for a sorority.

Later, in class, she fidgeted with her pen, messed with her fingernails, and paid little attention to the professor's talk of the Holy Roman Empire. She snapped out of her daze in time to hear the professor announce, "And due next Wednesday, I want your five-page essays on the Political Evolution to Periclean Athens from the Ancient Greece and Hellenistic Civilization."

Jenna flipped her notebook over and furiously wrote down what the teacher had said. How did Latimer University expect students to have a social life, participate in extracurricular activities, *and* write papers on Ancient Greece and the Hellenistic

Civilization? Thank heavens she still had her papers from high school; she remembered touching upon that senior year.

When the clock hit 9:50 A.M., she gathered her books and followed the flow of students out of Tennison Hall and onto the quad. She crossed the one-way street in front of her classroom, slipped up the small hillside between the language building and the business school, and walked along the side of the quad. Upperclassmen hung out at Major Bigby Hall, the main building for the business students, chatting, smoking cigarettes, and snacking before their next class. There were a lot of athletes standing around and many frat guys. She'd heard that Bigby was *the place* to see all the hot guys on campus. So far, she hadn't been disappointed.

"Nice bruise," someone said.

Ugh . . . she hadn't covered it up well enough this morning when she was running out of her room. She didn't look up, but quickened her pace. *Great . . . pick on the freshman.*

"You're Jenna, right?"

He knows me? Jenna stopped, pivoted, and met the blue-eyed stare of David "Tiger" Harrison from Billado Hall the other day. David "Tiger" Harrison of Phi Omicron Chi. David "Tiger" Harrison from the depths of ultimate cuteness.

"Oh, hi! Sorry . . . I was in my own world."

He pointed to her forehead. "What happened to you? Nothing serious, I hope."

She couldn't tell him the real story. That she'd been checking out his fine behind and lost her balance. "Dorm mishap, you know."

He laughed and smiled. "Bet it's fun going through sorority recruitment with that, huh? All the houses remember you, I'm sure."

"Something like that," she said, feeling her cheeks warm. "My friends have helped me with some makeup to cover it up. I'll certainly need it tonight."

David looked confused for a moment. "Oh right! Pref Night. Which houses are you going to?"

She stopped short of biting her lip again, not wanting to show her nervousness to this foxy Phi Omicron Chi. "I put down Delta Kappa and ZZT, but I haven't gotten my invites yet."

"Solid. Cute girls in both houses."

Not knowing how to answer that, she nodded.

"And after tonight . . . one of them will have another cute girl," he added.

Okay, that made her blush again. *Whew!* "Thanks."

He kicked at the ground with his sneakered foot. "Why don't you bring some of your new sisters over to the Phi Omicron Chi house on Saturday night? It's our Open House for fraternity Rush, and we'll have a band and burgers and hot dogs." He leaned in and whispered, "After the formal Rush ends, we'll be tapping a keg in the basement."

"Well, that all depends on whether I have sisters."

"You? Of course you will!"

"Thanks, David."

"Tiger, remember?"

"Right . . . Tiger. Thanks." Kinda cute and cuddly, she mused.

"Yo! Tiger! Let's motor," a blond guy in an LU sweatshirt yelled out at him.

"I gotta go. Good luck tonight, Jenna. See ya Saturday night."

She hoped she would have news to share with him.

"Kiersten, I have a big problem." Roni sat cross-legged on the quad, enjoying the midmorning sunshine as she spoke to her friend on her cell phone. There was nothing she couldn't talk to Kiersten about.

"Talk to me," Kiersten said across the long distance.

"So, you know tonight is the last night of recruitment."

"Right. So what's this problem? You've made it this far, Roni."

Roni's eyes darted around at the gathering of students on the quad. There were some guys tossing a football, two girls playing with a dog, and a couple making out like bandits under one of the trees. Even though Roni was surrounded by fellow LUers, she felt comfortable enough to tell Kiersten all that was bottled inside.

"I think I found a home."

Kiersten squealed. "Oh, Roni, I'm so happy! I know you'll make the perfect sorority sister."

Roni took a deep breath and continued, "Thing is, I'm not sure they want me."

"How could they not want you?"

"Well, there are a lot of girls still left in recruitment and only so many spots available."

Kiersten sighed. "But you know where you absolutely want to go?"

"Yes." Roni saw the three letters, emblazoned on her brain. The three Greek letters she wanted adorning her for the next four years . . . forever. "Is there a way to ensure that I get in?"

"It's all a numbers game. Who needs how many people. Lists and preferences and matching up."

"I know."

Silence reverberated for a moment. Roni tossed her hair over her shoulder and switched phone ears, waiting for Kiersten's wisdom. *She's never let me down before.* "Kiersten?"

"Look Roni . . . I don't want to give you bad advice, so you probably need to talk to your Rho Gamma about this."

"I will, but I wanted to talk to you. You know so much more about all of this."

"I went through it a while ago, though, Roni."

"Yeah," she said, feeling a tightness in her throat. "Isn't there a way to really ensure I'll get into the house that I want?"

She could almost hear Kiersten thinking on the other end of the phone. "I don't want you to seem anxious at your parties tonight, sweetie."

"I'm not," Roni insisted, although she seemed to be covered in the stench of desperation. "I just know what I like and what I want. If I can't join this house, then I don't see what the point is. They're the people I want to be with. It's just . . . perfect."

A sigh sounded over the cellular device in the form of static. "You know what? You remind me of my next-door neighbor, Annabeth, from my freshman year at Emerson. She totally loved the Alpha Sigs, to the point where she suicided. I couldn't believe she did that."

Roni gasped hard. "She committed suicide over a sorority? Oh, my God!"

"No, no, no," Kiersten corrected. "She didn't *commit* suicide; she *suicided* the sorority she wanted the most."

"What does that mean?"

Kiersten laughed. "It's an old term. Suiciding. It means putting one house down as your first, second, only preference. That way, if you're on their first bid list, you automatically get in. If you're not and are on their second preference list, you get in, if there's room. My aunt did it, too, but these days they call it 'intentional single preference.'"

Roni's pulse skipped a beat. "And this works?"

"It worked for Annabeth. But it's risky, Roni. You could end up cut from recruitment, with nowhere to go."

Was that a chance she was willing to take to get into the sorority of her choice?

"Roni?"

She wet her lips and stared off into the distance, focusing on the geology building across the quad. "I'm here, Kiersten."

"You're not going to do it, are you? I was just telling you about Annabeth. I certainly wasn't suggesting you should—"

Her call waiting beeped, interrupting her thoughts. "Shoot, Kiersten, I've got to go. I've got another call."

"But Roni—"

"Wish me luck . . . and thanks for everything!"

"Good luck . . . call me!"

She clicked her phone and put it back to her ear. "Hello."

"Veronic'er?"

"Oh, hi, Mother." Roni rolled her eyes and flung herself back onto the cool, freshly cut grass of the quad. "What's going on?" She counted to five, waiting for her mother to say something. "Is there something you wanted, Mother?"

"As a matter of fact, there was. Your father and I are going to the Pops this evening with the Georgoudises. You know John Georgoudis is on the Admissions Committee at Harvard, and I wanted to let you know we're going to ask him about delaying your entry to Harvard for a year so you can get this . . . rebellion out of your system."

"I'm not going to Harvard, Mother."

"You say that now, Veronic'er—"

"Mother, I'm at Latimer. I'm going through sorority recruitment. I'm happy."

Her mother paused for a moment. "You know, John's wife, Penelope, was a sorority girl back in her day—best on her campus. I hope you have the good sense to join the *right* sorority."

The right sorority. At that moment, Roni had never been surer of what sorority she wanted to join and how she would do it.

"Don't worry, Mother. I know *exactly* what I'm doing."

At noon, just when Jenna was starting to relax, it happened. The worst thing possible.

Knock. Knock. Knock.

"Holy crap," she whispered.

"Wh-uh? Huh?" came the mumbled sound from Amber's corner. She'd gone back to sleep in her pillow fort and comforter tent after her two morning classes.

Jenna couldn't think. She couldn't move. She was sure her heart had stopped. And the tears had already started to form in her eyes. Here she'd been enjoying recruitment and all that it meant, and now this.

Knock. Knock. Knock.

"Amber... someone's knocking at the door."

"No shit, Sherlock." Amber, now fully awake, swung up and sat on the edge of her bed.

"Are you going to answer it?"

"Hell no!"

"Someone has to!"

Knock. Knock. Knock.

"I'll get it," Jenna said bravely. She'd faced worse things in her life than being dropped from sorority recruitment. Slowly she opened the large wooden door only to see a girl wearing a Rho Gamma T-shirt standing there, sad and solemn.

I'm getting cut. She could deal. She'd *have* to. But she wished Darcy were here to lean on. Swallowing hard, she said, "Hey."

"I'm Justine." The girl looked at her clipboard and then hugged it to her chest. "May I come in, please?"

"Sure."

Justine stepped inside. Jenna's chest hurt, wanting this over and done with.

"Justine," Amber asked quietly, "what are you doing here?"

The Rho Gamma nodded at Jenna. "Would you mind giving Amber and me a minute?"

It's not me? It's not me! It's not me!

"Shit," she muttered under her breath. It was Amber. And Justine must be *her* Rho Gamma.

Not able to look at her roommate, Jenna picked up her room key and a book, and headed out the door. The last thing she heard was Justine saying… "Amber, I'm sorry to tell you this, but you didn't receive any invitations for Preference Night. You've been dropped from sorority recruitment."

Jenna leaned against the wall in the hallway, her heart drilling a staccato beat in her chest. Poor Amber! Nausea overcame Jenna just thinking about the conversation going on in the room behind her. How in the world would Amber go on when she had been completely convinced she'd get an automatic bid? As Jenna paced the hall carpet, she was devastated for her roommate, but, selfishly, she breathed a sigh of relief for herself.

I'm okay.

A few minutes later, Justine stepped out of the room and made her way down the hall for her next visit. Jenna walked back into her room and saw Amber doubled over on her bed, sobbing. She went to her roommate and tried to hug her.

"Oh, Amber, I'm so sorry."

Amber merely whimpered.

"It's going to be okay," Jenna said, trying to comfort her. "I promise, it'll be okay."

Jerking up, Amber gritted her teeth together and glared at Jenna. "It's so *not* going to be okay. I just got cut! I'm going to be the laughingstock of all my friends back home."

"No one's going to—"

"What do you know?" Tears poured from Amber's eyes. "You didn't even want to do this, yet you're still in. Guess the joke's on me."

"Amber, I—" Jenna stopped herself because she had no idea how to make this better for her roommate. "I'm...sorry."

Wiping her cheeks, Amber turned away. "Yeah. Whatever."

"Can I...do anything?"

"I just want to be alone."

Jenna stood silently for a moment, thinking Amber might change her mind. But it was apparent she wanted to be alone. "Okay...I'll be in Roni's room if you need me."

Jenna slipped out of the room and headed down the hall. She only hoped that she, Roni, and Lora-Leigh would make the cut.

A knock on Roni's door completely freaked out Lora-Leigh. She opened the door to Roni's private room with great anticipation. She saw not a Rho Gamma but a ridiculously pale Jenna Driscoll.

"Jesus, Jenna...you scared the hell and four dollars out of us!"

Roni peeled herself from her bed where she'd been curled up. "I was about to vomit hearing someone knock on the door."

"God, y'all are so dramatic," Jenna said. "I'm sorry, I'm a little freaked out. Amber just got cut from recruitment. I tried to console her afterward, but she told me to go away."

"That sucks big time. Amber was so sure she'd get in," Lora-Leigh said.

"I'm safe, aren't I?" Jenna asked with concern. "I mean, Justine and Darcy would have told us together if we were both out. Right?"

Roni pulled her hair into a high ponytail. "I'm next, I just know it."

Lora-Leigh rolled her eyes. This was the third time in the last hour that Roni had started with the negative attitude. Honestly, these girls were putting too much into this whole thing. Life went on. If they made it, they made it; if not, who cared?

Strangely, Lora-Leigh realized *she* cared.

"Aren't you supposed to be in your room, Lora-Leigh?" Jenna asked, grabbing hold of a stuffed penguin Roni had on her bed.

"I told Goth Virginia where I'd be in case a Rho Gamma came a callin'."

Roni picked at the end of her satin pillow. "How *cahn* you be so calm?"

Lora-Leigh pulled at her hair even though it was secured in a ponytail. "Y'all, there's nothing we can do. We've had four days to show these chicks who we are and what we're about. I don't have to prove myself to anyone. We'll just form our own sisterhood. The Tuthill Sorority."

Both Jenna and Roni laughed, but Lora-Leigh knew she was talking a big game.

"Look, y'all," Lora-Leigh started, trying to be brave for her friends and not let on that she was just as freaked out about hearing The Knock as the next person. "We need to do something to humor ourselves. Boston, you've got this huge room; we can play cards or something." Her mother always played solitaire whenever she stressed out over something. Lora-Leigh liked to hem or baste, but she didn't want to go down to her room and . . . wait.

"I don't have any cards, sorry," Roni said in a quivering voice.

"Then let's work on homework, surf our class message boards, call home . . . anything!"

"I couldn't study now if my life depended on it," Roni said.

Lora-Leigh blew a tuft of hair out of her face and tried not to sigh too hard. Instead, she moved to Roni's armoire closet, like every dorm room had. "Okay, let's play 'How Do I Look?'"

Roni looked confused. "Play what?"

"What's that?" Jenna asked, getting comfortable next to Roni on the bed.

"It's something my best friend at home and I used to do all the time." Opening the wooden doors, Lora-Leigh almost gasped at what she saw but held back. "Um, you know, *How Do I Look?* is that show on the Style Network where friends rummage through each other's closet and help them redo their look."

Roni was on her feet and next to Lora-Leigh in a heartbeat. "That's okay, we can do something else."

Too late, Lora-Leigh was foraging through the labels. Designer, all of them. Dolce & Gabbana coat, Marc Jacobs skirt-and-top combo (cute!), Gucci purse and belt, BCBG tailored pants, Nicole Miller blouse, and—*holy shit!*—a real Zac Posen gown. And was that a Metsy Joanz dress? Metsy Joanz was her *absolute* favorite designer above all others. The woman Lora-Leigh modeled her own work after. Veronica Van Gelderen had some deep financial pockets. But Lora-Leigh could sense discomfort beaming out of Roni's gigantic eyes.

Lora-Leigh stepped back and closed the closet. "On second thought, Boston, you're okay with your own style." She winked at her friend, and a silent understanding passed between them.

"Maybe one day you'll have a Lora-Leigh Sorenstein original hanging in there."

Roni smiled at her. "I'd love one."

Over the next couple of hours, the girls calmed down and talked to one another about their classes, their intended majors, and what they were looking forward to about the school year. Lora-Leigh learned that Jenna was the oldest of four girls and that Roni was an only child. Jenna was a trumpet player and Roni was a swimmer. And she shared her fashion-designer dream with her new friends, feeling comfortable and secure in the camaraderie they'd formed in such a quick time.

"Hey, look!" Jenna pointed at a crystal clock on Roni's bedside table. "It's ten after three!"

Roni jumped up off the floor and screamed. "We're safe! We're still in!"

Lora-Leigh couldn't stop herself from hopping to her feet as well, joining in the impromptu crumping going on in the middle of the room. They'd all made it. They were going to Preference Night. One step closer. Just one more round of parties before they knew which house they'd land in. Lora-Leigh was absolutely breathless, shaking. *Get a grip!*

Then Jenna stopped. "What if we all get in different houses and quit being friends?"

"That won't happen, Jenna. I like you for you, not the letters you wear on your chest," Roni answered.

Lora-Leigh nodded her agreement. "What Boston said."

"You're right, you're right. The important thing is we all find the house that's best for us."

"Come on," Roni said. "Let's go get something to eat while we can. We'll need the energy for later."

As they walked out of the room, Lora-Leigh hoped something magical would happen tonight to show her what to do. She just hoped she didn't barf somewhere along the way from nerves. Plus, her mom would be at the Tri-Omega house, which would be... weird. Biting her lip, Lora-Leigh secretly sent up a prayer asking for her sign. Whether it would come, she didn't know....

Twilight set across Latimer University as the freshmen girls poured from their dorms out onto Sorority Row in their finest formal attire. Taffetas and silks. Lace and chiffon. Everyone and everything was fashionable and beautiful this September Thursday evening.

Preference Night had begun.

Roni took a deep sip of the night air, tinted with honeysuckle and roses. Every house on the row seemed to teem with the fresh scent of summer flowers, mixed with the tension and nerves already in the atmosphere. She clutched her small handbag to her (she was wearing the Zac Posen dress Lora-Leigh had been admiring in her closet) and continued in the flow of pedestrian traffic along Sorority Row. After her friends had left her room earlier, she'd swiftly removed the tags from most of her clothes—realizing her behavior bordered on manic—to hide the fact that they were expensive, designer, and... different. She just wanted to blend in.

The first Preference Party Roni went to was at the Omicron Chi Omega house, full of ceremony and song, celebration and... a hard sell. She hadn't expected them to come after her so full force about how she would be a great asset to the house. They tried to convince her that O Chi O was where she belonged. She liked them—and had picked their invitation over Tri-Omega's—but she didn't think it was where she wanted to spend the next four years of her life. She didn't feel a connection to any of them. Her decision was made. It was just a matter of going through the motions to make it so.

Now she looked up at the elegant, yellow, Spanish-designed house with the gold letters ZZT emblazoned proudly above the front double doors. The house she wanted to belong to.

"Hey, Boston! Check it out. We're here at the same time," Lora-Leigh said, seemingly unaffected by the frenzied movement going on around her.

"That's awesome that we're going to the same party." Roni toyed with the strap of her Kate Spade bag and switched it from her left to right shoulder. "I hope they like me."

Lora-Leigh's brows crooked at Roni. "You're here, aren't you? They obviously like you."

"You're right. I'm being a dork."

"You're being you, Boston," Lora-Leigh said with a smile.

"How was the Tri-Omega party?"

Lora-Leigh shrugged, noncommittal. "It is what it is."

Roni snickered at her friend. "I see you've finally accepted that recruitment is happening around you and you're part of it."

Lora-Leigh tugged at her dress and stared at the ground. The outfit was a gorgeous creation, Roni thought, worthy of the racks of the finest department stores. It was made of black charmeuse, plunging a little in the front, and had a cinched waist. "Yeah, whatever," Lora-Leigh said. "I actually had a good time at the Tri-Omega house. My mom was there serving the punch. It was sort of cool to see her and know we could be sisters. But I didn't get my sign."

"Your sign?"

"Yeah, I need one big frickin' sign before this night is over."

Don't we all. Roni opened her mouth to speak just when Jenna and a couple more girls joined their group. "Isn't this the best night ever, y'all?" Jenna sang out. She even added a twirl as punctuation.

Roni looked at the three of them; they were quite a trio. She in her designer label, Lora-Leigh in her amazing homemade creation, and Jenna in her prom dress. All of them in black, all of them elegant in her own way.

The rest of the nervous girls gathered around, and a Rho Gamma motioned them to line up on the sidewalk in front of the ZZT house.

To the left, Roni noted the local television station's van. People lined the streets, as well, admiring the young girls clothed in their finest and ready to make one of the principal decisions of their lives (thus far).

"Local TV?" she asked Lora-Leigh. "Are you kidding me?"

"Slow news night," Lora-Leigh quipped. "People here take sorority recruitment seriously, and Preference Night and Bid Day are huge human-interest pieces for the local media."

"I suppose so," Roni said, thinking of how at home, the stations focused only on the Red Sox, Patriots, or Bruins and certainly not something as trivial as sorority recruitment.

Jenna grabbed Roni's elbow and squeezed. "It's starting!"

Chills sped up and down Roni's bare arms as the sisters of ZZT exited their darkened house in their black cocktail dresses, each of a different design, but complementing one another all the same. The girls carried white candles with them. When the sisters poured out onto the grassy green lawn, the light from the candles tossed a soft glow on the close-cropped landscape.

"Oh my God, they look amazing," Lora-Leigh said with a gasp.

They were an array of glamour, sophistication, and beauty as they gathered around and began softly singing. The girl who'd been escorting Roni around the house, Beverly Chang, stepped forward and welcomed her into the candle glow. Beverly took her hand and ushered Roni up the walkway. As the ZZT's distinctively harmonized melody reached out to her, Roni took a deep breath and stepped into the house.

Lora-Leigh couldn't control the absolute freaking out of her heart as they headed into the ZZT house, which smelled sweetly of roses and orangey incense.

Immediately, Camille was at her side. "Is this another Lora-Leigh Sorenstein original?"

"It is . . . do you like it?"

"Stunning. You look absolutely fabulous!"

She shivered slightly. Lora-Leigh appreciated the vote of confidence. Emily, the girl who'd hosted her at the Tri-Omega house, had been just as attentive, but it had been her mother's presence at the Preference Night ceremony that made Lora-Leigh realize how important all of this was. Now she almost felt guilty enjoying herself here at ZZT.

They moved around the formal living room, which was decorated with tall, white taper candles. The ceiling was covered in dark blue, gold, and white balloons, with curly ribbons hanging down. A true party atmosphere that made Lora-Leigh feel like she was at a 1920s flapper party—although she doubted there'd be any gin in the bathtub. She glanced over her shoulder to see Roni and Jenna being taken care of by sisters of ZZT, who were bringing them finger sandwiches and sparkling cider in flutes.

"We made all of the hors d'oeuvres ourselves," Camille told her. An alum dressed in wait-staff attire offered Lora-Leigh a plate of delicious-looking deviled eggs.

"Oh man, I've got to have one of these," she said, remembering how much she loved the deviled eggs her bubbe had made for her when she was a little girl.

Lora-Leigh then took a couple of finger sandwiches, an artichoke tart, and a mini strawberry cheesecake. She was here, so she might as well eat.

Camille continued explaining, "We have a cook here at the house... Miss Merry. She helped us in the kitchen today making food for the parties. The shrimp toasts were her idea."

"I'll have to get one of those!"

"Sure thing," Camille said, and then guided Lora-Leigh toward the cushions on the living room floor. "We'll get one after the ceremony. It's about to begin. Afterward, I'll show you around some, and then you and I can talk."

"I'd like that," Lora-Leigh said, and nibbled at the yummy treats.

"So where do you want to sit?"

Lora-Leigh pointed to near where Jenna and Roni sat with

their ZZT sponsors. "How about up there with those girls?"

Camille nodded.

They picked their way through the crowd and then sat carefully on the large royal blue crushed-velvet pillow on the floor. Roni tossed Lora-Leigh a confident look and winked at her. Jenna was too busy geeking out (in a good/cute way) to notice anyone else.

Then the lights went down, and the room was aglow in the warmth of candlelight. Lora-Leigh listened carefully to Marissa, the president of ZZT, who greeted them and told them how much it meant to the sisters to have them all here tonight.

"It's a special night," Marissa said. "And we welcome you with open arms to our home. We hope you can feel the special love and affection that we ZZTs have for one another. To show you, we asked a couple of sisters to talk about their time in ZZT. First up, Kwana Johnson."

Lora-Leigh was engrossed in Kwana's speech, in which she poked fun at her roommate's grooming habits, her big sister's encouraging gifts, and Marissa's guidance through her Marketing 301 class. A senior named Kelli Fletcher stood up next and read her tribute.

"Last year, I was a Rho Gamma during recruitment, which meant disaffiliating from Zeta Zeta Tau for the summer leading up to recruitment and having to be nonpartisan during the whole recruitment process. It's harder than it looks, you know... wearing different letters and not being able to talk about how amazing your sisters are and what your house means to you." Kelli's voice seemed to catch in her throat, and she stopped for a moment. She took a deep breath and continued,

"Being a Rho Gamma, I got to see sororities again from the outside, and it really made me realize even more what a huge part of my life my ZZT sisters are. They're my confidantes and the closest friends I've ever had. I'm a senior this year, and being involved in recruitment again from the inside, meeting all of the wonderful girls—like you—and hanging with my sisters again, singing the songs and having the chance to tell y'all how special this place is to me... it just helps me see how much ZZT and all of my sisters have made my overall college experience what it is. I love y'all, you know it!"

Everyone clapped, and suddenly, as Lora-Leigh looked around at all the sisters' genuine smiles she realized that these girls really meant what they were saying about one another.

After a couple of songs, some explanation of the sorority's history, and a few more testimonials by sisters from each class year, the girls then invited the potential new members to take some time to see the house.

Camille turned to Lora-Leigh. "You wanna walk around?"

"Sure," Lora-Leigh said, smoothing her dress as she stood.

They stopped for a refill of sparkling cider and then went through the TV room, the dining room, and into the front hallway, where the entrance to their housemother's apartment was.

"There's more to the house, but I think this will give you an idea of what it's like to live here," Camille said. "New members aren't allowed upstairs until they're initiated, and then sophomore year you're eligible to move into the house, if there's room."

"This is great," Lora-Leigh said. "Kind of like the dorm, but kind of like my parents' house, too."

"Exactly."

Camille led her into the study hall. It was a large room with tables and chairs, desks, couches, and nooks where sisters could hole up and cram for an exam or simply get some textbook reading done. Lora-Leigh took it all in, although she was starting to feel the itch of frustration under her skin.

I need my sign, dammit.

"You want to sit and chat?"

"I'd like that," Lora-Leigh said, wringing her hands together more than she'd have liked.

They went around and sat on one of the couches. Another freshman and ZZT sister sat opposite from them, across the magazine-laden coffee table, on the matching couch.

"I won't lie to you, Lora-Leigh," Camille said, her smooth skin appearing almost bronze in the low light of the study room. "The sisters think you're a perfect fit. You're unique and really together, and you could add a lot to the house. I know you have another choice, but I hope you feel the same way about us and will consider ZZT for your new home."

In the back of her head, Lora-Leigh heard her mother's voice telling her not to give up too much information or seem "desperate" to get a bid. *Always keep them guessing and don't let them know your true feelings.*

Lora-Leigh ignored her mother's words.

"Thanks, Camille. I think y'all are great, too."

She couldn't get attached, though. In a year, she'd be gone to L.A. or New York. Off to design school. She didn't want to make a four-year commitment and then back out of it. Lora-Leigh almost choked on the emotional lump threatening her. She coughed slightly, and Camille took notice.

"Sorry, dry throat."

"That's okay. Let me run and get you something else to drink. I'll be right back."

Lora-Leigh nodded, then rolled her eyes at her own outburst. Wanting to have something to do while waiting for Camille, she rummaged through the stack of magazines on the table in front of her.

One magazine in particular caught her eye: "*The Mighty Sword*," she muttered, reading the title. Oh, it was the Zeta Zeta Tau magazine. Lora-Leigh had to remind herself that not only were you a member of your university's chapter, but you were connected with a network of women all over the United States. A sister worldwide in ZZT.

As Lora-Leigh thumbed through the pages, she was fascinated by the women smiling back at her. An article featuring Famous Alumnae showcased Sondra Pickett, of the Court of Appeals for the Ninth Circuit in San Francisco. There was also a picture of Mary-Louise Hightower, the woman from that makeover dating reality show her mother watched all the time.

"I see you found our magazine." Camille sat next to her and handed her a flute of cider.

Lora-Leigh sipped it quickly, hoping to ease the ache in her throat. "Thanks for the drink. Your magazine is really well done." The layout was nice, and the colors were inviting, both things Lora-Leigh could appreciate with her designer's eye.

Pointing at other pictures in the magazine, Camille said, "We have an astronaut, two congresswomen, an ambassador to Iceland, plenty of beauty queens—Miss United States in 1999—and oh, you'll like this one...look..."

When Camille flipped the page, Lora-Leigh almost fell off the couch. "Is that Metsy Joanz? No way!"

"It is! She went to Syracuse back in the late sixties. Course, she was Margaret Johansen back then. She changed her name to Metsy Joanz when she moved to Manhattan and started her first clothing line."

Lora-Leigh could hardly believe it! Metsy Joanz. *The* Metsy Joanz was a sorority girl? And a ZZT at that! "Did she spend all four years in college?" she asked.

"Sure she did. Served as president of the Gamma Eta chapter. She was a business major and then went on to design school after her undergraduate years." Camille turned. "You know, our ZZT national conference is in San Diego this summer, and Metsy is designing the conference bag for us. Cool, huh?"

"A-a-amazing," Lora-Leigh managed to get out. Metsy Joanz had been a sorority girl *and* had managed to get her undergraduate degree *and* then go on to be a kick-ass designer.

Could Lora-Leigh really stay at Latimer four years, get a good—and basically free—education, and then follow in her idol's footsteps to success?

And then it hit her. *Of course, the magazine was her sign!* The one she'd been waiting for.

"We should get back to the others. Come on."

Lora-Leigh followed her hostess back through the house to where they came out in the front foyer. Unbelievable! She'd gotten her sign. But as happy as she was, Lora-Leigh knew her mother wanted her down the street in the horseshoe-shaped house.

Lora-Leigh lifted her eyes to Camille's and felt the onset of tears begin. *What is wrong with me?* Why was she getting choked up? *Come on, Sorenstein... toughen up!* This was the most emotional thing she'd ever experienced. It didn't help that the sisters here were all so damn cute and sweet and supportive. And Metsy Joanz was one of them! But her mom was...well... her *mom*. And as much as she was annoying, she didn't want to disappoint her.

She swallowed. "How will I know?" she asked Camille.

"Know what?"

"How will I know I've made the right choice?"

The lights flickered, indicating the end of the party.

Camille wrapped her arm around Lora-Leigh and escorted her to the door. Right before they parted, the ZZT leaned in and whispered close to Lora-Leigh's ear... "Lora-Leigh, follow your heart."

Outside the ZZT house, Jenna found Roni and Lora-Leigh and joined them. Roni, who seemed a tad emotional, laced her fingers through Jenna's and then Jenna reached for Lora-Leigh. The three of them stood there together—united—as the ZZTs spilled out onto the lawn with their candles once again to bid them farewell...

"Remember...Zeta Zeta Tau,
Remember...when we part,
Remember...how proud you would be to wear our silver
sword o'er your heart.
Remember...whatever happens, our sisterhood is true.
Remember...Zeta Zeta Tar...and we will remember you."

Jenna's heart was totally going to explode in her chest from the sheer pain of her happiness. Sure, it was *très* cool at the Delta Kappa house, and the sisters there were wonderful; however, the emotions that poured out through these singing sisters moved Jenna like nothing ever before.

But Darcy's a Delta Kappa.

She kept repeating that to herself while the ZZTs continued humming and singing...

" *... and we will remember you.*"

If she chose Zeta Zeta Tau over Darcy's Delta Kappa, would it be the right thing for her? The ZZT house seemed like such a good fit, full of a wide array of interesting girls. She'd met a sister who was a clarinet in the marching band. She met another girl from Buckhead, near where her family lived in Marietta, Georgia. And one sister who wore a medical alert bracelet (what it was for, she wasn't sure).

The ZZTs' song ended, and they blew out their candles and stepped slowly back into their house.

"Y'all! What am I going to do?" Jenna cried out to her two friends.

Roni squeezed her hand. "Shhh... we're supposed to be silent."

"What for?" she asked.

Lora-Leigh whispered, "We're supposed to be thinking about our choices as we walk across campus to the Student Union."

"Who said that?"

"The Rho Gammas this afternoon. Weren't you listening?"

"That's totally stupid," Jenna said with a pout. She needed to talk to her girls and see what they were going to do. Who were they going to pick?

They moved slowly up Sorority Row, joined by girls exiting other houses, all quiet as proverbial church mice.

"I need to talk to y'all," Jenna hissed, frustrated by the silly rules.

Roni's eyes grew big, and Lora-Leigh appeared lost in her own thoughts.

Still Jenna begged. "Y'all. This is creeping me out. Big time! I need help."

Darcy slid up beside them and placed her forefinger over her lips. "Shhhh. Silence, girls. You've got a lot of thinking to do and a nice long walk to do it." Her eyes connected with Jenna's, and she winked. "All of you."

It was the longest walk of Jenna's life, around and down Sorority Row, across to the grassy quad, past the library, and down the pedestrian walkway to the student union. There, the Rho Gammas continued to enforce the silence as the girls headed up the grand staircase and filed into the ballroom full of chairs with white cards and pens on them.

Preference cards.

Jenna had been informed all about these cards by Darcy and Tricia in their last Group 7 meeting. However, talking about it and actually doing it were two different things.

I have to make a choice.

Roni and Lora-Leigh slipped by her and took seats. They all knew not even to try to look at one another's cards because the Rho Gammas would scold them.

Jenna heard many voices coming together in her head—
Amber and her plethora of advice; her mother, who'd been
encouraging her through e-mail; Darcy, with her experiential
wisdom; the chats with Roni and Lora-Leigh. Jenna knew there
was only one voice she could heed now.

This is my decision.

Looking at the card in her hand, she thought of her friends
sitting next to her in the ballroom. Which houses would they
choose? Would they all end up as sisters? Or would they go
three separate ways?

She loved the time she'd spent at the ZZT house, like *really*
loved it, and both Roni and Lora-Leigh were up for that house,
too. However, knowing Darcy was a Delta Kappa made her
thoughts sway there.

How do I know if I'm making the right choice?

This was messed up. Why couldn't she join both? Her mom
had told her that with becoming an adult, she'd have to make a
lot of grown-up decisions—on her own. This was the biggest so
far, and she didn't want to screw it up.

Taking her pen, she colored in the bubble next to Delta
Kappa as her first choice. Smiling confidently as her heart went
crack-a-lack under her skin, she colored in the bubble next to
Zeta Zeta Tau as her second choice.

Well, it's done.

She stood and glanced at Lora-Leigh, who appeared to be
struggling with her own choice. The two friends locked eyes,
and Lora-Leigh winked up at Jenna. She noticed Roni, slumped
in her chair, and swore she was crying. The houses really jerked
on the emotional heartstrings this evening, and Roni seemed

not to be handling it well. Jenna didn't understand the difficulty for her. Roni would totally be a popular girl on campus. Any house would be lucky to have her. Still, her friend seemed perplexed as she looked at her preference card... hopefully making the decision that was best for her.

Most of Jenna's life, she'd made decisions for others. Tonight was about *her* decision. Her first big choice. And she'd made it.

She slid out of the row, careful not to snag her skirt on any of the chairs, thus revealing her insulin pump. When she made her way to the back of the room, Darcy and Tricia were standing there with the rest of the Rho Gammas. Jenna turned her card in. Darcy spread her arms wide and gave Jenna a great big bear hug.

"I hope recruitment has been special for you, Jenna," Darcy whispered to her.

Jenna had never felt so at home. "It was awesome. I couldn't have done it without all of your encouragement."

Darcy smiled down at her and stepped back. "Go home and get some rest. Hopefully, tomorrow, you'll be part of a wonderful new family."

Jenna beamed, and tears formed in her eyes for the first time. She'd staved them off through the emotional candlelight ceremonies at both ZZT and Delta Kappa, but now, knowing how close she actually was to having a home away from home, well, it was all a bit overwhelming.

She gathered her wits about her, headed down the staircase to the main level, and took a seat on the bench to wait for her friends.

A few moments later, Jenna glanced up and saw Lora-Leigh bounding down the stairs confidently to the first-floor lobby.

"Well?" Jenna asked. "What did you do?"

Lora-Leigh didn't seem confused or upset. In fact, quite the opposite. She heaved a massive sigh as she sat down next to Jenna. "I did as I was told."

"You picked your mom's sorority?"

Lora-Leigh shook her head. "I followed my heart."

CHAPTER
9

Lora-Leigh sat in the Red Raider Café, just off campus on The Strip—a stretch of road where all of the clubs and bars were—munching on her double-cheeseburger with extra mayonnaise and fries and waiting for the waitress to refill her Dr Pepper.

"Here you go, honey," the waitress said, delivering a second Dr Pepper with condensation already rolling down the side. "Sorry for the wait."

Lora-Leigh sipped generously, haphazardly sketching a man's face on her pad, and thought about where she'd be in a few hours: at the Strumann Center receiving her bid. She hoped like hell it was the invitation she so desperately wanted.

Desperately. That was a strong word to use. But after hearing of Metsy Joanz's history and background, it made Lora-Leigh only more determined to slice her own path and be a rockingly successful fashion designer.

"Nice drawing. He looks kinda familiar," someone said near her booth.

Lora-Leigh looked down at her sketch and then up at the guy she was somehow unconsciously drawing. *Oh. My. God.*

"Oh, hey, DeShawn. What's up?" she asked, trying to play it cool. She moved her elbow over the sketch, but it was too late. The star athlete from her history and art classes had already seen it.

"Not much." DeShawn Pritchard was standing there with his friends, grinning at her like a fool. She couldn't believe she'd been drawing him . . . and that he'd seen it. And his friends had seen it, too. Specifically an offensive tackle, a fullback, and one of the defensive backs. LU football players tended to travel in packs.

"You missed a scintillating lecture today in Western Civ," she said casually, although her pulse picked up.

"Yeah, I was wiped. Coach had me running the stairs this morning, and I had to go spend extra time with the trainer. What's up with you?"

"Just trying to avoid the dorm food."

"You got that right." When she peered past him at his friends, he added, "Yo, Lora-Leigh, these are my boys . . . Filbert here, D-Rock, and Little John."

Filbert was Antonio Filbert, LU's all-conference defensive back. D-Rock was Derrick Rockingham, fullback; and Little John was John Danforth—all six feet eleven inches and three hundred plus pounds of him. *Little, my ass.*

"Hey guys," she said. "Nice to meet cha."

"Lora-Leigh's in my art and Western Civ classes," he said to the guys. "Which reminds me . . . can I borrow your notes from today?"

"Sure." Then she asked, "What's in it for me?"

He laughed. A deep, rolling laugh that obviously started in his stomach and bubbled up. "My eternal thanks?"

She might have been disappointed had he not winked at her. "No problem. I'll make a copy and bring them on Monday."

He scratched his closely trimmed hair and looked at the drawing again. "You must have missed me today."

She didn't want to admit that she had, so she shrugged it off. "You know, just working on facial shadowing and stuff."

"And you picked me as a subject?"

Think fast, Sorenstein. "I saw your picture in the *Raider Gazette.*" That worked. He was *always* in the campus newspaper.

"You're really good, you know?"

Feeling a ridiculous blush come on, she said, "Thanks, I try."

Little John laughed heartily. "Y'all just gonna stand there flirting or are you gonna ask her out, dawg?"

"No kidding," D-Rock echoed.

DeShawn spoke up. "We're just talking, man."

She wanted to be annoyed with him, but she could see that he was . . . *he was blushing!*

D-Rock hung his head. "Whatever. Look, we're gonna get a table. We gotta practice soon, and I need to scarf somethin' down, pronto, G."

Lora-Leigh watched DeShawn nod at his buddies as they took the corner booth by the window. (Of course, so everyone could see them sitting there.) As much as she was enjoying hanging out with him, she thought she needed to go see her mother. Her mom wasn't going to be happy about Lora-Leigh's choice, so Lora-Leigh needed to break the news in person. Who knew what would happen once she got her bid?

She slid out of the booth and stood; her head barely coming to DeShawn's chest. "I've got to get going. Like I said, I'll bring the notes on Monday."

Leaning back to get her sketch, she lost her balance. DeShawn reached out and encircled her waist with his hand. His green eyes shone brightly when she lifted her eyes to him. "Good thing I was here to catch you."

"Oh . . . thanks," she said, feeling like the entire Red Raider defense was scrimmaging on her chest from the building pressure. His touch sent ridiculous schoolgirl-crush-like flares up and down her arms.

She moved to walk away, and he called out to her.

"We're having a party at the athletic dorm tomorrow night . . . you know, last hurrah before the football season starts. You should come . . . bring some of your friends."

Not exactly a request for a date, but it was a start.

Lora-Leigh smiled. "Thanks, DeShawn. Maybe I will." And then she strolled out of the café.

Okay, so maybe this day was turning out better than she thought it would when she first woke up. While walking back toward campus, she realized she couldn't wait to get to Strumann and see if she had an invitation on her bid card.

But first, she had to deal with her mother.

"Why don't any of your clothes have tags in them, Roni?" Jenna asked as she helped her friend with her laundry on Friday.

Roni bit her bottom lip to keep from telling Jenna she didn't want everyone on the floor to know there was some rich girl with designer clothes on the hall with them. "I got them all at this discount place that pulls the designer tags out." That sounded good, didn't it? There was a place in the Boston suburbs that had sales like that every season, so it wasn't a total lie.

"That's weird." Jenna screwed her nose up and laughed.

"I have to admit, I don't know the first thing about washing any of this stuff." Especially since she'd pulled all the instructional tags off. Roni had taken a lot of her clothes to the dry cleaners next to Tuthill, but she couldn't very well send out her pajamas, jeans, and undies.

Jenna cocked her head to the side. "It's easy once you learn to separate the different colors."

Roni shrugged. "Why do you have to do that?"

Rolling her eyes, Jenna dove right into the laundry pile. "You don't want to have a red sock in with your whites, or it'll turn everything pink. We won't let that happen to you, though, Roni."

"I'm so lame," Roni said. "Sorry... we always had someone, umm, take care of the laundry." *God, that sounds pretentious.*

"Yeah, so did we," Jenna laughed. "Me!"

Roni reached for the Tide and poured the directed amount into the bottom of the washer and then piled her whites in there. "Is that right?"

Jenna dove into the washer. "No! Are you crazy?"

"What? What's wrong?"

"You can*not* put your bras and panties in the machine like that." Jenna peered at the tags that were actually there. "These are like *way* nice! If you put your underwear in, it'll chew it up and spit it out. You have to do this stuff by hand."

"Sorry," Roni said with a frown. Excellent. Not only would she have to operate a washer, but she'd have to do stuff by hand, too. Would her mother freak out now, or what? "You really know what you're doing, don't you?"

"When you've got three little sisters and your parents work like dogs, you sort of have to learn this stuff, or you end up going to school in bedsheets."

Roni envied Jenna her wonderful, loving family. "It must be great to have little sisters. I bet they love you a lot."

Jenna smiled at Roni and watched her as she put the quarters in and hit the "start" button. "Tons and tons. My Little Js are great. All of them. I love them so much."

"And you miss them, too, don't you?" Roni knew she would . . . if she had any siblings.

"Like, big time. I'm so used to being around them. I don't know how they're getting along without me."

Roni was confused. "Haven't you talked to them?"

"Oh, sure," Jenna said. "I've had a couple of e-mails from them, but I'm sure I'm not getting the full stories. Like they're really going to tell me what it's like now that I'm not there. My mom had to hire this lady to help out in the afternoons." She played with her hair for a moment. "Sometimes I feel guilty for going off to school. I got this band scholarship that is helping to pay for a lot of it, so I'd be stupid not to come here, right?"

"Absolutely," Roni said with great conviction.

Roni paused a moment and listened to the gentle *zug-a-zug-a-zug* of the washing machine. She thought of this afternoon's activities and wondered what her friend was thinking. "Are you...nervous about Bid Day?"

Jenna thought for a moment and then said, "No, I mean, what's the point? We can't change the outcome now."

"You sound like Lora-Leigh!"

They laughed together. "You know what I mean," Jenna said. "We've made our choices, and we just have to see how the computer matches us up."

Suddenly, Roni wanted to hyperventilate. Sure, she'd kept busy since last night: doing homework, going to class, looking for that amazing Adonis of the Pool in the face of every cute guy she saw, and now futzing with the laundry. She hadn't taken the time to let it *really* sink in what she'd done last night when she'd filled out her preference card. Nothing meant more to her than getting into a sorority. Had she screwed it up?

"Roni, I need to run. Are you gonna be okay with this?" Jenna asked.

"Sure. No problem," she said, her throat completely dry.

Jenna leaned in and hugged her. "I'll see you around three, okay? Come to my room, and we'll walk over to Strumann together," Jenna said.

Roni nodded, trying to hold back the choking feeling in her

chest that threatened to consume her. Swallowing hard, she said, "Fine. I'll see you later."

And then Jenna was off.

Roni hoped she hadn't ruined her college experience just as it was getting started.

Lora-Leigh put her Jetta into "park" in the driveway of her parents' house. Two BMWs, one Lexus, and a Mercedes were parked on the street in front. That meant her mother was entertaining this afternoon. Like most afternoons.

She wasn't going to want to hear what Lora-Leigh had to tell her.

Shit...

In all the excitement of getting through Preference Night and making her selection, Lora-Leigh had totally forgotten her mother would be expecting to see her at Tri-Omega's Bid Day party this afternoon. She purposely hadn't talked to her after Preference Night last night because she was too emotional and raw and too set on what she'd chosen. Her mother would only have confused her more, pressuring her with Tri-Omega talk. Lora-Leigh knew she'd made the right decision. The one that was best for her. Sure, the Tri-Omegas had their good points— every sorority did—but she never would've fit in there.

She'd fit in with the Zeta Zeta Taus.

Using her key in the back door, she slipped in, took a sip of water from the pitcher of purified water in the fridge for courage, and then moved into the living room, where the entourage sat: the Tri-Omega triumvirate consisting of her mother, Bunny Crenshaw, Cousin Lucy—and two other women whom she didn't recognize. They drank tea and lemonade and snacked on her mother's homemade scones with apple butter and real clotted cream. Nothing but the best for the ΩΩΩ sisters.

"Look who's here!" her mother shouted out. "Our newest sister."

The other women clapped, and Lora-Leigh walked awkwardly into the room. Sure, it wasn't a done deal that she *wasn't* a Tri-Omega, but even if they offered her a bid, she'd more than likely turn it down.

Lora-Leigh waved and went to hug her mother. "Hey, everyone. Hey, Lucy, how's married life?"

"You don't want to hear about that! We're here to talk about you. Come sit."

That was the last thing Lora-Leigh wanted to do.

"That's okay," she said, standing next to her mother. "I can stay only a minute. I have to get ready for Bid Day."

Bunny Crenshaw, dressed to the hilt in her white linen pantsuit, waved a heavily diamonded hand in front of her. "I was just at the Tri-Omega house, and let me tell y'all, the party is going to be fabulous. Cornelia Hunter told me the canapés and hors d'oeuvres were special-ordered just for the party. And the Bid Day T-shirts are a-dor-a-ble!"

"Hey, Mom," Lora-Leigh said tentatively, interrupting before Bunny Crenshaw could get cranking any further. "I really need to talk to you for a minute."

"Well, certainly, dear."

"In private."

Mrs. Sorenstein reached up and took Lora-Leigh's hand. "Is everything all right?"

Lora-Leigh indicated with her head that she wanted to leave the living room. "Can we just talk?"

"Would you ladies excuse me?" her mother said as she stood. "I'll be right back with some fresh tea."

"Take your time," Bunny said.

Lora-Leigh dragged her mother through the kitchen and out onto the Sorensteins' screened-in back porch. "Look, I need to say this, and I need you not to say anything back. Just listen."

"You're scaring me—"

Lora-Leigh's heart pounded like a drum and bugle corps in her head. "I put Tri-Omega as my second choice on my preference card last night."

"You what?"

"Mom, listen!"

"I will not. All we talked about this summer. All the preparation. I had Bunny go to bat for you in the house." Mrs. Sorenstein looked Lora-Leigh up one side and down the other, flattening her mouth into a nonsmile. "I'm very disappointed in you."

Lora-Leigh creased her brows together firmly. "What do you mean 'go to bat' for me? They didn't like me?"

"They don't take every legacy, you know. You were special."

She couldn't hear this. She didn't want it spelled out to her how different and special she was, compared to the initiated Tri-Omegas. "Look, I made another choice, Mom," she said, trying not to rub anything in.

"What am I supposed to say to my sorority sisters in there? Women who've taken the time to be here for me when you join our sorority?"

Don't let her make this about her... it's my choice.

"You're the one who wanted me to go through recruitment. Don't you want me to join the house I identify with the most?"

"I wanted you to join *my* sorority, Lora."

Uh-oh. Her mom only referred to her by "Lora" when she was pissed off at her.

"Look, I admit I didn't want to go through sorority recruitment, but you made me do it, and I'm glad you did. I found a really awesome bunch of girls who are pretty frickin' cool, and they like me just the way I am and—"

Mrs. Sorenstein held up a perfectly manicured hand. "You don't owe me an explanation."

"Yes, I do, Mom." Lora-Leigh bit her lip again, feeling the dissatisfaction seeping from her mother. She always seemed to be a disappointment to her parents no matter what she did. Her chest felt heavy, like a gigantic elephant was sitting on it, punishing her for making a choice that was best for her.

Her mother was on the verge of tears. "I don't know what you want from me, Lora."

Chest pains. Actual chest pains over this. Why couldn't her mother be happy for her? "I wanted to see you and . . . thank you."

"Thank me?"

"Yeah." Lora-Leigh stepped forward, made the bold move, and wrapped her arms around her mother. "You made me do this."

"I—I—I didn't make you do what you did," her mother said. "Second choice? No one puts Tri-Omega second. How *could* you? Oh, don't answer that. What sorority did you put first?"

"Zeta Zeta Tau."

Mrs. Sorenstein clicked her tongue against her teeth. "Merciful heavens. Hardly any girls from Latimer; they never win at Greek Week; and what is their overall GPA like?"

Lora-Leigh straightened, standing tall. "I don't know. I didn't ask."

"Your father can find out."

"Mom! I'm sure it's fine."

Her mother took a deep breath and stepped away. Disappointment misted the space between them, and Lora-Leigh knew this was going to be a bone of contention for a while.

"You may not get your first choice," her mother said.

Lora-Leigh shrugged. "You're right. I might not. But I won't accept an invitation from Tri-Omega."

"Why not?"

"Look at me, Mom! What do you think? I don't *fit in* there."

"Don't be silly, you'd fit in just fine. The girls loved you once they got to know you."

Ignoring the backhanded compliment, Lora-Leigh said, "I did what I wanted to, Mom. Please be happy for me."

Silence.

"Please, Mom . . ."

Mrs. Sorenstein inhaled deeply again but wouldn't meet Lora-Leigh's eyes. After a few moments, she said, "I really need to go put the tea kettle on."

"Mom . . ."

"You run along now, dear. I don't know what I'll tell the girls in there. I'll figure it out. They don't have to know, really, until the bids are out," she muttered to herself. "I'll, ummm, tell your father he missed you."

"Sure . . . okay. Mom, are you all right?"

Mrs. Sorenstein turned away from her and moved back into the living room, laughing boisterously to her friends. "Tea in a moment, ladies." She was in serious denial, and that stabbed Lora-Leigh in the chest. It didn't matter, though. She'd come here to thank her mother, and she'd done it. Without her mother's insistence, Lora-Leigh never would have gone through sorority recruitment. Sure, her mom was mad now—embarrassed, probably—but it wouldn't last long.

She'll get over it.

But would Lora-Leigh?

Jenna hustled into her room, excited about the festivities that would begin soon. She was going to take a quick shower, put her hair up (it was going to be hot, hot, hot outside), and get dressed to go to Strumann. Something stopped her, though, as she dumped her purse on the bed. There, on her pillow, was a note pinned to one of her Care Bears like a stake to the heart:

Driving home for the weekend.
Enjoy sorority life.

"Oh, Amber . . . ," Jenna said as she looked at the note.
She hates me.

And for that, Jenna almost hated herself. This totally sucked. Yeah, Amber got dropped from recruitment, but it wasn't

Jenna's fault. Why did her roommate have to add that dig about enjoying sorority life? So stupid.

Needing some positive reinforcement, she booted up her computer and checked her e-mail. Knowing her mom and sisters, there would be *something* there to make her feel better and counter the Amber sneak attack.

As the e-mails downloaded, Jenna saw a joke from her sister, Jessica, something from her mom, and one other with the subject line "Tomorrow." She clicked on it and nearly wigged out when she saw:

From: david.j.harrison@latimeruniversity.edu
Date: Fri, 18 Sep 14:40:32
To: jenna.m.driscoll@latimeruniversity.edu
Subject: Tomorrow

Hope I got the right Jenna Driscoll. It's me, Tiger. Good luck with Bid Day today. Remember to bring your new sisters to the ΦOX house tomorrow night for the open house party.
See ya then,
Tiger

Jenna squealed and danced around the room. David "Tiger" Harrison, the most adorable guy she'd seen on campus, had sought her out and *e-mailed* her! She was completely freaking out! Suddenly, charged by his words—and the prospect of her first fraternity party—Jenna grabbed her shower equipment and headed off to get ready.

She wasn't going to let Amber's attitude ruin this for her. Not tonight.

CHAPTER
10

Lora-Leigh entered Jenna's dorm room cautiously. "Anyone home?"

"Hey Lora-Leigh, come on in."

That hyper chick, Amber, wasn't around, so Lora-Leigh made herself at home on the foot of Jenna's bed while her friend scrounged around on her hands and knees looking for the mate to her sandal. A Kenneth Cole knock-off, Lora-Leigh noted, scrutinizing the slip-on, black, strappy item.

"Where's your roommate?" Lora-Leigh asked.

Jenna stared up through the blonde hair that had fallen in her eyes. "She went home for the weekend. She was seriously freaked about getting dropped from recruitment."

Lora-Leigh sighed. "Especially when there were people like me who weren't jazzed about it to begin with and didn't get dropped." She knew there were more deserving girls, those a helluva lot more excited about this whole sorority thing than she'd been at the start.

"Here it is!" Jenna announced, holding up the left sandal. "As soon as Roni comes down, we can get going."

Staring at her friend, Lora-Leigh scrunched up her face. "Don't you think you're a little overdressed, Jenna? I mean, the skirt is cute, but this is Bid Day. It's casual. You're supposed to be in a T-shirt and shorts." The blouse hung off Jenna in a way baggy fashion, like she was trying to hide fat or something. Lora-Leigh couldn't help noticing things like that because how clothing draped on the body was as serious to her as . . . deciding on a sorority.

Jenna pointed the found sandal at her. "You're one to talk. Look at you, Lora-Leigh. You're obviously not trying to impress anyone."

"What's wrong with the way I'm dressed?" Lora-Leigh asked, tugging on her almost-too-tight T-shirt that read IF YOU'RE LOOKING FOR TROUBLE, YOU FOUND IT. The copper color of the tee blended well with her hair and eye coloring. Pairing the novelty shirt with khaki shorts and tennis shoes was a no-brainer on a day like today. She knew what was going to happen, thanks to hearing her mom's recruitment education and having lived in Latimer all of her life. Lora-Leigh remembered the times she and her friends biked over for the Running of the new members, laughing her ass off at the display and thinking how utterly ridiculous the girls looked. Today, she couldn't wait for the adrenaline rush that was sure to propel her down Sorority Row. Hopefully. "Besides," Lora-Leigh added, "once we get our bids, they'll give us Bid Day shirts at our new houses."

"*If* we get bids," Jenna corrected.

Lora-Leigh's heart throbbed too hard. The two of them

would have to wait a-whole-nother hour—until four—to find out which house, if any, they received bids from.

"Well, I'm going to look my best for my new sisters," Jenna said, now attacking her rosy cheeks with a large makeup brush. "See, I'm thinking positively."

Scrutinizing her friend, she realized something was up. "This sunny disposition has to do with more than getting your bid, doesn't it?"

Jenna jumped up and down in place. "You know that cute Phi Omicron Chi I told you about?"

"The Fox you were gawking at when you took your header down the stairs?"

"No! Yes... anyway. He sent me an e-mail wishing me luck. And he wants all of us to come to the Phi Omicron Chi house tomorrow night for their Open House Rush party."

"Cool," Lora-Leigh said. "I've been invited to a football party, too." Before she could say anything else, she glanced down at Jenna's feet. "Dude, your feet are gonna hurt like blue-blazing bullshit when you have to run from the student union to Sorority Row in the heat."

Jenna dropped her head to view her shoes and pouted. "Oh."

"Yeah. Sandals ain't gonna cut it, hon."

With a sigh, Jenna tugged off the shoes and reached for her Nikes.

A soft knock on the door made Lora-Leigh's heart flip up in the air and land in her lap, even though the Rho Gammas weren't coming to visit today. They were all at the student union getting the bid cards in place.

"Hey guys," Roni said, peeking in. "Are you ready to go?"

"As ready as I'll ever be," Jenna announced.

Lora-Leigh tried to remain casual. After all, she had an image to uphold with these two. She didn't want them to know how anxious she was to read her bid card and view the three letters she was hoping to see.

"Take a load off," she said, patting the bed next to her.

Roni was dressed in an aqua sleeveless shirt and a black miniskirt. It was a cute design that Lora-Leigh would have to remember for future knockoff sewing. The plunging neckline revealed Roni's tanned skin and a silver Tiffany necklace on a long chain. There was a paleness in her face and sadness in her eyes that didn't match the carefree, fashionable outfit. Roni sniffed a bit. "You gettin' sick on us, Boston?"

"No. Sorry. It's just—" she said, choking up.

Jenna kneeled in front of Roni. "What's wrong?" she asked as Roni started shaking.

"I—I did a wicked stupid thing last night," she eked out.

No more stupid than me, Lora-Leigh thought, but didn't say. "What did you do?" she asked.

Roni took a deep breath of air and rolled her head from side to side, causing her black hair to fall into her face. "I put down only one choice on my preference card last night."

"You what?" Jenna exclaimed.

"Oh, Boston."

Jenna pressed. "Did you get dropped?"

Lora-Leigh couldn't imagine any sorority not having Roni Van Gelderen on their first-choice list. She had everything: looks, personality... and money. One didn't get asked back to

Tri-Omega unless their parents were influential... or a legacy, like her.

"No, I didn't get dropped yet, but Darcy and Tricia told me my bid card could be blank. They told us the computers match our choices with the sororities' lists. So, if ZZT didn't put me on their first-choice list... one incorrectly bubbled-in circle on a preference card may mean social disaster and ostracism for the next four years."

"Good Lord, it's not that bad," Lora-Leigh said.

"But it could be," Roni pleaded.

"Chillax, Roni," Jenna said.

"Huh?"

"Chillax—chill... relax..."

After a long pause, Lora-Leigh said, "You've got balls, Boston." She swallowed at the thought of what her friend *actually* did. "I can't believe you frickin' suicided."

Jenna looked confused. "She what?"

"What she did... it's called suiciding. Picking one house as your first, second, and only preference, and not having another choice. You're hoping to be on their first-choice list and if not, you're betting you're on their fill-in list. Suiciding. My mom told me all about it."

"My friend Kiersten told me about it," Roni said with a sniff.

"Do a lot of people do it?" Jenna asked.

"It's risky," Lora-Leigh said, "but it can work. My mom did it when she wanted to get in to Tri-Omega."

Roni blotted her eyes. "So I may not have screwed up?"

Lora-Leigh looked at the beautiful, dark-haired girl before

her. So quiet and unassuming. What would make a girl like Roni suicide? Lora-Leigh had no clue. There was only one thing to do to ease this situation for all of them.

"Why don't we mosey over to the student union and see what they've got in store for us."

They should call it Torture Day instead of Bid Day.

Jenna sat on the sticky, hot, plastic ballroom chair in potential new member number order. Underneath her bottom was a small envelope with a card in it.

Does it say KΔ? Does it say ZZT?

The suspense was killing her.

"When can we open them?" she asked the girl next to her.

"Oh, the Rho Gammas do a skit or something for us to reveal their houses, and then I think we, like, get to open the cards. I don't know. I'm too freaked out."

"Me, too," Jenna said.

Music filled the room as the whole host of Rho Gammas scurried in with gigantic balloon bouquets of all hues and shades—the colors of the sororities—with them. Jenna began clapping along, feeling the electricity and excitement in the air.

Across the aisle and up about ten rows, she could see Roni's dark head bobbing along to the techno beat pounding out in the ballroom. Eight rows behind her was Lora-Leigh. The two exchanged a smile, and Lora-Leigh held up crossed fingers.

"Whooo-hoooo! I'm Heather. Welcome to Bid Day!" the head Rho Gamma shouted over the P.A. system.

A roar elevated from the group of girls, all eager to find

out their individual news. More clapping and squealing commenced, and Jenna found it hard to contain her own glee. The Rho Gammas hurtled through the room, passing out balloons and cheering boisterously, causing a frenzied fury in the apprehensive audience.

Jenna wiggled in her seat, feeling the bid card underneath her. *What does it say? Which house is it? Is it Darcy's?*

"Are y'all excited?" Heather shouted out through the microphone. "This is the moment you've been waiting for—all week, all summer! Y'all've done a fantastic job, have shown your true personalities, and have put your best foot forward to impress the many wonderful houses we have here on campus. You've seen true friendship, cherished sisterhood, exemplary philanthropic work, and the general good-feeling atmosphere associated with Greek life. The Panhellenic Association here at Latimer University is pleased we've had such a successful week, and we look forward to welcoming you into our ranks."

"Then let us open our bids," someone yelled out from in front of Jenna.

She giggled along, but then clasped her hands together to keep from fiddling with her shirt. Her feet tapped out a nervous rhythm on the floor, wanting to know what was in her envelope.

"Patience, ladies," Heather instructed. "You won't have to wait much longer."

"Good, 'cause I'm about to pee my pants," the girl next to Jenna said.

Jenna tried to concentrate on the stage show, but it was one heck of a challenging endeavor. She didn't know what she was more curious to know: confirmation of Darcy's affiliation, or who her bid was from.

Heather continued. "Okay, ladies. Before you open your bids, we want to reveal the Greek affiliation of our fantabulous Rho Gammas who have helped you, kept you informed, and done all of the work to get you set in your new homes."

Jenna sat tall in her seat, trying to see both Tricia and Darcy. She *knew* Darcy was a Delta Kappa. Of course, everyone in Group 7 thought that she was a Delta Kappa and that Tricia was an O Chi O. Actually, at this moment, it didn't matter because Jenna knew!

Let me open my card!

The laughter ceased, and Heather said, "We don't want to keep you from getting to your new house. After the Rho Gammas reveal their affiliations, we'll let you open your cards, and then you can bolt! Be prepared to make the run through hordes of students and locals who gather to watch the running of the new sorority members. Especially the fraternities and the guys going out for Rush. This is your time to shine and have fun. Enjoy it for all it's worth!"

It was a long haul across campus; Jenna hoped she could run that far without losing her breath. Thank God Lora-Leigh had told her to put on tennies. She looked at her watch as the minutes continued to drag along.

Why are they torturing us?

"Once you get home, the Bid Day parties will be in full swing," Heather said. "Let me be the first to congratulate you for making it through sorority recruitment!"

The music pumped up, and the lights shone brightly on

the girls gathered up front. The Rho Gammas moved around the stage, singing along with an old eighties song called "Celebration."

"'Celebrate good times, come on!'"

As the music got louder, the Rho Gammas paired off in front of them, singing along and clapping. Jenna pounded her hands together along with the beat, not taking her eyes off Darcy as she stood next to the head Rho Gamma, Heather. That probably meant they were in the same house.

More applause.

More singing.

"Come on, come on, come on . . . ," Jenna muttered.

"On the count of three . . . One. Two." A long pause for drama. *"Three!"*

Screams and yelps rippled from the many voices in the ballroom as the Rho Gammas revealed their Greek letters to the assemblage. Jenna smiled when she saw Tricia's Theta Beta Rho (*Wow . . . no one guessed that!*) shirt, but she got a nauseating kick in the gut when she saw Darcy's letters.

They weren't Delta Kappa.

"Ladies, you may open your bids!" said Heather, who was standing next to her sorority sister, Darcy.

As the melee around her fell like raindrops, Jenna felt the hot, salty tears well in her eyes. Her card, unopened, lay lifeless in her hands while she took in what she had seen on the stage.

Darcy's a ZZT!

But Jenna had chosen Delta Kappa on the assumption that Darcy was a Delta Kappa. "That's completely messed up," she muttered. How could she have been so wrong? She'd *seen*

Darcy coming out of the Delta Kappa house with her own eyes. Yet, Darcy was wearing the blue letters of ZZT?

Slowly, torturously so, she peeled the flap of the envelope away to reveal the white card. Her pulse machine-gunned away in her temples, almost deafening her to the screams, cheers, and cries around her.

She'd be happy as a Delta Kappa. She knew she would. Nothing wrong with being in the Delta Bunch. They were obviously a great group of girls who'd made her feel really welcome. Jenna would make it her home.

Why did her heart feel so heavy, though?

The room was becoming less and less full as all around her crazed girls were peeling out and running to their new homes. She didn't see Roni or Lora-Leigh, so they must be on their way as well.

Get it over with . . .

Jenna slid the card out and turned it over. Her breath caught in her throat, and she thought she was going to choke on her happiness.

"Shut up! Like, no way . . ."

The letters on her card read: ZZT. She'd gotten her second choice. "I got my second choice!" Spinning around to face the stage, she tried to locate Darcy—a ZZT, too!—so they could go to the house together.

I got in Zeta Zeta Tau!

Instead of running out of the ballroom, Jenna ran up to the front of the stage, waving her bid card up at Darcy. "Darcy! I'm a ZZT!"

Darcy fell to her knees, leaned down over the stage, and

awkwardly hugged Jenna. "I'm soooooooooo happy for you! We're sisters now."

Jenna's tears fell, but out of joy and happiness. "What do I do now?"

Grabbing Jenna's hands and swinging them back and forth, Darcy said, "Run. Run to the house. I'll be there to meet you when you get home."

Home. She'd found a home. Then what was she doing standing here when she had new sisters to meet?

Without hesitation, she waved at Darcy, stepped into the aisle, and took off on a dead run out of the Strumann Student Union on her way to Sorority Row.

Roni was about to have a major organ breakdown over all of this. Lungs collapsing. Brain aneurism. Heart attack. All of it at once.

The room was abuzz with chatter, laughter, and the slightest tremor of near mania. Roni could feel it emanating from her skin, shooting out the ends of her fingertips, and reaching out to everyone around her. An almost supernatural energy sizzled throughout the room. This was it. Her social D-Day. Had she completely mucked this up by suiciding?

What she craved more than anything, though, was a place to belong. A family to fit into. People who would support her, encourage her . . . love her, even. And she believed that connection materialized through the sisters at Zeta Zeta Tau.

She only hoped they sensed it, too.

The harriedness of the opening of the bids had crescendoed

to a near maelstrom of emotions. Chairs scuffed across the ballroom floor, paper was ripped, howls of joy reverberated up to the ceilings as well as cries of the brokenhearted who hadn't gotten what they wanted.

"Beta Xi!"

"Oh my God, I got Phi Epsilon Chi!"

"Tri-Omega picked me!"

"I'm a Delta Kappa!"

"ZZT! I got in ZZT!"

Hearing all this, Roni got over her trepidation, grabbed her card out from underneath her, and blinked hard as her trembling hands tugged at the sealed envelope. "Dammit!" Two rips and one hell of a paper cut... didn't matter. It was open! She jerked out the card and flipped it over, eyes growing wide.

For two seconds, her heartbeat stopped altogether, and then it was as if she'd been immediately resuscitated on much-needed life support when the emboldened letters on her card burned into her eyes.

"*Yes!*"

"Don't just sit there," the girl next to her said. "We've got to go!"

Without having to think twice, Roni headed for the stairs. She took them two at a time, holding on to the railing as she made her way through the Strumann lobby, out the door, and into the late-afternoon sunshine, peeling off to the left with the pack.

Plenty of other girls were running along with her as they sped through the pedestrian mall toward the library that sat at the heart of the Latimer campus. The group rounded the big oak tree on the corner and then burst onto the one-way street that had been closed off especially for them. Hordes of people from town and campus lined the quad, cheering them on, but Roni heard nothing. Everything was one big colorful blur. All she wanted to do was reach Sorority Row. Reach the ZZT house, where her new family would be! And maybe even Jenna and Lora-Leigh!

A local Latimer policeman had the intersection of University Drive and Sorority Row blocked off to allow them full access to their new houses. The first house was Theta Beta Gamma, where two girls who were running with her stopped only to be scooped into welcoming embraces. Next, the O Chi O's front yard was decorated in red, white, and yellow balloons and streamers with a huge WELCOME HOME banner awaiting the girls jumping around the yard. Roni let out a yelp of frustration, hoping her tired legs would get her all the way around the corner to the gargantuan yellow Spanish house—her new home.

Delta Kappas out on their lawn waved on the rest of them, and the Pi Eps had music cranked to decibel eleven as their lawn party was rocking away. While these were all great sororities and Roni had enjoyed visiting them and getting to know them, she felt no disappointment or regret over not selecting them. Especially when she rounded the corner and saw the second-to-last house on the right. *Her* house.

Zeta Zeta Tau!

A tall girl carrying her flip-flops and running barefooted glanced at her. "Are you a ZZT?"

"I am now!" Roni shouted.

"Me, too!" The taller girl grabbed Roni's left hand and pulled her along. "Come on . . . we're almost home."

Roni's body was on fire, exuberant and jazzed from the run to the house. Especially when she saw the white, gold, and blue balloons all over the yard. Over the door was a ginormous hand-painted banner that read ZZT Loves Their New Members!

She stumbled to a stop like a cartoon character as she took in everything. A chubby black-haired girl she remembered from Four Party greeted her with a hug and handed her a blue T-shirt and a gift bag. "Welcome home, Roni!"

She knows me?

The tall girl got a hug and bag, too. "Welcome home, Sandy!"

The tall girl is Sandy. My new sister . . . Sandy.

"I'm Lexie, the Recruitment Chairman. Go on in the house real quick to change, use the ladies' room, if needed, and grab some water. Then come on outside. Everyone's waiting for you!"

Making her way up onto the porch, Roni took in the scenery. She thought she was going to faint from all of the excitement. In front of her, the lawn teemed with girls in shorts and jeans and ZZT attire. There were some older ladies, whom Roni recognized from recruitment as alumnae, there to help out. All of them were ZZTs, though. And so was she!

This was the best day of her life. Roni had done what was best for her, and it had paid off. She couldn't wait to call Kiersten and tell her!

Jenna looked around her, almost overwhelmed by all the craziness. She held her T-shirt in one hand and a gift bag in the other. But where was Darcy? She said she'd be here.

"Come on inside and change," a girl named Lexie instructed.

Inside the house, squealing girls ripped off their various tops and tugged on their Bid Day shirts. Jenna was afraid of whipping off her shirt and revealing her insulin pump to her new sisters, so instead, she slid into a back corner, pulled her T-shirt on over her head, and then wrenched the bottom shirt off through the sleeves, just like she'd done a thousand times on the high school band bus. Fortunately, her T-shirt was a large, and it hung off her with plenty of room to hide her pump.

"Jenna Driscoll! Glad you could join the festivities!"

Jenna spun around to see not only Lora-Leigh standing there—in a T-shirt that read I SAID IT'S GREAT TO BE A ZZT!—but Roni was there too!

"Oh, my God, y'all! We're sisters!"

Roni ran up and hugged her like all get-out, followed by Lora-Leigh crushing them like she was an LU linebacker. "Friggin'-aye right we're sisters," Lora-Leigh said, ever the potty mouth.

"I can't believe my suiciding paid off! Holy freakin' shit!" Roni exclaimed, and then clamped her hand over her mouth and laughed.

"Boston... didn't know you had it in you, you foul-mouthed demon," Lora-Leigh said. "I'm totally corrupting both of you!"

The three of them jumped around screaming and reveling in the fact that they'd found a home, new friends, and forever sisters.

They peeked inside their gift bags to see a water bottle with ZZT letters on it, as well as pens, pencils, notepads, a key chain, and a welcome note.

The new members were directed out to the side lawn, where the party was in full swing. Digital cameras appeared from everywhere, and Jenna was being swept into one small group after the next to get her picture taken.

"I think I've smiled myself a headache," Roni said with a laugh.

Lora-Leigh picked Jenna up from behind and hugged her. "Live it up, girls! We deserve this."

Jenna grabbed a diet soda, barely able to comprehend everything going on around her. She and Roni and Lora-Leigh were sisters! How cool was that?

"You don't know how happy I am to see you in those letters, Jenna," a sweet voice said. Roni and Lora-Leigh parted to reveal Darcy, their Rho Gamma. She spread her arms wide, and Jenna ran forward, hugging her new...*sister.*

"There you are, Darcy!"

"Sorry, Heather and I had to drive through all the traffic from Strumann."

Jenna squealed. "You're a ZZT!"

"So are you, Jenna."

"I thought you were a Delta Kappa," Jenna said, her voice muffled in Darcy's Bid Day T-shirt.

"What made you think that?"

"I saw you coming out of their house the other day."

Darcy threw her head back and laughed. "Oh, my roommate, Jeanine, is a Delta Kap, and I was taking her cell phone to her. I'm a ZZT, just like you."

"I *am* a ZZT!" Jenna said, feeling her brain was going to explode from the merriment. She pointed at her buddies standing there. "We all are!"

Lora-Leigh smirked slightly. "Recruitment Group Seven stays intact."

After tons of pictures—a group shot where everyone gathered around—Jenna, Darcy, Lora-Leigh, and Roni moved over to a pit barbecue where they were grilling burgers, hot dogs, and chicken breasts to go with the potato salad, coleslaw, and desserts spread out on the tables. Digital cameras continued to flash and click away as the new members gathered for more pictures. Jenna couldn't stop smiling.

She met other sisters she'd talked to throughout the week, fellow new members, alum, and the housemother, Mrs. Walsh, who had been a ZZT back in her college days in the late fifties. The girls danced to the DJ who spun House music on the lawn (competing with the other houses).

Jenna was told that when the sun set and the party was over, the sisters would go inside for a special ceremony. There, the thirty new members would together take an oath of loyalty to Zeta Zeta Tau and the sisterhood they had now formed.

She spun around and absorbed everything going on around her.

"Who knew second choice could be this amazing?"

Lora-Leigh finished up her third hot dog and wiped her mouth with a napkin. She glanced across the street at the Beta Xi house, where their Bid Day party was in full force, as well. Girls were jumping around, hugging, and posing for pictures. Seemed that everyone over there made the right choice, just like she had.

She knew her mother was down the street at the Tri-Omega house—with Bunny Crenshaw, Cousin Lucy, and the others—but she didn't have *one* single regret. She'd made the best decision she ever could have.

"Lora-Leigh, there you are!"

She turned to see Camille, the sister who had ushered her through recruitment so wonderfully. "Hey, Camille! Where have you been?"

"I just got off work at the mall. Look at you in your ZZT shirt. You're a sister now."

Camille hugged her, and Lora-Leigh felt welcomed and included into the Latimer community. She was okay with being at LU now that she'd realized she could have a good education and move into a design career. After all, there was more to fashion than just the clothes. There was marketing and publicity and accounting and... She'd learn all of that here at Latimer. Right now, she wasn't upset about the fact that she wasn't in California or New York because she'd found a place where she seemed to fit. She squeezed back to let Camille know her true emotions.

"So," Camille said. "Looks like your heart made the decision for you?"

"Yeah," Lora-Leigh said, with a lump in her throat. "You were right. This is the place for me."

"Everyone loves you, Lora-Leigh. You're going to make a great sister."

"I have to tell you, the ZZT trump card was Metsy Joanz. I can't believe that!"

Camille shrugged. "See, it was kismet, Lora-Leigh. We're

going to have a great year!"

Her heart hammered megahard underneath her Bid Day shirt. Today, there'd been no comments about her earrings or crazy curly hair that was behaving quite well despite the typical Florida humidity. "I want to really give something back to the house, Camille. I promise y'all won't regret picking me."

Camille smiled wide. "And no regrets for you, either." She laid her hand on Lora-Leigh's arm. "Have you spoken to your mother?"

"I went home after class today and told her I hadn't picked her sorority."

"How'd she take it?"

"Not very well," Lora-Leigh said. That was saying it lightly. Her mother was going to stew on this for a while and Lora-Leigh knew it.

"You know, my mom wanted me to join one of the traditionally African American sororities. They're fantastic, but I really wanted to fit into a place where so many different girls from so many unique backgrounds could come together. My mom was disappointed, but she understood I did what was best for me. Yours will, too."

"I hope so." Lora-Leigh hated not being in her mom's good graces. In time, her mother would come around.

Camille steered her back toward the party, where some of the sisters were already teaching the new girls one of the ZZT songs. "Let's get back to the fun. Today's about you."

"Damn straight!"

She squeezed her way into the middle of the gathered

group, feeling the friendship surrounding her immediately here with the ZZTs. Her new home. Make no bones about it; they'd chosen her and she'd chosen them. No one—*not even Mom!*—could take that from her.

At eight P.M., the parties ended, and Sorority Row became quiet as sisters and new members retired into their respective homes for their sisterhood ceremonies. Lora-Leigh followed the others inside the house and into the formal living room, lit in the golden glow of candles. She stood with Roni on her left and Jenna on her right, among the wonderful crowd of thirty other new members who were all individuals with something to share and offer ZZT. Lora-Leigh couldn't wait to see what their new member time would be like and how they could all blend into the activities, the life... the house.

Marissa, the president, called the new members forward. "Welcome to Zeta Zeta Tau, ladies. We couldn't be happier to include you in our sisterhood. Tonight is the first step on your journey to becoming a full-fledged ZZT. To know our history, to understand our purpose, and to share in our ritual and secrets. We are a family from this day forward."

Lora-Leigh's chest actually hurt—in a good way—as the ZZT members started singing to them. Something sweet and harmonized about "... shining bright... oh ZZT, we're one."

To her, the songs, the ceremony, the camaraderie weren't silly anymore. There was no longer the bitterness over how she thought all sororities made you conform to their ways. The message here was clear: *Everyone belongs.* Even Lora-Leigh

Sorenstein. The kooky fashion-designer wannabe from Latimer. She fit in well with the bubbly blonde from Marietta, Georgia, and the rich girl from Boston.

Lexie, who'd greeted her at the door with her T-shirt and gift bag, stepped through the girls, pinning tiny white, blue, and gold ribbons on their chests. "These are our colors, which run true. Wear them with pride and always honor their meaning: sisterhood, friendship, and charity."

Candles were then passed out to each of the new members, and Lexie brought a tall white taper down from where the officers stood at the front of the room. "From this one unity candle, we all light our way in the world. Coming together as women in the bonds of sisterhood. To strengthen our souls, to refresh our spirit, to give back to the community as a whole, and to enrich our college campus. Come, light your candle and spread the warmth around the room."

Lora-Leigh followed her new sisters and touched the wick of her candle to the larger one. The new members walked around the room, lighting the candles of the other members gathered. Lora-Leigh made a point to go straight to Camille, who had been so kind and supportive of her throughout recruitment. She couldn't wait to get to know her better.

Through the flickering white-orange candlelight, the unshed tears in Lora-Leigh's began to fall as Marissa pinned her with the official new member pin: a white enamel rose with ZZT written in tiny letters. "The new member pin is a symbol of your newfound family. The pin must be worn at all times throughout your new member period. Keep it close to your heart."

"Always," Lora-Leigh mouthed.

"A sisterhood so true," Marissa said, smiling at Lora-Leigh.

Lora-Leigh looked over at Roni and Jenna. Nothing about this could be wrong. They were home. They were *sisters*.

GREEK ALPHABET

ENGLISH SPELLING	GREEK LETTER	PRONUNCIATION
Alpha	A	*Al-fah*
Beta	B	*Bay-tah*
Gamma	Γ	*Gam-ah*
Delta	Δ	*Del-tah*
Epsilon	E	*Ep-si-lon*
Zeta	Z	*Zay-tah*
Eta	H	*A-tah*
Theta	Θ	*Thay-tah*
Iota	I	*Eye-o-tah*
Kappa	K	*Cap-ah*
Lambda	Λ	*Lamb-dah*
Mu	M	*Mew*
Nu	N	*New*
Xi	Ξ	*Zigh*
Omicron	O	*Ohm-i-kron*
Pi	Π	*Pie*
Rho	P	*Roe*
Sigma	Σ	*Sig-mah*
Tau	T	*Taw*
Upsilon	Υ	*Oop-si-lon*
Phi	Φ	*Fie*
Chi	X	*Kie*
Psi	Ψ	*Sigh*
Omega	Ω	*O-may-gah*

GREEK ORGANIZATIONS
——————LATIMER UNIVERSITY——————
Latimer, Florida

ORGANIZATION	GREEK LETTER	CLASSIFICATION
Alpha Sigma Gamma	ΑΣΓ	Sorority
Alpha Mu	ΑΜ	Fraternity
Beta Eta Psi	ΒΗΨ	Fraternity
Beta Xi	ΒΞ	Sorority
Chi Pi	ΧΠ	Fraternity
Delta Kappa	ΔΚ	Sorority
Delta Sigma Nu	ΔΣΝ	Fraternity
Eta Lamba Nu	ΗΛΝ	Sorority
Gamma Gamma Rho	ΓΓΡ	Fraternity
Kappa Omega	ΚΩ	Fraternity
Kappa Tau Omicron	ΚΤΟ	Fraternity
Omega Omega Omega	ΩΩΩ	Sorority
Omega Phi	ΩΦ	Fraternity
Omicron Chi Omega	ΟΧΩ	Sorority
Phi Omicron Chi	ΦΟΧ	Fraternity
Pi Epsilon Chi	ΠΕΧ	Sorority
Pi Theta Epsilon	ΠΘΕ	Fraternity
Psi Kappa Upsilon	ΨΚΥ	Sorority
Sigma Sigma	ΣΣ	Fraternity
Tau Delta Iota	ΤΔΙ	Fraternity
Theta Beta Gamma	ΘΒΓ	Sorority
Zeta Theta Mu	ΖΘΜ	Fraternity
Zeta Zeta Tau	ΖΖΤ	Sorority

For more about
the sisters of
Zeta Zeta Tau, read

SORORITY 101:
The New Sisters

SORORITY
101

CHAPTER
1

Jenna Driscoll studied the pearly white new member pin in her hand. The dime-size pin was shaped like a blooming white rose with three Greek letters in the middle: ZZT. It was crazy to think that only yesterday she'd been officially pinned as a Zeta Zeta Tau at the conclusion of sorority recruitment.

She lifted her gaze from her new jewelry to the dorm mirror in front of her. She'd changed her outfit at least four times, stripping off her smart black pants and finally opting for the low-rise Seven jeans she'd picked up by some unbelievable stroke of good luck at Goodwill in Atlanta. They weren't too tight in the hips and allowed her to wear her insulin pump, which monitored her diabetes, on the inside of her pants. She paired the jeans with a top that showed off her shoulders and neck but was loose at her waist and wouldn't give away the secret of her medical condition. No one needed to know about *that* just yet.

Right before she headed for the door, she clipped her pin onto her shirt.

She couldn't wait to show it to Tiger tonight!

She'd met David "Tiger" Harrison on her first day of classes at Latimer University. They'd bumped into each other (literally). And when they'd run into each other again during the week, he'd invited her to come to the Phi Omicron Chi party this Saturday night.

Just as she grabbed her jacket and small purse, the dorm-room door opened.

"Oh. You're here," her roommate mumbled, barely glancing at her.

"Hey, Amber." Her roommate's face was just as sad-looking as it had been when she'd gotten the word a couple of days ago that she'd been dropped from sorority recruitment. It was a heartbreaking crush for her. "I thought you went home for the weekend."

Amber flopped down on her bed with a long, hard sigh. "I did, but my parents were driving me crazy. They wouldn't stop hovering and babying me. It made me feel worse about . . . everything."

Instinctively, Jenna tugged the collar of her jacket over her pin. The motion didn't escape Amber's attention.

"So, which house did you get into?"

"Zeta Zeta Tau."

Amber merely nodded.

"You know," Jenna said optimistically, "I heard that if any houses weren't full, there would be an open recruitment time, and more bids might be offered."

"Only losers go out for open recruitment," Amber said emphatically.

"That's not true." Jenna sighed. "Amber, look, I know—"

She held up her hand. "Don't. Just don't go there, Jenna." She tossed her fiery red hair over her shoulder. "I know you're trying to help, but I'll be fine. Don't cheerlead. Leave that to the Latimer pom-pom squad."

Jenna's heart raced at the tension swirling around the room. When they'd first moved in together, Amber had been so sweet. She even wanted to decorate their room and get matching comforters for their beds. Now she was like a different person entirely. Jenna kept hoping it was only temporary. It *had* to be temporary, right?

She shook off the negative vibes. Her new sisters were waiting for her, and having fun with them tonight would help soothe her nerves. "Look, Amber . . . I gotta go." She hesitated at the door, hating to leave her roommate like this, even if she was in a pissy mood. "Are you okay?"

"Where are you going?"

Jenna bit her bottom lip slightly, wondering how Amber would take this information. "Umm . . . a few new ZZT sisters and I are going to some frat Rush parties."

Amber frowned. "Of course you are. That's just perfect."

Thinking quickly, Jenna blurted, "Do you want to come?"

"I don't think so. I'm not a charity case." Amber turned into her pillows, and Jenna swore she heard a sob. She didn't know what to do. If she stayed with Amber, she'd miss seeing Tiger at the Phi Omicron Chi house.

No . . . I'm not the big sister here, Jenna reminded herself, thinking about her younger siblings in Marietta, Georgia. She'd worked hard to get into ZZT, so she deserved to have some fun. Amber could take care of herself tonight, and tomorrow Jenna would see if she wanted to go get a coffee together or something.

"Okay," Jenna said. "I'll see you later, then. I'll try to be quiet when I get in."

Amber rolled over and faced the wall. "Whatev."

Jenna felt a heaviness in her chest, but she tried her best to ignore it as she walked to the elevator to meet up with her two new ZZT sisters and friends, Lora-Leigh Sorenstein and Roni Van Gelderen. The three of them had been in the same sorority recruitment group together, and now they were pretty much inseparable.

"Hey!" Lora-Leigh said. "How's the Roommate from Hell?"

"Be nice," Jenna scolded. "She's not that bad."

"Yet." Lora-Leigh adjusted one of the half-dozen earrings dangling from her left ear. Lora-Leigh was outspoken and blunt, with a raw sense of humor that Jenna usually loved, except right now, when it was making her even more nervous about Amber.

Roni seemed to read her mind, because she put her hand on Jenna's arm and said gently, "She'll be all right. Just give her some time."

"Thanks," Jenna said, smiling. Tall, beautiful Roni always seemed to know the right things to say.

"Okay, that's enough Amber-angsting for tonight," Lora-Leigh decided. "Now what do you think of the top I made today?" she asked, pointing to her stunning silk azure halter. "Am I ready for *Project Runway*?"

"You're too good for *Project Runway*," Roni said with a smile.

"Ooh, I like the way you talk. Hopefully the guys tonight will like my style, too."

Jenna giggled. "Something tells me your outfit is for more than just random frat guys."

"Yeah, well, if we just *happen* to stop by the athletic dorm for their party later, and we just *happen* to see DeShawn Pritchard there, *la culpa no es mía.*" DeShawn was the junior star running back for the Latimer University football team and Lora-Leigh's current "friend with flirt privileges." There was enough chemistry between them to fuel a bonfire, whether Lora-Leigh would ever admit it or not.

Lora-Leigh pushed the "down" button on the elevator. "Well, ladies, we have a very aggressive social agenda this evening. Let's get started."

Jenna's heart raced as the elevator dropped down to ground level. She couldn't believe she was going to her first frat party tonight! Suddenly, she felt a whole universe away from the relatively quiet social life she'd had with her friends in Georgia. Without her parents around to check her curfew (What curfew? Ha!), she was going to step her social life up a notch.

"Hey, y'all! There you are," a girl sang out when Jenna stepped from the elevator into the dorm lobby. It was her new ZZT sister Sandy Cobb.

"Ready to party tonight, Cobb?" Lora-Leigh shouted out.

"You know it." Sandy was tall for starters, but in her three-inch wedge sandals, she simply towered over Jenna. She motioned outside. "There's Danika. She's going to walk over with us." Danika, one of the other new members, waved from the other side of the glass door.

"Ready?" Roni asked.

"As ready as I'll ever be," Jenna said, following her friends.

"Which one is Phi Omicron Chi?" Jenna asked when they turned off University Boulevard onto Fraternity Row, which sat on the east side of campus.

"It's six down on the left," Lora-Leigh said without missing a beat. "The big Tudor mansion. They're right up there with the Tri-Os in their alumni funding, so they've got one of the poshest houses."

"For someone who started out being anti-Greek," Roni teased, "you sure seem to be our resident expert."

"Hey," Lora-Leigh said. "Have you forgotten that my currently estranged mother practically branded Tri-O on my forehead in utero? The notebook she gave me to study the Latimer Greek system weighed ten pounds. I couldn't help learning something." She grinned. "Besides, in high school my friends and I used to crash LU frat parties all the time. What else is a small-town Latimer renegade supposed to do with her time?"

Jenna laughed. "How are things going on the home front anyway?" Lora-Leigh's mom was a loyal Tri-Omega and had wanted more than anything for Lora-Leigh to join their sisterhood, too. But Lora-Leigh had opted for ZZT instead, and as far as Jenna knew, her mom hadn't gotten over it.

Lora-Leigh shrugged, letting out a small sigh. "I'm still blacklisted. Every time I call my mom's cell, I get her voice mail. She's doing the Hannah Sorenstein version of mourning, which involves a lot of tearful lunches with her Tri-O sisters. It could potentially take years of therapy or a dozen seasons of *Dr. Phil* for Mom to recover."

"We'll hope for a breakthrough," Sandy said jokingly.

"Hope for a miracle instead." Lora-Leigh laughed as she glanced over at the Pi Theta Ep house.

Jenna followed her gaze. While the other houses on Frat Row had well-groomed lawns with quiet exteriors, with rushees in dress shirts and ties coming and going, the Pi Theta Ep house was complete chaos. The front lawn of the stucco, tropical-villa-style house was littered with crushed plastic cups and empty beer cans. A group of rushees in sumo wrestler "diapers" were mud wrestling in a toddler pool as the PTE actives cheered them on.

"What are they doing?" Roni asked, looking slightly horrified at the display.

"Welcome to Rush on Frat Row. They call it 'open houses' and 'group activities,' but really it's just one ludicrous display of machismo. Male bonding at its best," Lora-Leigh said. "You've gotta love testosterone, if for its entertainment value alone."

"They're Neanderthals," Roni said.

"Regressing back to the age of primitive man is what the Pi Theta Eps are good at. They're like Latimer's resident *Animal House*. They have the least amount of funding but the most fun. And they throw some killer parties. They're way more fun than the Gamma Gamma Rhos." She nodded to the plantation-style house with the huge white columns in front. "They're so old school—a bunch of sports-coat donning, loafer-wearing academics."

"I almost feel like we shouldn't be here," Roni whispered as a few rushees passed them by. "Our recruitment was so . . . personal. It's like we're intruding on their agenda."

"Forget your sense of propriety for a sec, Boston." Lora-Leigh rolled her eyes. "Because we *are* their agenda. The more fab chicks the frats have at their parties, the better they look to the rushees. We, ladies, are one hot commodity."

Roni laughed. "Then I'm going to sit back and enjoy being in high demand."

Jenna laughed, too, but the only guy she was really hoping to impress tonight was waiting for her at the Phi Omicron house. When they walked up the steps to the front door, she took a deep breath. Roni must have picked up on her nervousness, because she gave her a quick hand-squeeze and a reassuring smile.

Lora-Leigh led the way, following some rushees as they went inside, and Jenna felt a thrill as soon as she walked into the foyer. The whole house was pounding with music, and at least a hundred guys were crowded into the living room and den. And, even better, a hundred pairs of eyes were turned in their direction, checking them out.

"I've died and gone to hottie heaven," Danika said above the loud music.

"Why didn't we have activities like this during our recruitment?" Sandy asked.

"Now, let us go forth, be flirtful, and partify," Lora-Leigh quipped.

"You heard her." Roni laughed as she pulled Jenna into the living room with Lora-Leigh following. "Come on."

The girls pressed their way through the hordes of actives and rushees, deeper into the house, to a larger denlike room. A wooden-railed staircase toward the back led upstairs. People sat on the steps, laughing and drinking from red plastic cups.

Guys in shirts and ties stood around making small talk with the brothers of the house, no doubt trying to see if they fit in. Much like Jenna and her friends had done last week. Jenna craned her neck for a glimpse of Tiger, but she couldn't make him out in the crowd. The Foxes—the nickname for Phi Omicron Chi—were all wearing shirts with their Greek letters on them, though, so that helped differentiate between the rushees and the actives.

Jenna noticed a trophy case along the wall filled with all sorts of cups, plaques, and awards. Tiger's name jumped out at her on one of the plaques, and on closer inspection she saw it was an award for coming in first at the NCAA championship golf tournament last spring. Impressive. He'd told her he was on the LU golf team, but she had no idea he was that good. She didn't have time to check for his name on any of the other trophies, though, because her view was blocked as another group of girls clustered around the case, giggling like devoted groupies as they admired the accolades.

Roni nudged Jenna and nodded her head at the girls. "Look, they have on new member pins. I wonder what sorority they're in."

Jenna tried not to be obvious as she scoped out the other girls. "I have no clue. I can't make out what's on their pins."

"It's a three. The symbol for Tri-Omega," Lora-Leigh said drily. "The pin that will be emblazoned in my brain forever, filed under 'Parental Disappointment Number Five Hundred and Fifty-three.'"

"Oh," Roni said. "In that case, I *hate* that pin."

Lora-Leigh laughed.

"Jenna!" a voice suddenly called out over the music. "You made it!"

Her heart accelerated as she spun around. "Tiger! Hey!" She smiled and waved, then scolded herself for not being more subtle. She didn't want the whole world to know she was crushing on Tiger. But, with those piercing blue eyes and sandy, flyaway curls, who wouldn't crush on him?

"That's Tiger?" Lora-Leigh whispered to Jenna. "Yummicious. He's like an Adam Brody sans surfboard."

Jenna felt a blush cover her like a blanket of sweat as Tiger walked toward her. But then he stopped a foot away, covering his eyes. "Wait. Don't tell me which sorority. You joined . . . ZZT!"

"Right!" Jenna said. "How'd you know?"

"Lucky guess. ZZT has some of the nicest girls," Tiger said, leaning in closer. "And some of the prettiest."

Jenna laughed. Okay, so that line had been the tiniest bit cheesy. But, hey, she'd take the compliment if he was offering. She didn't dare steal a glance at Lora-Leigh, though, 'cause she knew the sappy-alarm eye roll was probably going off by now. Hoping to divert the attention away from her, she introduced Tiger to Danika, Sandy, and the other girls.

"I'm so glad y'all made it," he said. "I want you to meet some of the other guys." He waved to a couple of guys from across the room, and they nodded, heading toward them. Jenna noticed them both sneaking subtle glances at Roni, but with her modelesque figure and Natalie Portman good looks, how could they not? They introduced themselves as Corey Hock and Chris Stevens.

"Y'all want some punch?" Corey asked, holding out plastic cups to the girls.

"Is it spiked?" Lora-Leigh asked.

Chris smiled. "You know it, but you didn't hear that from me. We're not supposed to break out the good stuff until after Rush officially ends. But since it's over in fifteen, we figured we could bend the rules a little."

"Works for me," Lora-Leigh said with a grin, and the other girls took cups, too.

But when Corey offered one to Jenna, she hesitated. Even though she'd been careful about what she ate today, she'd been jacked up about this party all day, too. And she knew even a little bit of alcohol might set off her 'betes.

"Um, I think I'll take a Diet Coke instead?" Jenna muttered hesitantly, keeping her eyes on the ground to avoid quizzical glances. She was positive an onslaught of questions, or at least a teasing remark about why she wasn't drinking, was sure to come from someone. And if it came from Tiger, she'd be committing social suicide right then and there. *Please don't say anything,* she chanted in her head.

"No prob," Tiger said quickly. "I'll get it!"

Jenna looked up as Tiger grabbed a can of Diet Coke from one of the ice buckets nearby and handed it to her with a smile.

"Thanks," she said, smiling gratefully as relief swept over her.

"Pacing yourself is smart," Tiger said. "You'll be way better off than the rest of us. Once the keg is tapped, it'll only be a matter of time before half the guys here are completely lit. Rush is hard work."

Jenna couldn't help laughing. "From what I've heard, the guys have it a lot easier than we did. No preference cards, no bid night, no door songs, no ice water teas. Guys just get invited to join the frats and then show up if they want to."

"Our activities are definitely different from sorority recruitment," Tiger said. "We're having a Texas Hold 'Em poker-a-thon later this week. The Psi Kappa Upsilons have a paintball tournament. And the Delta Sigma Nus do Demolition Day with sledgehammers to beat up an old car and old computers."

"That sounds kind of violent," Roni said.

"It's supposed to be, Boston," Lora-Leigh said. "These are guys we're talking about. No candles or singing here."

"It's more like testosterone-induced insanity," Tiger said with a laugh. "I won't deny it. And we have to set up all the functions and entertaining along the way."

"Of course, some of the entertaining isn't all that bad," Chris said, smiling at Roni. "It all depends on who the guests are."

As everyone kept talking, Jenna could already guess how the pairings were going to go. It turned out that Corey was from outside Houston, and since Danika was a Texan, too, the two of them immediately started swapping stories about their home state. Chris only had eyes for Roni, but she didn't seem to mind. Roni was smiling coyly as she played with her hair, a tactic Chris seemed mesmerized by. And Sandy was deep in conversation with a cute blond Rushee on the nearby couch.

"Uh-oh," Jenna said, realizing she knew that Rushee, "Sandy seems to be getting close to Brent Gleason."

"You know him?" Tiger asked.

Jenna nodded. "He's a bass drummer for the Marching Raiders. And he's dating the second clarinet, Lisa Stratford."

"Oh," Tiger said.

"I'll go give her the red light," Lora-Leigh volunteered. "I want to check out the rest of the scene here anyway."

Lora-Leigh headed in Sandy's direction, but not before smiling at Jenna and giving her the "he's all yours now" signal with her eyes. Jenna's heart fluttered as she turned back to Tiger.

"So how do you know who plays in the Marching Raiders band?" Tiger asked.

"Um, you're looking at the third trumpet," Jenna said. She cringed slightly as she said it, hoping that Tiger didn't have any preconceived notions about band geeks. That was always such a buzz kill at the start of any getting-to-know-you confab.

But Tiger just smiled. "That's cool. I heard brass players have great lips."

Jenna's heart stopped in her throat. Great lips for . . . kissing? Just the thought of kissing Tiger made her cheeks ignite.

"That's the theory," she said, trying to keep it light even though she was having a hard time finding her breath. "No one's ever told me if I live up to it, though."

"You'll have to test it out sometime, then," Tiger said with a laugh.

Omigod. Test it out with who? Him? "Right" was all she could manage to say.

"Well, what about dancing?" Tiger asked as the music cranked up a notch. "Are brass players good dancers?"

Jenna met his sparkling blue eyes and smiled. "Now that's a proven fact," she said.

"Then let's go," he said, leading her onto the dance floor.

Her skin nearly sizzled as Tiger's hand made contact with her shoulder. With her hip pressed to his, she worried that he might be able to feel her insulin pump, so she adjusted to put some space between them. But not too much. It didn't take her long (oh, maybe about five seconds) to decide that she could do this all night long and be totally and completely happy.

Roni felt the vibration of her BlackBerry in the front pocket of her jeans. She was only half-listening to Chris Stevens brag to a Rushee that they'd won the intramural football trophy last year and the two years before that. She'd enjoyed the harmless flirt session with Chris, but they'd run out of things to talk about after the first fifteen minutes, and now it was getting the teeny-tiniest bit awkward. Unfortunately, her parents had only taught her the fine art of schmoozing with people, not anything about the fine art of ditching them. (Where was Lora-Leigh when you needed her?) So when her BlackBerry buzzed, she took the opportunity to make a polite exit, excusing herself to duck onto the front terrace.

She glanced at her BlackBerry to see an e-mail from Kiersten, her best friend from back home. Roni scrolled down and read:

> Roni! I got your message about ZZT! So incredibly happy for you. Enjoy yourself and when you come down off your cloud, call me with the details. Can't wait to hear all about it!
> XOXO, Kiersten

Roni sat down in one of the rocking chairs that lined the Phi Omicron Chi porch and reread Kiersten's message. Roni had called Kiersten yesterday after the new member ceremony, but she'd missed her. Kiersten was the one who had encouraged her to go through sorority recruitment, since she, herself, had been a sorority girl during her time at Emerson University in Boston. Kiersten had been Roni's au pair growing up, but now she was her staunchest, most loyal supporter. More so than her parents, who hadn't even bothered to call and see which sorority she'd joined. Roni's choosing Latimer University—a state college, God forbid!—over her mother's Wellesley and her father's Harvard was unforgivable, apparently.

Roni had to get updates on her parents from their housekeeper. The latest Van Gelderen headlines were that her father, a prominent Boston attorney, was planning to run for an open state legislature seat, and her mother had been nominated for Wellesley Alumna of the Year. Surprise, surprise. She just wanted them to tell her the news themselves. No matter how hard she tried not to set herself up for disappointment, she couldn't help wishing that there was more of a connection between her and her parents. Like, maybe, familial love and affection?

Kiersten cared, though. She'd cared enough to e-mail and call Roni throughout the sorority recruitment process and give her advice on how to choose the right house. Roni would give her a buzz tomorrow afternoon, when she knew Kiersten would be home.

"I never would've figured you for a social pariah, Boston," a familiar voice said, and Roni looked up to see Lora-Leigh. "Didn't hobnobbing with New England's A-list teach you anything?"

"Yeah." Roni smiled. "It taught me to wish I *was* a social pariah."

Lora-Leigh laughed. "You're not getting your wish tonight. In case it's escaped your attention, there's a room full of gorgeous guys in there."

"I was just checking a message," she said, standing up and smoothing out her top.

"Messages can wait," Lora-Leigh said. "The party can't."

Roni let Lora-Leigh lead her back into the room; then they scanned the crowd. A lot of the Rushees were starting to leave, but there were about a dozen or so left in the room talking to the actives. Her heart nearly came to a complete halt when she saw . . . him.

It was the guy from the natatorium.

Earlier in the week, she'd swum in the lane next to him at the LU indoor swimming pool. They'd barely spoken, but they'd struck up a friendly race and had shared a smile before they went their separate ways. There had definitely been a brief flash of chemistry.

And now, here he was—across the room, standing with a Dr Pepper in one hand and the other tucked into the pocket of his jeans. Was he a Phi Omicron Chi? No, he wasn't wearing their letters. Definitely a Rushee. He was talking with a couple of the Foxes.

But as Roni was looking, he raised his eyes to hers and smiled in a flash of recognition, then motioned her to come over.

She smiled and turned to Lora-Leigh. "I'll catch up with you in a few, okay?"

"Sure," Lora-Leigh said. "I'll go see if I can track down Jenna and Lion."

"Tiger," Roni said with a giggle, then headed toward the mystery man.

When she reached him, he stepped away from the rest of his group and smiled. Roni swallowed down her hammering heart. What was wrong with her? She normally didn't have a problem talking to guys. In fact, in Boston, Roni'd had her fair share of "suitors," as her mom had called them. But the guys she'd dated had been boarding school preps stamped for Ivy League. They were mostly matches encouraged or (even worse!) arranged by her parents. Even though she'd never been without an escort for dances and dinner parties, she'd never connected with any of those guys. Playing the dating game without her parents' looming shadows was a different experience entirely. Here, Roni didn't have her impeccable family name to pave the way for conversation. Here, she was just like everyone else, and she was suddenly at a complete loss for words.

"I've been waiting for my rematch," he said.

"Are you sure you really want one?" Roni teased, finally finding her voice. "Most people don't like losing."

He laughed. "I was hoping I'd have a chance to redeem myself. You know, heal my wounded male ego, that sort of thing."

"I'm ready whenever you are," Roni challenged, tossing her hair over her shoulder and putting on a killer smile. The tactic had always worked to reel in the Boston preps, and she hoped it would have the same effect on this guy.

"Good," he said, extending a hand. "Lance McManus."

She felt a thrill as she took his hand and introduced herself.

He cocked his head to the side. "I assume from the accent that you're not from 'round here?"

"No, I'm from Boston."

"LU's a long way from home."

"Thankfully," she said with a twist of sarcasm. "What I mean is, it's nice to be somewhere different. Now I'm just trying to fit in and get used to the South."

"Oh, Florida's not really the South. It's . . . Florida."

"Are you from Florida?"

"I am now. My family has moved around a lot over the years. I was an army brat." He squinted at her closely. "Hey, aren't you taking Geography 101?"

She rolled her eyes. "Yeah, I have Dr. Sylvester. I can barely stay awake in his class."

His smile widened. "I *thought* I saw you in class! I have the Tuesday lab with you."

"You do?" Her pulse skittered. "But I haven't seen you . . . ." How could she *not* have seen him?

"You sit up front, but I sit way in the back." He peered down at her with his thick bangs falling nearly into his eyes. "Personally, I think I have the best view from the back row." He smiled at her, and her heart jumped to her throat.

"So I'm guessing if you're bored in Dr. Sylvester's class that you're not a Geography major."

"No way," Roni said emphatically. "I'm undeclared right now. I figured I'd get the core curriculum classes over with first and then see what interests me so I can start focusing junior year. But I think I can safely say Geography is out of the running." And she was *not* going to automatically do pre-law, either, just because that was what her father wanted . . . expected. "What about you?" she asked Lance.

"I'm thinking about going pre-med," Lance said. "Believe it or not, Anatomy 101 sounds way more interesting than Geography."

Roni laughed. "I think I'd choose studying earthquakes over cadavers, even if it means putting up with Dr. Sylvester. But the idea of helping to cure people of disease. That's an amazing thing."

"Plus, the doctors in *Grey's Anatomy* get all the cute girls," Lance said with a laugh. "Since I've always had bad luck in that area, I figured pre-med was worth it to see if I could improve my odds." He grinned at her.

"Are—are you having fun rushing?" she asked, having a mental fight with the blush she could feel creeping across her cheeks.

"I guess," he said. "My folks thought it would be a good way to get more involved here at Latimer, but I already have a full course load, and I'm on the LU swim team, too. I don't know if I'll have enough time to dedicate to a fraternity. But it's nice meeting everyone. Either way, I'll get some friends out of it, so it's all good."

"I just joined ZZT, and so far, Greek life is amazing. I've already met so many awesome people."

He leaned down to her—he had to be at least six-six—and said in a stage whisper, "Maybe I should join ZZT, too."

She smiled, glad that she seemed to be making some progress on the flirt front with him. Talking to Lance was easy. No mandatory polite inquiries about his family's health, no small talk about summering in the Hamptons. No, just a getting-to-know-you chat without the WASPy niceties. It was actually—what was the word?—fun!

Roni had no idea how much time had passed until Danika tapped her on the shoulder. "Here you are! Lora-Leigh and Jenna are waiting outside. We're heading over to the athletic dorm for their party. They've got a band and everything." Danika looked at Lance and back at Roni. "You coming?"

Reluctantly, Roni nodded. She didn't want to leave Lance, but she wasn't ready to stick it out solo at the party without the other girls. "I've got to go," she said to him. "It was great talking to you, Lance."

"Finally," he said.

She took two steps, stopped, and turned back to face him. "Maybe I'll see you at the pool again?"

"Definitely," Lance said. "I'll be waiting for that rematch."

His hazel eyes connected with hers, and he smiled one last time. As she stepped onto the front porch to catch up with the other girls, she couldn't stop smiling herself. Oh, yes. There'd be a rematch. She'd make sure of that.

Lora-Leigh could hear the pounding of the bass in the band long before the girls reached the athletic dorm, and her adrenaline picked up the pace as soon as she did. She'd been waiting all night for this party, biding her time while Roni, Jenna, and the other girls flirted with the frat boys. She could take or leave the frat guys she'd met so far, but she couldn't say the same for Jenna, who had been on a guy-high ever since she'd seen Tiger tonight.

"You keep smiling like that and you're going to pull a muscle," Lora-Leigh joked as they walked toward the end of Frat Row.

"I can't help it," Jenna said blissfully. "Tiger asked me to come to his next golf tournament. Did I tell you that?"

"About five hundred times," she said with a laugh.

"Sorry. I just can't believe he asked me to go."

"That's all right," Roni said. "It's your first date with an older college man. You *should* be excited."

"I sense a sordid, scandalous love affair in the works," Lora-Leigh teased.

"Sordid and scandalous?" Jenna laughed. "I'll settle for sweet with a little bit of sappy thrown in for good measure."

Lora-Leigh shrugged. "To each her own."

Personally, she thought scandalous might be fun, but Jenna was too softhearted for that. Lora-Leigh, on the other hand, had always had tons of guys as best friends, or even friends she dated casually like her bud Brian from high school. A big, long-term BF had always eluded her, and that was fine by her. But DeShawn Pritchard was different. He was a walking enigma—a die-hard jock with a serious art talent.

She and DeShawn had Western Civ and Art classes together. He spent most of his time in Western Civ snoozing behind his Ray-Ban sunglasses. But in Art, he came to life, so intensely absorbed in sketching and painting that half the time he didn't even stir from his seat until ten minutes after class ended. She'd snuck a few peeks at his canvases, and they were incredible.

He turned the brainless muscleman stereotype on its head, and she found that downright sexy.

"Well, ladies," Lora-Leigh said as the dorm courtyard came into view. "I think we've found the hot spot of the night."

There was no question about it. This party was hopping. The

band was pushing the amps to the max, and the courtyard was packed with people. The football players in the crowd were obvious, towering over everyone. The dorm sat at the end of Frat Row next to the Omega Phi house, so there were several dozen frat guys who had spilled over into the courtyard during the post-Rush party.

"I think I liked our odds at the Phi Omicron house better," Sandy said. "Look at all the girls here."

It was true. Unlike the girl/guy ratio at the frat parties, here the girls clearly outnumbered the guys.

"They're cleat chasers," Lora-Leigh said, rolling her eyes. "They know LU has a great athletics program with pro potential, so they come here to nab a future proball player. NFL, NBA, or MLB, doesn't matter. They're not picky, and they're all the same—a bunch of miniskirted, stiletto-wearing carbon copies."

"But you're here chasing one of LU's star athletes, too," Jenna pointed out with a good-natured, teasing smile.

"I never chase," Lora-Leigh said emphatically. "That's the act of only the truly desperate. *I'm* in a league of my own, girlfriend!"

"Is that so, Curly?" a rumbling voice said behind her.

Lora-Leigh froze. Oh, no. It couldn't be. There was no way that *he* had heard her say that. But he had. Because standing behind her was DeShawn Pritchard, grinning down at her, clearly enjoying the fact that he'd caught her off guard. Well, she wasn't going to let him revel in self-satisfaction for too long.

"You know it," Lora-Leigh said, recovering in time to throw him a chill smile. "But do you think you can handle it?"

"Not even a question," DeShawn said with a wink.